PEESDOV

The Peesdown Series
Book 1

CAROLE WILLIAMS

This is a work of fiction. Similarities to real people, places, or events are entirely coincidental.

PEESDOWN PARK

First edition. February 3, 2021.

THE PEESDOWN SERIES

PEESDOWN PARK

PANIC IN PEESDOWN

PASSION IN PEESDOWN

POISON IN PEESDOWN (coming soon)

FOREWORD

In 2005 I decided to form my own petsitting business, Pampered Pets, in Leeds, and have my wonderful clients, super assistants, especially Marion who was my right-hand woman, and Deborah, my secretarial help, not to mention all the fabulous dogs, cats, bunnies, guinea pigs, chickens, etc that we had the privilege to look after, to thank for this series.

A very special thank you, also, to my own precious pooches, Charlie, Dolly and Lucas who were absolutely brilliant with all the dogs we looked after. They never knew who was going to jump into the car on our walks or who was coming home with them to stay but there was never a cross word, just a warm welcome. They are all in doggie heaven now and I do miss them but while they were here, they had a fabulous life with all their friends on our many adventures in Roundhay, Temple Newsam, Golden Acre and Meanwood Parks and the beautiful woods and countryside around Leeds. I have superb memories and thousands of photographs of our time there.

My darling Charlie, whom I rescued when he was around six months old. I had ten wonderful years with him.

Dolly and Lucas, both of whom came to me from clients who unfortunately (but very fortunately for me) couldn't look after them any longer. I had walked Dolly (in the front) since she was a puppy and she came to me at 3 years old. She was 13 when she died. I had also walked Lucas from a puppy and he came to me when he was 18 months and was nearly 12 when he went to doggie heaven.

TABLE OF CONTENTS

PROLOGUE 3

CHAPTER 1...4

CHAPTER 2...15

CHAPTER 3...28

CHAPTER 4...55

CHAPTER 5...67

CHAPTER 6...80

CHAPTER 7...88

CHAPTER 8...100

CHAPTER 9...111

CHAPTER 10...117

CHAPTER 11...131

CHAPTER 12...144

CHAPTER 13...156

CHAPTER 14...169

REVIEWS..171

PROLOGUE

His father was watching television in the lounge and had his back to William as he entered the room, donned rubber gloves and pulled the cord from his pocket. In a flash, it was around his father's neck. Having taken him by surprise there wasn't much of a struggle and it was only a minute or two before the deed was done.

Breathless, his heart thudding loudly, William turned to walk upstairs. His mother was banging cupboards so she must be putting away laundry. He found her on the landing. She heard him and turned, opened her mouth to speak but screamed instead as she saw the look of grim determination on his face and the cord in his hand. He silenced her, hitting her hard in the face. As she slumped to the ground, he grabbed her, put the cord around her neck and pulled hard. Within a short space of time she had joined her husband in heaven. William would pray for them later.

CHAPTER 1

Anna Stapleton turned her cherry red Mini Clubman into the entrance to Peesdown Park and switched off the engine. The car park was empty. No people, no cars. Silence prevailed. It was late September; children were back at school and their parents at work. Loneliness engulfed her. Millions of people inhabited the earth but at that moment in time she felt completely alone, isolated from the hustle and bustle of everyday living. No-one knew she was there, no-one cared. She was so depressed, she wanted to die.

She had been driving around aimlessly for the last hour, just to get out of the house. The walls had been closing in, panic had taken hold and she had run away. She had driven to Wetherby, stopping for petrol on the way. She had thought about going to the coast but every town; Bridlington, Filey, Whitby ... they all held painful memories and she wasn't up to that yet. It was too soon. Instead, she had driven back to Leeds and onto the ring road, heading towards Temple Newsam. She thought vaguely about having a walk in the grounds or visiting the house. It was terribly old ... Tudor or Jacobean ... she wasn't sure. There was a café too where she could get a cup of tea. Then she had seen the sign for Peesdown. She couldn't ever remember having been there. There was another sign, indicating there was a park. She turned towards it, drove along the High Street, across Miller Lane and through the park gates.

She looked dully at her surroundings. On this chilly, wet day, the park looked uninviting, hence, no doubt, the lack of visitors. The overflowing litter bins, ravaged by hungry squirrels or foxes were upturned, their licked and chewed contents scattered untidily on the ground. The doors on the block of toilets were open but she would never enter on her own, however desperate she was. Anyone could be hiding in there. The tiny cafe in the corner of the car park was closed, a battered sign on its door of green peeling paint advertising a willingness to sell ice cream.

Anna shivered at the thought and looked at the little packet of digestive biscuits on the dashboard in front of her. She knew she should eat something but although she hadn't had breakfast and very little the previous day, she wasn't really hungry. She picked it up, undid the wrapper and nibbled on a biscuit. Nausea overwhelmed her and she thrust the remainder inside her jacket pocket. Desperate for fresh air, she opened the car door and got out, pondering on the wisdom of walking through the woods with no-one about. During the summer, a woman walking her dog had been raped here with no indication that her attacker had ever been caught.

She shrugged, locked the car and headed, with her hands deep in her jacket pockets and her hood over her head, for the path towards the lake. No doubt the man, whoever he was, was sensibly tucked up somewhere warm and dry and not lurking about in the cold and wet waiting for some silly woman to be wandering aimlessly about on her own.

Her feet, in comfy old black leather loafers, took her down the winding path, stepping neatly over the few leaves brought down by the rain, which made the tarmac slippery. She noticed the bushes of holly in amongst the trees. It made her realise how fast Christmas was approaching. Her heart sank even further. Christmas. She normally revelled in it; the present buying, the cooking, the partying. But no more. It would be a nightmare this year. How on earth was she going to get through it?

On reaching the lake she shivered again. It was grey and depressing on this drab morning and for a moment she wondered what on earth she was doing as she perched precariously on a broken damp wooden bench beside the murky water. Ever hungry ducks, followed by a couple of hopeful coots swam towards her but she had nothing for them. They swam away, leaving her alone to dwell on her loneliness.

"You shouldn't quit your job," her son, Brian, had said during his monthly dutiful telephone call from his big, brash house in Florida, where he had lived for ten years with his big, brash blonde-headed wife, Indiana. Anna had never taken to her and neither had Indiana to her. They had only met twice, once when Brian and Indiana had married and then again when the pair had paid a flying visit to England for a weekend, which hadn't been a success and the whole family were relieved when it was time for them to return to America.

"Why don't you take a long holiday? Come over here. Let us make a fuss of you for a while. Indiana would love to show you around," Brian had urged half-heartedly. He didn't want her there. She knew it and he knew it and as for Indiana, she certainly wouldn't want to nursemaid her mother-in-law and anyway, Anna was still angry with them. They hadn't come to the funeral and that was going to be a very hard thing to forgive.

Anna's only child, who should have given her total support at the burial of her beloved husband and his father, had been conspicuous in his absence. Naturally selfish and egotistical, the son Anna and her husband had so lovingly spawned, had pleaded business problems with his real estate company. He had no-one he could leave in charge, not even for the funeral of his father, from whom he had borrowed a great deal of money to set up his business in the first place. Oh, yes, Anna was angry and deeply hurt and at the present time wanted nothing less than to be in her son's company. No. She was better off here, in England, in Leeds, in Peesdown Park, grieving for the man she had loved and lost in such a brutal way.

"It's only a routine operation," the surgeon had said a year ago, when it was discovered Gerald had cataracts. "We'll remove one first and then the other a few months later. It will change your life."

How right he had been. Gerald had visited outpatients for the first operation six months ago. Anna was supposed to pick him up a few hours later. She duly arrived and was told by a breathless junior nurse that something had gone wrong and Gerald was in intensive care. He had suffered a massive stroke and was not expected to live long. Twenty-four hours later he was dead, not even having regained consciousness so that Anna could say goodbye.

Even now, six months later, she was still in shock. Numb with grief, unable to believe how her lovely, kind, caring husband could have been taken so quickly and so cruelly. If only there had been time to prepare. Perhaps it would have been easier to cope. Now she couldn't concentrate on anything. It was difficult enough with normal household chores but as for work. That was totally out of the question.

Financially she was secure. The mortgage had been paid off years ago and Gerald's life insurance was substantial and then there were their savings so she had no real need to work. She had never liked her part-time secretarial position in a small builder's merchants much anyway and she gained the impression that her bosses were pleased to see the back of her when she handed in her notice. They were embarrassed by her widowhood and had no idea what to say or how to treat her and she was of no use to them, unable to focus on her work, near to tears all the time, irritable and miserable. It was a relief to everyone when she finally resigned and it was just a matter of deciding on what to do with herself now and as she stared despondently over the lake, she simply had no idea at all.

* * *

It was raining. Good. He was itching to get into the park and see her ... Miranda ... the only person in the whole world with whom he had ever wanted a relationship. He had only met her a few months ago but she was becoming extremely important to him and he would have her to himself this morning as there wouldn't be anyone much about due to the bad weather. It was amazing how many dog owners were fair-weather friends. Goodness knows how their poor animals fared when their owners didn't go out in the rain. They didn't deserve dogs, those people. Miranda would be in the park though. She was a professional dog walker and had to go, whatever the weather.

He looked across the lawn at the gate he always kept chained up to prevent people gaining access to his home. The leaves on the trees and shrubbery in the garden were soaking wet and dripping onto the sodden grass below. He looked up at the sky. Was there a hint of brightness ... just a faint touch of blue behind the grey clouds?

He looked at the brass clock on the mantelpiece. It was time. She would be in the park at any moment and he wanted to be there too. He had to get ready. He looked around for his bald wig, his fake moustache, his glasses and his stick ... and his tiny digital camera. He liked to have that with him at all times ... it had served him well since he bought it. He had a nice collection of photos he had printed off, tucked away with his box of trophies so he could see what he had done, time and time again. It had all started with his parents ... taking pictures of their dead bodies. He hadn't wanted to forget that moment ... when he was finally free of them.

When he left his spacious detached Victorian house ten minutes later, he looked a completely different person to the one who had stood at the window earlier. He now appeared thirty years older, he walked with a limp, leaning heavily on his stick for support with one hand and a big black brolly in the other, his thinning brown hair was covered by the bald cap, his moustache was in place and the black-rimmed glasses on his nose gave him the appearance of an ageing intellectual.

He left the house he had bought just months ago, following his lengthy time abroad, walked down the gravel park and undid the padlock which kept the chain in place around the wrought iron gates. He didn't want anyone approaching his home unexpectedly so he always kept them locked. He didn't even have to worry about a postman as he used a box number and collected his mail from the post office down the road once a week.

He chained them up again once he was on the pavement outside, thinking how much better it would be when the wooden gates he had ordered were in situ. He would be able to bolt them from the inside and it would be impossible to see the house from the road at all as there was an eight-foot laurel hedge in front, which also grew between him and his nearest neighbour on the right. The boundary on the left was a mass of overgrown shrubbery and tall trees. He valued his privacy.

Miller Lane stretched out in front of him. His house was the last on this section. There were three more detached Victorian properties on his side of the road, then the gates for Peesdown Park, then two more Victorian houses, the Georgian Vicarage and right at the end and facing him, was the medieval St. Edmunds church. On the opposite side of the road to the Vicarage was the church hall, then Peesdown High Street, directly opposite the park gates. The Red Lion with a beer garden was on the corner and across from his house, there was a field upon which grazed a couple of Shetland ponies. He had no idea to whom they belonged but didn't care. They didn't bother him and made his part of Miller Lane quiet and private.

He headed down the road, slowly, always slowly. It wouldn't do to rush it and make people wonder how such an old and feeble man could walk very quickly. The park gates, big black wrought iron affairs, came into view. His heart began to thud, as it always did on his sorties. The itch was becoming stronger by the minute!

* * *

Miranda Denton entered the car park in her battered old dark green Volvo estate, sporting the information on both front door panels that she was Four Paws Petsitting Service, offering dog walking, home dog boarding, cat and small petsitting. She pulled up beside the little red Mini, pleased to see the park was virtually empty. She liked rainy days when she could practically have the park to herself and she could allow the dogs to run about freely without fear of them upsetting anyone and getting into trouble. Out of the six she had today, two were particularly naughty so it would be nice to have a relaxing walk for once instead of yelling her head off to get them back or have to keep them on a lead in case they upset someone. None of them walked very well when restrained. Their owners hadn't bothered to train them to walk to heel and as much as she tried to persuade them to teach their dogs some manners, advising her clients that she was a dog walker and not a trainer, it rarely worked but if she wanted the money, she had to put up with it.

She opened the boot and four jumped out, heading straight for the lake, knowing where they were going, noses to the ground, sniffing, always sniffing, eager to see who had been about and if they had left any food. She opened the rear door of the car and lifted the last two out, two little Shih Tzu's who their owner had insisted remain on extension leads.

Locking the vehicle, throwing four dog leads around her neck, clipping them all together so she didn't lose any as she had done in the past which cost her a pretty penny replacing them, zipping up all the house keys and her car keys in her pocket for safety, she and the Shih Tzu's followed the other four dogs along the path towards the lake, waiting for the inevitable poos which she would have to clean up. Thankfully there was a poo bin at the top of the path so she wouldn't have to carry them far. Then, to her dismay, she saw the woman sitting on the bench. Bugger. Nellie would be a little sod now.

* * *

A shrieking female voice behind Anna startled her out of her reverie.

"Nellie! Nellie! Come here! Do as you're told for once!"

Anna half turned to be accosted by the muddy, wet nose of a chocolate coloured Labrador pushing her nose forcefully into her jacket pocket where rested the packet of digestive biscuits.

"Oh, God! Oh, Nellie!" yelled a young woman with flowing blonde hair running behind, "Noooo!"

Nellie, however, was on a mission and ignored the instructions, hell-bent on foraging in Anna's pocket, blissfully mindless of Anna's unsuccessful attempts to push her away. The dog was strong and determined to get what she was after.

Tail wagging furiously, she thrust her nose deeper into Anna's pocket and triumphantly pulled out the digestive biscuits and wolfed them down in one go, eyes sparkling mischievously as she spat the wrapper on the ground.

Anna put out a hand and patted her silky brown coat.

Nellie wagged her tail harder and licked Anna's hand as if to say thank you.

"Oh, I'm so sorry," gasped Miranda, tumbling down the hill behind them, holding onto two small dogs pulling hard on extension leads while three others dashed up to join Nellie, desperate to see if Anna was the source of yet more unexpected treats. "Oh, God. It wasn't chocolate, was it? That's poisonous for dogs."

"No, don't worry. It was only digestive biscuits."

"Oh, Lord. They will make her poop even more," Miranda giggled.

Anna smiled and studied the young woman who possessed long, fair, wavy hair, was small in stature, tending towards plumpness, although it was difficult to tell with the amount of clothing she wore; mud-caked trousers and heavy walking boots, an old tatty wax jacket and a green woolly scarf around her neck.

She moved closer to Anna, gently cuffing Nellie and her friends away.

"Nellie is such a pig," she said. "No-one would ever think I fed her. Oh goodness. Just look at your jacket."

Anna looked. It was smeared with mud from Nellie's nose. She grinned ... actually grinned, for the first time in months.

"It doesn't matter. It'll wash," she replied, eager to soothe the dog walker's embarrassment.

"That's very reasonable of you," Miranda replied thankfully. "You wouldn't believe how uptight some people get, especially the non-doggy ones. Oh God. Roger! Nooo!" she yelled frantically at the black Labrador who was busy licking up Nellie's excrement. "Please. Don't look," she turned to Anna apologetically. "He's simply disgusting. I've tried everything to stop him doing it but nothing seems to work ... oh, Lord. Now Sammy's doing one and I've forgotten to bring any poo bags," she cried, rummaging in her pockets, the two small dogs on extension leads becoming tangled around her legs as they sprung into action, snapping loudly at a pair of swans swimming curiously towards them.

"Roger!" yelled Miranda but Roger, like Nellie before him, took no notice and dived into the fresh pile of poo with relish. "Oh heck," hissed Miranda. "Here comes old Fart Features ... trust him to turn up just as the dogs are all emptying ... and me with no poo bags ... hurry up, Roger," she urged, changing tactics, still rummaging frantically in her pockets. "Clean it up ... quickly."

Anna looked at the elderly man in a blue uniform approaching with glee in his eyes and a purposeful set to his mouth. He held his hands behind his back, reminding her of her old headmaster, a right stickler for correct behaviour at all times.

"Poo bags," muttered Miranda, looking imploringly at Anna. "You haven't any on you by any chance? Polly hasn't done one yet and Roger's not too partial to hers and I wouldn't put it past old Fart Features not to follow us. He'd like nothing better than to catch us out and have us fined. I do wonder why he's a park keeper... he loathes dogs and hasn't much time for many people either."

Anna rummaged in her pockets but all that emerged were a few tissues and an empty cheese and onion crisp packet. The digestive wrapper Nellie had spat out was at her feet.

"They'll do," Miranda whispered. "Thanks," as Anna handed them to her.

"Morning," said the park keeper, his eyes darting hither and thither over the dogs, watching their every move. Nellie approached him hopefully, tail wagging, eyes smiling but he brushed her aside and glared at Miranda.

"I do hope your animals are going to behave themselves today. I had a complaint yesterday from Mrs Smedley ... she said one of yours tried to attack her dog and then tried to bite her."

"Mrs Smedley is mistaken," said Miranda crossly. "Sammy was only trying to say hello ... he was just a bit boisterous about it, gave her dog a bit of a fright but certainly didn't attack it and when Mrs Smedley put her hand down, he went to lick it, not bite it. She really does exaggerate."

"Yes ... and ripped the lady's tights with his claws by all accounts."

"He only put up a paw to try and apologise and unfortunately made a tiny hole in them ... I did give her the money to buy another pair."

"Um," muttered Fart Features. "Well, I'm off ... it's too chilly to hang around today. I trust you've plenty of bags to clean up after your dogs."

"Of course," Miranda smiled sweetly. "I never go anywhere without them."

Anna stifled a giggle as Fart Features gave her a withering look, muttered something about the Dangerous Dogs Act and then moved on along the path towards the car park. He had only just marched out of earshot when Miranda was off again.

"Oh, bugger. There goes Sammy," she cried, tearing across the grass, brandishing the cheese and onion crisp packet in one hand and hauling the two small dogs on extension leads behind her towards a small black and tan dog busily unloading itself. Roger, now replete from two earlier helpings of poo eyed her progress with interest but made no attempt to beat her to it.

Miranda whipped up Sammy's offering with the crisp packet and deposited it into a bright red bin on the side of the path.

"Thank goodness. Only four to go now. I better dash back to the car before we continue. I've a pile of poo bags in there ... then
I can relax and enjoy the remainder of the walk ... I hope," she smiled.

Anna smiled back. "Do you ... do you need any help?" she asked hesitantly, hating the idea of the woman walking away and leaving her to her gloomy thoughts.

Miranda looked at Anna's forlorn face. She was obviously desperately sad about something as her eyes looked sore and the skin around them was swollen, indicating she had been doing a lot of crying recently. Miranda had known of two suicides in the park since she had been walking there regularly and she didn't want this woman to be another statistic. If she wanted company, she could certainly have hers and it may well be possible to cheer her up a bit.

"Contrary to what you've just witnessed, I don't need any help but I'd certainly like some company. I normally walk around the lake ... it takes about an hour ... but it can be muddy in places," she added, glancing at Anna's loafers.

"That's fine. I don't mind."

"Ok. Stay there and I'll be back in a minute," commanded Miranda, turning to hurry back to her car, all six dogs sticking with her with puzzled expressions on their faces wondering why they were heading back to the car so soon.

They were all back in minutes. "Are you sure about this?" asked Miranda, eyeing up Anna's smart blue anorak and neatly pressed navy trousers. "You'll be filthy by the time we've finished."

"What's a bit of mud?" Anna smiled, as she stood up. The seat of her trousers felt damp from the dilapidated bench which, as she moved away, gave a deep groan and collapsed on the ground at her feet.

Miranda roared with laughter, causing all the dogs to gather round to see what was so amusing. "Thank goodness old Fart Features didn't see that ... he'd accuse you of vandalism."

Her mirth was infectious and Anne giggled with her, her imagination running riot at just what the grumpy park keeper might have said. Her day was becoming just a little brighter.

* * *

He stood behind a tree on the opposite side of the lake to where Miranda and a woman he had never seen before, were conversing with the park keeper. They seemed to be the only people out this morning. The remainder of the lakeside path was deserted.

He stared at the small group, at Miranda in particular. He liked her. He liked her a lot. He had only been living in Peesdown for a few months and had taken to walking here every morning. Miranda had been one of the first people he had talked to and he looked forward to seeing her. She gave him a purpose for getting up in the morning and getting out of the house. He had never met anyone like her before and he wanted to get to know her better ... and it had begun to annoy him when she talked to anyone else.

The rain had eased. It was just a light drizzle now but he'd been in the park for nearly an hour and was growing cold standing still ... watching. He had been sheltered by his brolly and a flourishing holly tree from the worst of the weather but his trousers and shoes were becoming increasingly damp and unpleasant to wear.

This unknown woman was sticking like glue to Miranda as they began to walk around the lake so he wouldn't get her to himself this morning. He sighed. He had got wet for nothing. He would go home ... change his clothes ... get warm. He'd make some toast and coffee, then take out his scrapbook and titillate himself with the pictures he had pasted in ... of his dying parents ... of the women he had enjoyed during his years abroad in the sun; those two silly girls in Mataro ... then pretty little Ingrid with the pigtails, looking far younger than she really was. He licked his lips. She had been so silly, trusting him ... unlike Charlotte ... she had guessed what he was about to do ... had squealed like a pig and had to be silenced quicker than he intended. Michelle ... with the enormous breasts. He had taken pictures of them all; naked, tied up and terrified. Then there were the trophies ... the earrings, the bracelets, the locks of hair. He smiled and turned for home.

12

CHAPTER 2

Anna learned a great deal about Miranda that morning as her new acquaintance was willing to talk about herself without hesitation. She was twenty-eight, childless through design and divorced for the last two years.

"Beastly Bastard ran off with my best friend," she sighed with resignation. "But to be honest, I'm better off without him. He was the most unreliable person I have ever come across. No idea why I ever married him ... think it was just a sex thing ... but that soon wore off with the drudgery of everyday living and housework." She pulled a face. "He hated it and I hated it and the place was like a bloody pigsty. Then there was the financial mess he got us into and finally, the worst betrayal of all with the one person I trusted implicitly. Anyway, I chucked him out and thanks to a legacy from my grandmother, bought him out of the house. Nellie stayed with me, of course. Beastly Bastard was never a real dog lover, so at least we didn't wrangle over her."

"So, is this ... dog walking ... what you do for a living?" Anna asked, utterly fascinated. She had never met a professional dog walker before and it seemed utterly alien to her. How on earth did anyone keep a pack of dogs under any semblance of control in a public park?

Miranda smiled. "Oh, yes. I walk lots of little darlings whose parents haven't time to see to them ... I collect five to walk with Nellie mid-morning and then another five, with Nellie, at lunchtime. It's quite lucrative, keeps me and Nellie fit and I'm not stuck indoors all day like their poor owners in their offices, hospitals or factories. Yuk!"

"Gosh. You must get awfully tired."

"Sometimes ... but I enjoy it and the money keeps me going ... quite a bit of which the taxman knows nothing about."

"How do you know I'm not from the tax office?" Anna teased. Miranda's brown eyes twinkled merrily. "I don't but you look nothing like a tax inspector."

"What do I look like then?"

"Unhappy," Miranda said sorrowfully. "Lost and lonely ... as if the weight of the world is on your shoulders."

Anna gulped and blinked rapidly to prevent instant tears from gaining momentum. She took out a tissue from her jacket pocket. Nellie dashed up hopefully but wandered away despondently when nothing edible emerged.

"Sorry," Miranda said. "I didn't mean to upset you."

"You didn't. You were stating the obvious," Anna replied, dabbing at her eyes with her tissue.

Their steps had taken them halfway around the lake. A sturdy bench had been positioned so that people could rest and take in the splendid scenery. Exactly opposite, were the massive lawns with an enormous, attractive flower bed circled by a tarmac drive coming up from the main gates. Behind them was a dense wood full of enormous beech and oak trees.

"I usually sit here for a moment or two ... to admire the view," Miranda said, flopping onto the bench.

Anna sat down beside her. The dogs who weren't on leads decided to play chase. Roger had a stick. The others decided they wanted it. Anna wondered why. It couldn't taste very nice after his shenanigans with the poo. The two small dogs on extension leads settled at Miranda's feet. Both were elderly and one had a runny eye.

"It's my husband," Anna gulped back more tears.

"Ah," Miranda uttered. "I knew there had to be a man in it somewhere."

"No. Nothing like that. He died ... six months ago ... went into hospital to have a cataract removed, had a massive stroke ... and he died," Anna croaked.

"Oh no! Oh, poor you," cried Miranda. "What a dreadful, dreadful shock."

Anna nodded, unable to speak.

"Cry all you want," instructed Miranda. "Don't mind me. I take it he was a good husband? Unlike my Beastly Bastard."

"Wonderful," Anna whispered. "Kind, gentle, caring, generous ... I loved him very much and miss him terribly."

The tears flowed but she didn't feel embarrassed with Miranda, who held her tightly and allowed her to sob, the first time she had vented her feelings in public.

"Let it out," Miranda urged. "It'll do you the power of good … and there's no-one to see bar me."

Anna cried piteously, unable to stop now she had started, all the while Miranda hugging her closely. The two small dogs laid down and placed their heads on Anna's feet, doing their level best to provide comfort too.

"What a sight I must present," Anna gulped as the storm passed and Miranda could release her hold on her.

"Don't worry. Feel a bit better now?"

Anna nodded. "I am so sorry … I don't usually cry all over people I've just met."

Miranda grinned. "That's okay. I'll charge you a fiver for the privilege."

Anna smiled. She was beginning to really like Miranda.

"What's your name, by the way. Now you've sobbed all over me, I think I'm entitled to know."

"Anna … after Anna Pavlova … the famous ballerina … my mother wanted to be a ballet dancer … and then she wanted me to be one too when her dream died."

"Oh, I remember wanting that too when I was small … didn't we all?"

"Funnily enough, no. I always wanted to run a shop," Anna said, thinking how it had always been a dream of hers but had never become a reality.

"What sort of shop?"

"I'm not sure … sweets, clothes … I don't know," Anna shrugged.

Roger darted past with a huge stick resembling a small tree trunk. He charged around, waving it in the air at the other dogs who were now playing tug of war over the one he had abandoned earlier. They ignored him as they tussled fiercely.

"Do they fight?" Anna asked, a little alarmed, hearing the deep growls. The dogs were baring their teeth too, which was even more disconcerting.

"No," Miranda smiled. "It's just play. They all adore each other, although someone who doesn't know dogs very well might think the opposite."

Reassured, Anna patted the two at their feet. "I don't know much about dogs. I've always wanted one but Gerald was allergic so we couldn't."

"Get one now then."

Anna glanced at Miranda, mulling over the idea.

"I wouldn't know what to do," she said helplessly. "Feeding, walking ... how do you get them to come back to you when they're off the lead ... and don't they have to have injections and things? I really wouldn't know where to start."

Miranda laughed kindly. She did it so easily as if that's what she was born to do. "I'll help," she said. "Anything you want to know, just ask. You'll always know where to find me," she waved her arm around the park.

The idea began to appeal. Anna imagined herself walking here every day, a furry companion of her own at her side, chatting to Miranda and avoiding Fart Features. She'd have to remember to bring poo bags.

"Don't rush into it if you're not one hundred per cent sure," warned Miranda. "It's a huge responsibility and commitment, especially if you value your freedom and don't want to be tied. They can't be left at home alone for more than three to four hours at a time before they either need feeding or toileting and if you're one of those who like to go away a lot, you'll need either a good kennels or a petsitter who boards in their own home ... and neither come cheap."

She stood up. "Do you mind if we walk on? I've got to get these back to their respective homes and collect the next lot soon." They continued around the lake, doing their best to avoid the muddy parts as Anna's loafers proved totally inadequate and she frequently sank deep, the mud covering her shoes and socks. The dogs didn't help. They were filthy too, mud-splattered under their bellies, their legs and feet mucky and wet, although they didn't care as they galloped gaily through it, sending sprays of dirty water over the two women. Miranda picked up the elderly two and carried them through the worst patches.

"What are their names?" Anna asked, pondering on the wisdom of getting a small dog, although it wouldn't be much protection from rapists and the like but then she didn't quite see herself as the owner of a Rottweiler or Alsatian.

"Pongo and Purdy," announced Miranda.

"What! You are joking?"

"Not at all."

"But they don't like remotely like Dalmatians ... they're ... they're." Anna gave up. She hadn't a clue.

"Shih Tzu's," remarked Miranda helpfully.

"Pardon?" said Anna, wondering if there was something wrong with her hearing.

"Shih Tzu's," Miranda repeated. "Quite valuable, quite sweet and these two, in particular, even though they are elderly, are more than likely to bugger off if I let them off the lead."

"Really?" Anna looked down at the little dogs, plodding along quietly, neither looking as if they wanted to make a run for it.

"You'd be surprised what the little buggers can get up to ... they clear off into the woods and roll in dead and disgusting things
... and eat dead and disgusting things ...and completely ignore any attempt on my part to get them back to me ... and their delightful owner would string me up from the nearest lamp post if I lost her little darlings. She idolises and spoils them rotten ... lucky little devils," she said fondly, gazing down at two little dogs. She bent down to pat them and they wagged their tails in acknowledgement.

"Where could I get one?" Anna asked, wondering what sort she would like. A big one, a little one, a mongrel, a pedigree, a male or female. What a difficult decision to make. "Look in the papers I suppose."

"A Shih Tzu?"

"Oh no," Anna said quickly. Pongo and Purdy were sweet but the breed somehow didn't appeal to her. "Something a little bigger ... I don't know ... a Spaniel perhaps." She had often admired them from afar. They seemed such happy, lively little dogs.

"Um. Spaniels are gorgeous but so many people don't realise how much exercise and stimulation they need. It drives me crazy when I see people in the park keeping them on the lead ... then they wonder why they are a damned nuisance and quite often turn snappy because they are so frustrated. If you get one, you will have to train it properly … mind that goes for any dog … but Spaniels are really intelligent … after all, it is a working breed … and learn very, very quickly. Then you can have tremendous fun with them … but you will have to be prepared to walk for miles and miles and miles," she laughed. "However, I suggest, if you are serious about getting a dog, you visit a rescue centre. They're overflowing and are desperate for good people to take their dogs, who very often have had a dreadful start and need kind and caring people to give them a forever home."

"I don't think I'd like to go there," Anna remarked doubtfully. "Don't they put them down after a few days? I'd get so upset and want to bring them all home."

"Not at the Dogs Trust or Happylands … they keep healthy animals until they can rehome them."

They plodded on, Anna's head buzzing with the thought of having a dog of her own. The lakeside meandered in and out in gentle curves and it was on one of the bends that they encountered Harry and his four black Great Danes.

"Don't worry. It's only Heathcliffe … accompanied by the Hounds of the Baskervilles," Miranda giggled.

Anna smiled nervously. The description was so apt. The man was tall, dark, wearing a wax coat and high boots and carried a thick nobbled stick. With the dark cloudy sky behind him, he looked like the devil incarnate as he approached, the hounds milling at his side.

With trepidation, Anna watched as Roger and his mates tore up to the hounds and said hello. If a fight ensued, the bigger dogs would rip the others to pieces. Anna trembled for Pongo and Purdy and looked worriedly at Miranda, who was totally relaxed and smiling at Heathcliffe, who smiled back and then did the same to Anna. She felt too nervous to respond.

"Morning, Harry," said Miranda.

"Morning," he said gruffly.

"Anna this is Harry … Harry, Anna."

Harry and Anna shook hands, two of his enormous dogs pushing their noses in to lick her fingers. They were beautiful, sleek creatures with large heads and huge brown eyes. Magnificent but forbidding. She was reluctant to pat them even though they seemed gentle enough but as they gazed up at her with their soft, brown eyes, she began to relax.

Miranda's dogs had said their hello and skipped off into the woods above. Harry's group now stood quietly by his side. Nothing awful had happened. No growling and no baring of teeth.

"Anna's pondering on the wisdom of getting herself a dog," Miranda commented.

"Better company than humans any day," said Harry approvingly. "They don't talk back … and their love is unconditional … and that's definitely the best sort."

He'd been hurt. The pain in his eyes gave him away. Anna felt a pang of sympathy.

"Sorry, I can't stop to chat this morning, Harry," Miranda was saying. "I must get this lot home. See you tomorrow, maybe."

Harry nodded and wandered off in the opposite direction, his four dogs trotting obediently behind.

"Nice man … Harry … rescued those from a crazy woman," Miranda said. "Silly cow bought them as puppies. Goodness knows what she thought she was doing but it's the old, old story. She didn't attempt to train or exercise them, they grew too big, weed and messed everywhere and chewed her house to bits so she put them out into her shed where they barked and howled all day and annoyed the neighbours. Harry heard about it, marched around there, pretended he was from a Dog Welfare Association and demanded the woman hand them over. He took them home, fed them, trained them and walks miles with them every day … now look at them, happy and content. Wonderful man. Simply wonderful. I have a lot of time for Harry."

"Do I detect a note of interest there," Anna teased.

"Goodness, no. Perish the thought," Miranda exclaimed. "I might like Harry very much but after the Beastly Bastard, no man is going to curry favour with me again. I'm like Harry … I prefer the company of dogs … you know where you are with them."

They had walked full circle of the lake and were back where they had met. They turned up the path through the woods to the car park. Anna felt a lot safer with Miranda and the dogs than she had earlier.

A few more cars had joined theirs. "That's Harry's," said Miranda, pointing to a smart new Land Rover, "and that neat little Fiat is Mrs Smedley's. Thank goodness we didn't bump into her.
I can't stand the woman. All prissiness and 'don't let your dog touch mine' type. I've no time for her. No time at all."

She moved towards her battered Volvo, opened it up and the bigger dogs leapt in, all knowing exactly where they had to sit; Roger, Polly and Sammy in the rear, Nellie on the back seat. Miranda picked up Pongo and Purdy and plonked them down with Nellie, shut them in and turned to Anna.

"Thanks for your company this morning. I've enjoyed it."

"Thanks for yours," Anna replied, meaning every word.
Miranda had no idea how much better she had made her feel … and given her other things to think about.

Miranda reached into the glove compartment of her car and brought out a business card and handed it to Anna. "Here's my phone number … give me a ring if you want a chat … or need some doggy advice … and don't sit at home and brood. Feel welcome to join me, with or without a dog, as often as you please."

Anna glanced at the card and smiled at the picture of a woman, resembling Miranda, walking four dogs on a lead with the name of her business, Four Paws, in big letters at the top. A phone number and address, along with a list of services Four Paws provided, was printed on the reverse.

"Thanks. I will," Anna said, waving as Miranda jumped into the Volvo, turned it around and headed towards the main road.

Anna got into her car, looked at her mud-covered loafers, splattered trousers and her filthy jacket where Nellie had pushed her nose into the pocket. She looked at herself in the rear-view mirror. Her cheeks were rosy and her eyes didn't look as dull as they had earlier. She certainly felt better than she had a couple of hours ago and her tummy was rumbling. Goodness, was she actually feeling a bit peckish?

CHAPTER 3

Anna opened her eyes at 6.00 a.m. the next morning, amazed to have slept the whole night through, not having done so since Gerald died. Normally she tossed and turned for hours, resulting in at least a couple of trips to the kitchen to make tea and then to the loo. All this between long bouts of weeping.

But not last night. She had dropped off as soon as her head touched the pillow and was delighted to feel refreshed and clearheaded now she was awake. No doubt, she surmised, the walk in the fresh air the day before did her a lot of good.

She remained in bed for a little longer. Normally she wanted to get out straight away, unable to get used to having it all to herself, often putting a hand out to touch Gerald and then finding he wasn't there, when the awful deep grief would hit her again. She had thought about moving into one of the guest rooms permanently but although she had tried it for one night, she hadn't slept any better and missed the spaciousness of their king size bed.

Gerald's things were still in their bedroom too. She hadn't been able to get rid of them. His clothes were still in the wardrobe, his toiletries in the bathroom, his watch and wallet were on his bedside table, along with the war book he had been reading before he went into hospital ... and died.

This morning, however, instead of weeping for the husband she missed so badly, she lay listening to the rain slashing against the window and thought about Miranda. She would get a real soaking today if this kept up and the mud would be even worse.

She thought about Miranda's offer for her to join her. Had she meant it or was she just being polite? No, Miranda was open and honest and if she hadn't wanted to meet again, wouldn't have mentioned it ... or handed over her business card with all her details.

Her thoughts turned to the other people she had met on the walk yesterday. Fart Features ... oh, Miranda was terrible, calling the poor man that. Anna wondered what his real name was. Then there was Harry ... what a tremendously kind person he was to have rescued all those big dogs. They must be eating him out of house and home. That made her think again about having her own dog. She rather liked the idea, having a furry companion to cuddle up to, to go out with every day, to have a living creature to care for and to care for her … but she needed to think about it a little longer. She didn't want to jump in on impulse and make the wrong decision … for her or the dog.

She got out of bed, showered, did some housework, wrote a couple of letters and looked at the clock. 10.15 a.m. Miranda would be at the park around 11.00 a.m. and it took half an hour to drive to Peesdown. She dashed around the house looking for her wellies. Loafers would certainly not do today, especially as it had taken nearly half an hour to clean them yesterday. She didn't want a repeat of that.

She found the wellies, remembering the last time they were worn, nearly a year ago, when Gerald had helped her clear up the leaves in the garden during the autumn. She looked out of the window. She had neglected the normally well-tended lawn and flowerbeds shamefully since Gerald had died. She really would have to pull herself together and do something about it very soon, before the winter arrived.

She pulled on the wellies and a waterproof jacket and for good measure, pushed several small plastic bags into her pocket … just in case Miranda forgot the poo bags again.

Miranda's empty Volvo was in the car park, as was Harry's Landrover and two other cars without occupants. Hoping one didn't belong to a lurking rapist, Anna hurried through the trees, hoping Miranda wasn't too far ahead. She wasn't. She was by the collapsed bench in deep discussion with Fart Features whose pockets Nellie was doing her best to delve into.

"Will you get away!" yelled Fart Features angrily, flapping his arms about in a state of panic, which did nothing to dissuade Nellie from her mission. To her, it was a splendid game and she was determined to win. She darted back and forth, barking loudly and then charged at her quarry, front paws landing smack on the top of his legs, leaving two beautifully muddy pawprints on his nice smart trousers.

"Bloody dog! Bloody, bloody dog!" Fart Features shouted. "It should be put down. It's out of control."

Miranda, trying desperately not to laugh, was attempting to grab Nellie and put her on the lead. She saw Anna approach and her eyes widened with pleasure.

"I'm so sorry ... I don't know what's come over her," she said to Fart Features, who was angrily rubbing the dirty patches on his trousers with his handkerchief and making them worse. "Hello, Anna," she added, looking up at her new acquaintance. "Glad you could make it today ... perhaps you could shed some light on what we've been discussing ... the bench."

She prodded the rotten wood on the ground with her foot. "It seems it's been vandalised ... not long after we were in the vicinity yesterday ... but we didn't see anyone doing anything, did we?"

Her face was expressionless and Anna tried hard to keep hers the same as she shook her head, unable to trust herself to speak.

"Kids, I expect," spat Fart Features. "Bloody kids. They're always doing it. No respect these days. Bring back National Service, that's what I say ... sort the little buggers out in no time that would," he muttered darkly, staring with dismay at his filthy trousers and his white handkerchief which was now an interesting shade of brown. He pulled a face and pushed it back into his pocket.

"Well," Miranda said, "it's nice chatting but I really must get on. I do hope you find the culprit. A good flogging wouldn't come amiss," she added as she and Anna marched away, leaving Fart Features studying the pile of wood with venom in his eyes.

They hurried along the path, not daring to look at each other until out of earshot of the park keeper. Then they collapsed into a fit of giggles.

"Oh God," blasphemed Miranda, gasping for breath. "You should have heard him going on and on and on. You'd think it was the crime of the century and the damned thing was rotten anyway."

"Your face," Anna laughed. "You were so dead-pan ... how on earth did you manage it?"

"Years of practice with the Beastly Bastard."

They wiped the tears of laughter from their eyes and continued at a slower pace along the path circling the lake. Sammy, Roger, Polly and Nellie went off to play chase through the trees while Pongo and Purdy plodded along on their extension leads. Anna bent down to pat them and they smiled at her with their eyes.

"I'm glad you decided to join us again," Miranda said. "I wasn't sure if you would."

"I'm glad you're glad," Anna smiled. "The walk with you did me the power of good yesterday. I felt so much better when I woke up this morning ... I think I shall have to make this a regular occurrence."

"Well, you know what they say. Walking releases happy endorphins ... and I must admit, even after all the hassle with the Beastly Bastard, I've never felt too down for too long."

The rain had stopped and the sun was coming out as they reached the bench where Anna had broken down the day before.

"Should we?" enquired Miranda.

Anna nodded and they sat down and gazed out over the lake. Further along, swans, coots, moorhens and ducks swam over to an elderly couple who were throwing bread towards the hungry birds.

"Hope Nellie doesn't notice or she'll be over there in a flash and they'll never get rid of her," groaned Miranda.

Luckily, Nellie was otherwise engaged, sniffing madly around a nearby bin, into which something obviously nice and tasty had been thrown. She sat down and stared at the receptacle, obviously pondering on how she was going to get whatever it was out of there and into her mouth.

Miranda laughed. "It must be something very delicious ... look ... she's drooling."

Anna grinned. The expression on Nellie's face was a picture of massive concentration but unless she physically leapt into the bin, she had no hope of retrieving what she desired.

"Had any more thoughts about having a dog?" asked Miranda, turning to Anna.

"I'd love one ... and I do have time for one. Heavens knows, I have nothing else to occupy my time as I've given up my job."

She told Miranda about the builders' merchants and how she had packed it in. "I didn't enjoy it anyway but I'm not qualified to do anything apart from being a secretary. There's no urgency in having to find work, financially that is, but I can't sit around forever. I need some kind of occupation to get me out of the house … even if it's only part-time … which would mean I could have a dog as it wouldn't be left for long."

"How about a shop then? You said it was a dream … it could be a reality … then you could have your dog with you all day … keep it in the back … shut the shop at lunchtime and take it for a walk."

Anna glanced at Miranda with surprise, imagining herself behind a counter, chatting happily to customers, dispensing … dispensing what?

"I don't know what to sell."

"Oh, I don't know … something different perhaps. Something not many people do … how about …. how about," Miranda was biting her lip and looking up into the sky as if for inspiration, "I know … how about a pet shop which doesn't sell animals?"

Anna thought about it. "Well, yes … I wouldn't want to sell animals anyway. I hate to see them in pet shops … not that I go in many but I did have to once for a friend when she was too ill to go out and needed some chews for her dog. I was appalled to see rabbits and kittens for sale."

"Exactly … there are a huge number of people who think the same thing but have to go in the places to get what they need. If you had a pet shop without the animals, I bet that would be a massive draw and you'd get loads of happy customers. You'd be so busy you might not have time to walk your dog," Miranda continued with a grin, "So I can do it for you."

Anna laughed. "Touting for business already?"

"Worth a try," Miranda giggled, looking at her watch and realising it was time to move on.

They stood up and continued along the lakeside path, Anna's thoughts in a whirl. Yesterday at this time she had been in the depths of despair, now she had a new friend, was contemplating getting a dog and maybe, just maybe, a shop!

"If you don't mind, we'll do a slight detour … up here … through the trees," Miranda whispered, looking anxiously at an old lady holding a bottle green brolly, mincing along the path towards them. A small white poodle in a pretty pink coat trotted neatly at her side. "It's Mrs Smedley," Miranda hissed.

"Ah," Anna acknowledged, remembering the conversation with Fart Features the day before. She followed Miranda and her gang of undesirables, as far as Mrs Smedley was concerned, up another path leading away from the lake. Deep in conversation, they were both startled a few moments later by a squeal of horror emanating from the lakeside path they had just left. Miranda whirled around, counting her charges quickly.

"Oh, blast!" she exclaimed. "Sammy's missing ... I bet the little bugger's sneaked back to annoy the Smedley woman."

Miranda streaked down the hill, Pongo and Purdy having no choice but to follow her in hot pursuit. Roger, Polly and Nellie dashed behind. Anna followed at a slightly more sedate pace.

Mrs Smedley, an older lady in her early seventies, dressed in a cream anorak, a black skirt and wellingtons was leaning by a tree, holding tightly to her brolly, her carefully made-up face a mask of fury. Her poodle was trembling by her side, its coat a sodden mess. The poor animal looked dazed and bedraggled. Sammy barked madly at the pair but on Miranda's furious yell, decided it was better to scarper and disappeared rapidly into the bushes.

Roger, Polly and Nellie decided to join him. They didn't like it when Miranda showed her authority as leader of their pack.

"Your dogs are a menace, my girl," screamed Mrs Smedley, eyeing up Pongo and Purdy, standing at Miranda's side, wondering what all the fuss was about. "They're nothing short of total hooligans."

"Whatever happened, Mrs Smedley?" asked Miranda, anxiously biting her lip.

Mrs Smedley heaved herself upright, dusted down her clothes and pointed to her poodle.

"Just look what that horrid dog did to my little Precious ... it charged straight at him and tipped him into the lake ... he hates the water ... he can't swim ... he could have drowned ... . and if he catches a cold, I'll expect you to pay the veterinary bills."

"I'm so sorry, Mrs Smedley," grovelled Miranda. "Sammy's a very naughty dog and when I catch up with him, I'll give him a good talking to ... and it goes without saying that I'll pay for any vet bills."

"Hum!" snorted Mrs Smedley. "I'm taking Precious home and as soon as I see the park keeper, I'm reporting you … yet again. In my opinion, you and your dogs should be banned from all the parks in Leeds, permanently!"

"I don't think the Council would ban us just because one of my dogs pushed yours into the lake, Mrs Smedley."

"Maybe not, Miss, but just remember Peesdown Park doesn't belong to the Council, does it? I could easily write to the owners and ask them to ban you from here, at least."

With that as her parting shot, Mrs Smedley turned and marched back the way she had come, a dejected looking 'Precious' following behind.

"Oh, Lord … that's torn it," moaned Miranda. "The damned woman used to be a hospital matron … she must have been a tyrant to work for … and now she wants to bring her disciplinary procedures to the damned park. If she does tell the owners, I'm not quite sure what they will say. Hopefully, they won't take any notice as I do like walking in Peesdown … it's more convenient for me than the other parks and saves so much petrol and time coming here."

"Who does the park belong to," Anna asked curiously. "I thought all the parks in Leeds belonged to the Council."

"No, not this one. The Pee family used to own it … lived in a big house in the centre of the park since the seventeenth or eighteenth century, I'm not sure which. There was a terrible fire early in the nineteenth century, in the middle of the night, and all the family were wiped out and the place burnt beyond repair. The wider family, who live in Ireland, demolished what was left and decided to open the rest of the place for the residents of Leeds to enjoy. They pay for the upkeep and Fart Features."

"How very sad, the whole family being wiped out … how many were there?"

"Oh, the parents, five children, a nanny and some other servants, I believe."

"Gosh, how awful."

"Yes … did you notice the huge flower garden just on your right off the path as you walked down to the lake?"

Anna nodded. She had noticed it and thought how lovely it looked.

"Well, that's where the house used to be. It's supposed to be haunted at night. Children can be heard playing apparently. I don't know how true it is. I've no intentions of coming to find out."

"No, I don't think I shall either," shuddered Anna.

Their conversation turned lighter again as they headed back to the car park, not noticing an elderly man with a walking stick and brolly standing in the trees watching them.

"Will I see you tomorrow?" asked Miranda, opening the boot and back doors of her Volvo, allowing the bigger dogs to jump in and picking up Pongo and Purdy to place them with Nellie on the back seat.

Anna smiled. "Yes. I think you probably will."

"Good ... enjoy the rest of your day then," Miranda waved as she jumped into her car and headed out of the car park, leaving Anna alone as Harry's Landrover had disappeared, as had the other two cars which had been there when she arrived. Anna sat in her car, wound down the window and listened. The rain had stopped half an hour ago and the birds were singing in the trees as watery sunshine began to spread over the park. It was so calming here ... she was beginning to fall in love with it ... the peace ... the birdsong ... the gentle breeze through the trees ... the smell of damp earth. It was all having a wonderful effect on her. She could feel her spirits lifting. Gerald was still with her and always would be but there was just a flicker of hope in her soul now, a wish to see what she could achieve on her own. She drove out of the car park with a smile on her face.

* * *

William was disappointed ... again. He had so hoped to spend some time with Miranda today. That damned woman she had started talking to yesterday was becoming a bloody nuisance. He hoped they weren't going to start walking together every day but then the woman hadn't got a dog so could have just been a casual visitor. He'd certainly not seen her before.

He might as well go home. Miranda would go to Golden Acre Park with her second pack of dogs. He knew her routine as she had told him on one of their chats where she went and on what days. He had followed her there once, minus his disguise in case she noticed him but she wouldn't be there for at least another couple of hours, which wouldn't be convenient for him. The Vicar of St. Edmunds, the pretty little church at the far end of Miller Lane, where William attended morning service every Sunday, had invited him and some other parishioners to afternoon tea to discuss arrangements for the Christmas bazaar, which William had said he would help with. Speaking to Miranda would have to wait until tomorrow. Drat!

He looked at his watch. He had a couple of hours before he had to walk down to the Vicarage. He went home, changed his damp clothes, made a hot coffee, toasted two slices of bread, buttered them well and piled on his favourite thick marmalade.

He took his snack through to the lounge and sat down on the sofa with his scrapbook to look at all his achievements over the past few years since his parents had died and he was let loose to do as he liked on the world … and the women … oh those women. He licked his lips as he turned the pages. Pictures of them before they died, vibrant young things, laughing as they joked with their friends on a night out, laying on the beach showing off their bodies in gay abandon or just walking in the parks. He had taken pictures of all those he fancied without them knowing. They had been so busy doing what they were doing, they hadn't noticed.

He had chosen those he attacked carefully, spending weeks stalking them. He had followed them back to their homes, making sure they didn't have husbands, partners, children or parents. He checked there were no other lights on in their houses once they went to bed, no other cars in the drives, no dogs, no anything. Just them. All alone. Then he had pounced.

* * *

Anna had a lot to think about following her walk at the park. She still felt desperately sad and depressed about losing Gerald but there was just a flicker, just a small glimmer of hope following her talk with Miranda. Something had stirred within her, a tiny feeling of excitement at the possibility of totally

29

changing her life by opening a shop and having a new companion if she visited the local sanctuaries in search of a dog.

She, like William, changed her clothes and made coffee and then, with little hope of finding anything, she idly picked up the local advertising rag which she rarely glanced at, most copies usually ending up in the recycling bin unread, and turned to the businesses for sale page. There were newsagents, sweet shops and a hairdresser in Leeds but right at the bottom, was something that did perk her interest. 'Retail outlet for sale in Peesdown. Needs attention. Further details from Mr J. Cross'. There was also a telephone number.

Anna stared into the distance. Peesdown … where she had been for the past two days. She tried to visualise the shops she drove by to get to the park but couldn't remember seeing an empty one for sale. She glanced outside. The sun was becoming stronger and it was turning into a pleasant afternoon. Should she go back to Peesdown and have a walk around? Her hand hovered over the telephone. Should she ring this Mr Cross first? The tiny pinprick of excitement in her tummy began to grow. She looked at the card Miranda had given her. Should she call her and ask her to come with her when she had finished walking the dogs? No, it was a bit previous. She should go and have a look first and see if she could find it. Peesdown wasn't that big and she needed a few things anyway. She could pop into the greengrocers and the butchers while she was out. She finished her coffee, grabbed her mac and handbag and left the house.

She drove around the ring road and found a space in the car park at the shopping centre on Peesdown High Street. She locked the car and made her way to the row of shops and looked up and down the street, trying to see the one for sale. There was a good selection of retail outlets; a small Tesco, a butcher, greengrocer and hairdresser, along with a post office, library, a small casino, a selection of charity shops, a bank, a chemist, a doctor and a vet. Peesdown was certainly well catered for.

Then Anna saw it, further along on the opposite side of the High Street in the direction of the park. An empty shop with a 'for sale' sign in the boarded-up window. She strolled towards it, remaining on her side of the road so she could get a better view, then stood and studied it. It was a good size with a central door and large windows on either side and two floors above with sash windows. She crossed the road and walked around the corner into Baker Lane. There was a six-foot wall circling the outside of what appeared to be a large garden at the rear of the shop. No doubt the previous owners had lived there … maybe they still did. Curtains were hanging in the windows on the upper floors.

She walked back to the front and studied it. It needed a new door but the windows appeared okay and the brickwork looked in good nick, as did the roof. Frustratingly, she couldn't see inside because of the boarded-up windows and all of a sudden there was nothing she wanted more than to find out exactly what the building contained and if it were feasible for her to invest in it and maybe, just maybe open the shop she had always fancied having.

She had brought the newspaper advert with her. She fiddled in her handbag and pulled it out, along with her mobile phone. With a beating heart, she rang the number for Mr Cross. It rang repeatedly and for a second she thought there would be no answer but suddenly the dialling tone stopped.

"Cross!" came a sharp retort.

"Oh," said Anna, taken aback. "Mr Cross," she said, taking a deep breath. She had started so she had to finish. "My name is Anna Stapleton. I've seen your advert … for the shop … and I was wondering … would it be possible to have a look around please."

"Oh, right. Yes, yes, of course. When would you like to view it?" His answer was a little softer.

"Well, actually, I'm standing right outside now … I don't suppose …"

"You suppose correctly. I'm only down the road, at the post office. I'll be with you in two ticks."

The phone went dead, leaving Anna holding it and wondering what on earth she was letting herself in for. She should have asked Miranda to come with her. She shouldn't be going into a boarded- up shop with a strange man. It was crazy. Her imagination began to run riot and for a second she nearly made a dash back to her car but then he was there. Mr Cross. She saw him hurrying up the road towards her. A nice-looking man, around her age, dressed casually in jeans and a dark green jacket, which complemented his blonde hair. His face was square and rugged looking and his smile was wide as he approached her.

"Anna … I'm so sorry … I must have sounded so rude on the phone. I was having a tussle with the post office assistant who was having difficulty understanding what I wanted. I'm not the most patient of people and she was certainly testing mine. Now," he said, taking a bunch of keys out of his jacket pocket, "let me show you around. The premises were my father's. He has had a shoe shop here for around 20 years but he died last year and left it all to me and my sister, Daphne. I'm in the Army and away a lot and Daphne produced twins not long ago and has been far too busy to concern herself with selling the shop. I'm home on leave, so thought I better get things sorted."

He opened the door and gestured for Anna to step inside.

Reassured by his manner, she did so. He snapped on a switch by the door and the whole floor was flooded with light. It was a big, empty area, needing a lick of paint to brighten it up and fixtures and fittings installed but Anna could certainly see herself here, dispensing items to her customers. She smiled.

"What do you intend selling?" asked Mr Cross, "and please call me Jeremy. Mr Cross or Major Cross sounds so damned formal."

"Major? You've done well … "

"Yes. It's my life. Can't imagine doing anything else. But you didn't answer my question."

"Oh … well, to be honest, I'm not sure. I've always wanted to own a shop you see but it wasn't something my husband was interested in … but he died a few months ago … and … well, I have to get on with my life and someone suggested I give it a go … and then I saw your advertisement."

"I see. But you must have some idea … of what you would like to sell."

"A pet shop," Anna said, realising there wasn't one in the area. "I think I would like a pet shop … one that doesn't sell animals," she continued, remembering the earlier conversation with Miranda.

"That's a splendid idea," Jeremy agreed. "I loathe those that sell pets. People buy them on a whim and then very often get bored and neglect them. I've entered one or two in the past and

32

walked out again without buying anything when I've seen kittens or rabbits on display. It makes me angry, especially when there are so many who desperately need a good home and can be found at rescue centres and the like."

"Yes … yes, that's what I think … and so does Miranda … my friend who suggested I run a pet shop."

"Sensible girl, your friend. Now … would you like to see the rest of the place? There are a few areas of interest at the back." He walked towards a door facing them, a little to the left. "This is a stock room," he said. It was only half the size of the main shop area but would be perfectly adequate for storage.

"And there is a toilet, here, just before the stairs," Jeremy continued, heading back into the shop and then turning immediately left into what could only be described as a hall, with a lovely stained glass window sporting two red roses and green leaves in what looked to be a relatively new UPVC back door.

"And this," he said, throwing open a door on their right, "could be delightful. Dad used it mainly as a place to dump all his junk I'm afraid. Goodness knows why as it could be fabulous with the right care and attention. He stored his gardening tools and other bits and pieces in the corner and he had an old sofa and table near the window. He spent his breaks in here to save going upstairs.
There's a kitchen through there," he pointed to a door at the far end.

"Oh, wow," breathed Anna. The room was, as Jeremy said, absolutely delightful, with big windows overlooking the lovely garden, which consisted of an enormous square lawn with an ancient apple tree in the centre, its leaves beginning to turn a lovely lime green, and flower beds along all three sides of the sixfoot wall she had seen from Baker Lane, which were covered with clematis and honeysuckle. The wall was the boundary with the outside area of the house at the far end and the adjoining shop to the left,

"Gosh. This is really lovely. I can see why your father wanted to sit in here, looking out at that. I should too," she smiled.

"It's a bit noisy out there during the day with people and cars up and down Baker Lane but in the evenings, it's relatively peaceful."

Anna peered into the kitchen. It was a decent sized room and a lot could be done with it apart from filling a kettle for a cup of tea.

"Upstairs there's another stock room and an office on the first floor and the accommodation is on the second," Jeremy said helpfully.

Anna loved it all. The whole place had a nice homely feel, even though all the furniture and stock had been removed. The first floor contained two large rooms, running the full length of the first floor, both overlooking the high street at the front and the garden at the back.

"A gardener comes in the summer," Jeremy remarked as Anna peered out of the window of what had once been the office and would certainly be hers with all the light from each end and a splendid view of the garden. "Twice a month he mows the lawn and keeps the rest of it tidy. My father used to potter around out there in the evenings. He kept it immaculate," he added wistfully.

"Did he live here?" Anna asked as they mounted the stairs to the top floor.

"After my mother died, yes. They used to have a lovely house … it was where my sister and I grew up … but he sold it. He couldn't bear to live there without Mother … and to be fair it was far too big for him on his own. So, he moved in here. It seemed the sensible thing to do and saved him travelling and he did love the garden … and he made lots of friends locally … so he was relatively happy."

"Good. I'm glad," replied Anna, knowing how ghastly life could be without the most special person in one's life. She had toyed with the idea of selling her home too but hadn't garnered the energy to do it and anyway, she wasn't certain where she wanted to go.

The accommodation on the top floor was simple and cosy. As they reached the top of the stairs, Jeremy opened the door on their right.

"This is the bedroom, which I'm afraid only has a view of the street below. The bathroom is through there, at the back," he pointed to a door.

Anna had a quick look. The empty room was spacious and could easily accommodate a big bed and other necessary bedroom furniture. The bathroom contained a reasonably new white suite and turquoise and white tiles on the walls.

"And this," Jeremy continued, "is the lounge and kitchen," opening a door exactly opposite the bedroom.

Anna stepped into the well-proportioned open plan kitchen and lounge, again, like the first floor, with views over the street and the garden.

"It's really pleasant in here in the morning and evening as the sun comes up in the east at the front and goes down in the west at the back. It does tend to get a little chilly during the day but as Father was always occupied in the shop at that time, it didn't matter," commented Jeremy.

"It has quite a nice view, considering it's in the middle of town," Anna remarked, staring out over the lawn and flower beds below at the semi-detached houses with their neat gardens along Baker Lane.

Jeremy leaned against the door frame and smiled. "I know. If I was interested in running a shop, I might well have moved in myself. It would be perfect for me."

"Where do you stay when you come back to Leeds ... now the family home has been sold?" Anna was curious. She liked Jeremy. She didn't feel at all uneasy with him. He was so natural with no airs or graces and hadn't given her cause for concern at all in the short time they had spent in the building. She had begun to relax and was enjoying herself.

"With Daphne ... she lives in Headingley ... handy for the cricket," he grinned. "She's been married for years, is a successful barrister who had no intentions of ever having children and then became pregnant and has landed herself with twins, whom she adores. She, and her husband, Nigel, who is also a barrister, own a five bedroomed house and she always keeps a room there for me when I need it. It's only a couple of times a year, if that, so
I'm not too much of a bother."

Somehow Anna couldn't envisage him being any bother at all. He was far too nice and being in the Army was sure to be neat and tidy and more than capable of looking after himself.

"So, what do you think of the place then? Are you interested?" he asked.

"To be honest, I don't know. This has all been so sudden. I need a little time to think about it … if that's okay with you?"

He nodded. "That's fine. I realise it's a big decision and there's no hurry."

"Would it … would it be okay to bring my friend … Miranda … for a second viewing. I would value her opinion?"

"Yes, of course. You have my number. Just give me a ring and I'll pop over again and let you both in. I'll leave you to it too so you can chat without feeling intimidated by my presence."

"That's very kind," Anna smiled.

He smiled back, his grey eyes twinkling merrily. "Oh yes. That's me. Very kind."

* * *

Anna drove home, her mind in a whirl. What a day it had been, waking up that morning with no idea a second conversation with Miranda would result in scuttling off to look at a shop!

For the first time in a long while she felt ravenous and wanted to eat a proper meal. She had existed on snacks and fruit since Gerald died, and often not even bothering with them. As a consequence, she had lost quite a bit of weight and all her clothes hung on her. Glancing in the rear-view mirror, she realised her face was looking gaunt too.

She was wondering what she could rustle up from the few items in her freezer when she passed the local fish and chip shop, situated in the street before the turning into her cul-de-sac. The delicious aroma hit her and her stomach flipped over. Funnily enough, the smell had made her feel nauseous over the last few months but now she knew she could enjoy a portion. She stopped the car, grabbed her purse out of her handbag and joined the queue of people in the shop, all chatting and laughing with Donna, the owner, a jolly tubby woman in her sixties who had owned the shop for as long as Anna could remember. When Gerald was alive, he and Anna had bought fish and chips at least once a week from Donna's Plaice and became good friends with

Donna and her husband, Terry, often spending an evening at the local Conservative Club together. However, Donna had lost Terry three years ago. Anna and Gerald had done their best to look after her and be there for her and when Gerald died, knowing exactly how Anna felt, Donna had reciprocated, often popping round to see if Anna was okay, bringing flowers, books and in the early days, keeping her company between shifts in the shop.

Donna saw Anna in the queue and smiled warmly.

"It's good to see you, gal. Feeling hungry?"

Anna nodded. "Starving, for once … cod and chips, please, Donna."

"Good. Well, get that down you," Donna said, wrapping up the meal in a sheet of newspaper and handing it to Anna. "You'll feel a whole lot better … I'll pop over tomorrow if you're not doing anything … for a chat and a cup of your Yorkshire tea."

Anna grinned. "That would be lovely … and I might have something to tell you too."

"Oh, what's that, then? Don't keep me in suspense," Donna said, leaving her assistant to deal with the queue of people and walking outside with Anna.

"Well, it's … well, I might be buying a shop," Anna said excitedly, clutching onto the wrapped-up fish and chips, the aroma making her belly rumble and her taste buds water.

"Oh, Anna. That's a great idea. You need to get your teeth into something and if you need any help or advice, you know where to come. Where is it and what will you sell?"

"I've only just been to see it … and I'm hoping to go back tomorrow for a second viewing. It's in Peesdown and I think … I think it will become a pet shop."

"Oh. Well, that will keep you busy my dear. Good luck with it all and I can't wait to hear all about it. Oh damn," she added, seeing her assistant waving frantically, "I shall have to go. I'll ring you tomorrow to see if you're in before I pop over and hear more about it. The best of luck, Anna. You deserve it."

* * *

William strolled back to his home from the Vicarage later than he had thought he would. The meeting at the lovely old rambling Georgian house next to the pretty little thirteenth century church hadn't started on time as two people were late turning up, breathlessly explaining that they had been held up in traffic due to an accident on the ring road. Then, when the meeting did get under way, the Vicar had to leave the room to answer a phone call from a distressed parishioner who had recently lost her husband and needed a visit later that evening.

Finally, when everyone had settled on the tatty but exceedingly comfortable sofas and chairs in the Vicar's lounge, the five elderly ladies and two other gentlemen, along with the Vicar and his lovely young wife, Samantha, began a lengthy discussion on the Christmas festivities, mainly the bazaar which they hoped would raise a good deal of money for Happylands, the local animal sanctuary.

"I thought it would be nice to choose a slightly different charity this year," said the Vicar. "After all, animals are God's creatures
too and deserve as much help as we can give them."

As everyone present, apart from William, were pet owners, noone raised any objections so they moved on to discussing what stalls they would have, who was going to play Father Christmas, what refreshments they would offer, who was going to decorate the church hall, who was going to be in charge of the raffle. The list went on and on and William began to think it would never end, even though he was enjoying the cups of tea and fancy cakes Samantha provided.

"Would you mind being in charge of the raffle, William?" the Vicar asked.

William didn't mind at all. "I should be delighted … absolutely anything I can do to help," he answered with a smile.

"Do have another slice of chocolate cake," insisted Samantha, liking this nice old gentleman who had recently joined their congregation.

"Thank you … I will," he said, smiling back at her, thinking how lucky the Vicar was to have found such a pretty young woman for a wife. Samantha was petite and slim with long blonde hair tucked up into a bun. She didn't wear any make-up but then she didn't need to. Her skin was flawless and her bright blue eyes, her best feature, sparkled at everyone she turned them on. She was well liked in Peesdown, always keen to stop and chat, especially in the park when she was walking the two little mongrels her and her husband had taken in from Happylands. It was rare the Vicar was seen out with them as he was always so busy.

The afternoon wore on. Arrangements for the bazaar dealt with, the Vicar listed what else was being proposed for the festive period. There would be a local choir presenting Handel's Messiah two weeks before Christmas and he needed help to sell tickets and look after people on the evening. William volunteered. He would be there anyway as he thoroughly enjoyed listening to Handel and always attended a performance of The Messiah every year, just as he had with his parents before they died. Then there was the Christmas lunch for senior citizens which was always held in the church hall and needed volunteers for kitchen and waitressing duties and ferrying guests without transport back and forth to their homes. William said he was willing to assist with laying the tables and the washing up afterwards.

Finally, the Vicar listed the services he would be conducting, Samantha offered them a last cup of tea and they all chatted for another hour before leaving.

"How are you enjoying living in Peesdown," asked Samantha, who was sitting beside William.

"It's very nice … very nice indeed," he smiled.

"Where did you live before?"

"Um … oh, Liverpool … but I've been abroad for years."

"Oh, how lovely for you. Whereabouts?"

He hesitated for a second, not wanting anyone to know he had spent a considerable amount of time in Spain as well as other parts of Europe… he had left a few bodies behind and didn't want linking with any of them. "America … and Canada," he said quickly.

"So how did you end up in Peesdown," Samantha asked. "Do you have relatives here?"

He laughed. If he told her, she wouldn't believe him but he was going to anyway. "I circled my finger over a map of

England and it fell onto Peesdown so to Peesdown I have come."
She laughed. She didn't believe him.

"And no, no relatives," he added. "My parents … in Liverpool
… they died a few years ago."

"Oh, no. I am so sorry, William. How awful for you."

"Yes. It was … you see, they were murdered."

He grinned now, as he reached his home, pushed open the
gates, locked them with the chain and padlock and crunched over
the gravel to his front door. He loved telling people his parents
had been murdered … just to see their reaction. Samantha's
hadn't been any different. She had gasped and then touched his
arm and said how very sorry she was. He wasn't. He was glad.
They had driven him nuts and it was the best thing he had ever
done, despatching them and sending them to join the God they
had gone on and on about for all of his young life. They were
surely far happier with him than down here and he was far
happier without them.

He went into the kitchen, heated up a ready meal consisting
of cottage pie and a few vegetables that resembled carrots and
cauliflower, placed it on a tray with a mug of tea and took it
through to the lounge. He drew the curtains, turned on the light
and sat down on the sofa to eat his tea.

Telling Samantha about his parents, Katherine and Ronald
Brownlow, had brought back the memories of his childhood and
his teenage years. Being their only child, he had been spoilt and
received virtually anything he asked for … and he asked for a
lot. On every visit to the shops, he came home with new toys,
new clothes and lots of nice things to eat. As he grew older, he
had all the latest equipment in his spacious bedroom; new
televisions, computers, stereo systems, as soon as whatever he
desired was released to the general public. When he reached
seventeen years old, he had driving lessons and after he passed
his test, a new BMW, but once he was free to go where he
pleased, when he pleased, the trouble began.

William knew his parents adored him and would have done
anything for him but they didn't understand him and as a result
he frequently disappointed them. They were wealthy. They
owned a chain of restaurants across the north of England which
were doing well. They had worked hard to get where they were

and were keen for William to join them in the business, especially as they would be leaving it all to him in the event of their deaths. William had other ideas. He had no interest in catering, no interest in business, no interest in anything much ... apart from girls ... but for some reason, girls didn't like him.

He had also been aware his parents wondered if he was gay. He never took a girl home, never seemed to go on a date. Once he had the car, he went out most evenings but would never tell them where and what he was up to. He left them to wonder and worry.

Then, one night, as he and his father were relaxing in front of the television, his mother discovered he wasn't gay. Unbeknown to him, she had ventured into his bedroom in search of dirty crockery as so much seemed to disappear into his room and never made it back to the kitchen.

She entered the lounge, her eyes ablaze with fury. William had taken one look at what she had in her hand and froze. His well- thumbed magazine was one of the worst he possessed; pictures of unclad women in disgusting poses ... women together and then with men, doing it ... actually doing it ... in front of cameras for all the world to see. He certainly hadn't wanted his mother to see that.

She had shaken with rage and threw it at his father.

"Look at this!" she had hissed angrily. "This is what our precious son gets up to in his bedroom ... staring at this ... this obscene smut."

She had turned furiously on William. "I'm utterly disgusted with you. Your father and I have brought you up as a Christian ... we all attend church every Sunday ... we have tried hard to teach you right from wrong and now here you are, disrespecting women in the most appalling, deplorable way. I won't have you spending money on such vulgarity and I certainly don't want it in the house. I want your bedroom cleaned out thoroughly ... tonight ... and the whole lot burned. Make sure he does, Ronald. I have to go out
... I have a meeting of the Women's Institute to attend."

His father had picked up the magazine and began to leaf through it.

"Ronald!" William's mother had shrieked.

41

Ronald had shut the magazine quickly. "Yes, all right, dear. Leave it with me. You go and enjoy your meeting."

Katherine had left the house, banging the door behind her. His father had sighed and handed the magazine to William.

"You heard your mother," was all he said as he turned back to the television.

William removed all the offending content and pretended to set fire to it on a bonfire in the bottom of the garden. At least, it appeared he did, what actually went up in smoke were old newspapers. He wouldn't get rid of his precious stash of porn whatever they said.

When his parents had bought him his car, there wasn't room for it in their double garage so Ronald had another built, specifically for William. William had liked his garage. No-one ever went in there because there was no reason for them to so he could store things which he needed to keep secret. The day after his bonfire, when his parents were at work, he took all his magazines and pornographic films down to his garage and stashed them in a lockable cabinet he had bought at a car boot sale. He had kept the key on his keyring and never let it out of his sight.

His next sin was walking out of school. He had always hated it. The teachers hadn't warmed to him and the kids he had journeyed through his education with, kept their distance. He was a loner and didn't care. He hadn't wanted their company either ... at least not the boys. He had tried to engage some of the girls in conversation over the years but after many false starts, they soon backed off and any hope of a relationship, let alone a sexual one, receded quickly. He was better off with his magazines and films.

Those women were always there for him ... they wanted him to ogle them, pretend they were in his bed, doing things to him, allowing him to do things to them. His parents simply had no idea how important these women were to him.

He walked out of school two months after his seventeenth birthday. No-one could stop him. He was of age and that was that. His parents were aghast, having hoped he would achieve good results in his A levels, attend university and then join them in the business.

"You're not going to lounge around here all day," Katherine had warned. "If you aren't going to school, you will have to work ... and when you do find employment, don't think you're going to live here free of charge. You'll have to start paying rent once you're earning."

William was horrified and puzzled as to why, after having had his own way and whatever he wanted for all of his life, the brakes had suddenly come on and his parents weren't playing ball any longer. "But ... but you're loaded ... why the hell should I?" he had yelled.

"Because, William, it's all part and parcel of being a responsible adult. I'll talk to your father to decide on exactly how much we should charge you."

William had no choice but to concede. "Okay, if I must. I'll go down to the job centre ... see what they have ... but I flatly refuse to go back to school. It's a complete and utter waste of time," he had said determinedly.

He obtained a job stacking shelves in a local supermarket. He hated that almost as much as school. The staff were all older, and although they attempted to be friendly, like others before them, soon retreated when they discovered he didn't want to reciprocate. The only conversation was work-related and they were never allowed a glimpse of his personal life.

He lasted three weeks. His parents always left for work early in the morning. He wasn't due at the supermarket until an hour later. He overslept regularly or just couldn't be bothered to turn up at all. The manager admonished him and after repeated warnings, sacked him. William didn't tell his parents until the end of the month, when they asked for his rent and found out he had no wages.

There was an almighty row. He had walked out, got into his car and cruised the rougher areas of the city. He picked up a young white girl with long, fair hair and intriguingly long legs. He had driven her to a dereliction site but it was no use, whatever she did, he couldn't perform. He threw her out of the car, chucking a twenty-pound note at her as he drove away, utterly ashamed and humiliated.

The rows continued at home. He got another job. The same thing happened. He was frequently late and then sacked for not turning up.

The rows grew worse. He began to find his parents exceedingly annoying and wished they weren't there to keep on at him. He debated on leaving home but would then have to pay proper rent and bills. He couldn't hold down a job and they wouldn't fund it. He was stuck … at home … with them.

Then he had an idea, which would keep his parents off his back   ...   and give him job satisfaction. He had sat in his car one day outside the cinema, watching a man on a ladder, cleaning windows of the upper storey of a smart detached house on the opposite side of the road. William had been intrigued. It must be possible to see all sorts of things that people got up to. He liked the idea. He wanted to see how other people lived, what their bedrooms looked like, maybe see a real naked female if he was lucky.

"I'm going to start my own business," he told his parents over dinner. "I'm going to use some of the savings you've put away for me and buy a van and then I'm going to set up as a window cleaner … concentrate on all the posh houses in the neighbourhood … the more windows, the more money I shall make."

He had known his parents were disappointed in his choice of career but he didn't care. The next day he bought a white van, ladders and washing equipment and printed out leaflets on his computer. He spent hours posting them through letterboxes of all the houses in the immediate vicinity, received a few enquiries and arranged when to do the work. His parents had been amazed when he sprang out of bed early in the mornings, hell-bent on making a start. What they didn't realise was that he hoped to catch people, especially women, still in their night attire … or less.

He had. Unfortunately, he met their husbands too and was reported to the police as being a pervert. His parents were horrified. The police had given him a caution. He had given up being a window cleaner. He had kept the van.

More rows ensued. It became a daily occurrence as he idled away the days and weeks at home, not working, just lazing about watching the television in his bedroom when his parents were there, watching porn when they weren't. He dreamed of being alone all the time, imagining what it would be like if they didn't come home after work … if he had the house to himself permanently … with no-one to nag, nag, nag at him, day after day … to be able to do exactly as he pleased, when he wanted. The idea had been most appealing.

His parents were wealthy people with a house in a highly sort after area. He went online and checked prices, astonished to learn it was worth around three million. Then there were the businesses

… five restaurants, all owned outright. Another few million there.

His mind had leapt into overdrive. Being their sole heir, he imagined having all that money at his disposal and never having to work again. He would be made for life. Invested wisely, the money would keep him in luxury, allow him to travel where and when he wanted. With no real love for his parents, he had started to plan.

* * *

Anna dashed home, hungrily devoured the fish and chips and then rang Miranda, who was surprised and delighted at her news.

"Gosh, Anna. You don't let the grass grow. That's simply amazing … and yes, of course, I'll come with you for a second viewing of the shop. It does sound perfect though, in the right place and big enough to do quite a bit with. I can't wait to see it. I'm free tomorrow afternoon between three and five. I have cats to visit and feed after that and then I have to interview a woman who has answered my advert for a dog walker later."

"Oh, I didn't know you were advertising for people to help you."

"Somehow it didn't crop up in conversation when we met but yes, I'm hoping to expand. I'm up to my quota on my walks but still receiving lots of requests from potential clients and as I don't want to turn anyone down, I need someone to help me, maybe more than one person … especially on the dog boarding side. So many people don't want their dogs to go to kennels these days, preferring their pooches to enjoy home boarding so I'm going to have to find people to help me on that front too."

"Gosh. You will be busy. You'll have your own little empire," Anna laughed.

"You too by the sound of it," agreed Miranda. "You could do very well with a little, well perhaps not quite so little, shop in Peesdown ... and if you intend turning it into a pet shop, we could very well help each other ... I can recommend you and you can recommend me ... that's if you want to after this morning's performance," she giggled.

"I think that's a very good idea," agreed Anna. "I'll ring Mr Cross ... Jeremy ... and see if he can let us have a viewing tomorrow afternoon. I'll text you and let you know ... and thanks so much, Miranda. I really appreciate this."

"Don't be daft. It's a pleasure."

Jeremy was delighted to hear from Anna again so quickly. "Yes, I can meet you at the shop at 3.30 p.m. and as I promised, I'll leave you both to have a good look around and discuss it properly. Take as long as you like and just pop the keys through the door when you leave. I have a spare set so that's not a problem."

Anna sent Miranda the text as promised. Miranda sent a text back. "Oooooh. So excited for you. See you tomorrow. Can't wait to view it. Xx"

* * *

Anna spent a restless night. Not as she usually did, grieving for Gerald, but excitedly going over and over in her head, plans for her shop. Her shop! Wow. She would never have given the idea any credence if it hadn't been for Miranda. That chance meeting in the park this week was changing her life because she was almost 100% sure she was going to buy the shop. It had a lovely feel to it. It was positioned perfectly for footfall. There was no other immediate competition if she turned it into a pet shop. She had the money to buy it outright without any kind of loan or mortgage and stock it too, thanks to Gerald's generous life insurance and their savings and she hadn't any other commitments so was completely free to concentrate solely on her business. Her business. A thrill shot through her.

Unable to sleep, she got up, made a hot chocolate and sat down in the lounge with a pen and notepad and started making notes about what she would sell, her opening times, where she would advertise, and all the other things that she would need such as insurance. Gosh, there was a lot to think about and she might need some advice. Thank goodness Donna had offered to help. She had owned the fish and chip shop for a long time and would know all the ins and outs of running a business.

Eventually, she began to feel tired. No doubt the hot chocolate had helped. With her eyelids drooping, she returned to bed and turned off the light.

* * *

William was pacing his lounge. He needed to get out of the house. He needed to find a woman. He debated on driving to the streets where he knew prostitutes were plying their trade but he was always reluctant to do that. He had never forgotten his first experience, which had wounded him so badly … that young girl, who had jeered at him, leaving him utterly ashamed and humiliated.

The experience had scarred him deeply … until those two girls in Mataro … friends who were on holiday. Raping and killing them had sorted out his ego with a vengeance; made him feel powerful, in control, a real man … and it had gone on from there

Anyway, you never knew what you might catch from prostitutes. Dirty little buggers. He had often watched them, jumping in and out of men's cars. No. He preferred the more respectable women. He wasn't into tarts and in the middle of the night, it was doubtful if he would find anyone remotely decent walking the streets … and it was dodgy with someone who didn't trust you. They might scream … alert other people … he might get caught. No. He would have to live with the itch for now.

He went upstairs, intending to go to bed and watch a porn film. He paused at the door of the bedroom next to his. He went inside

47

... his studio he liked to call it. He had a desk in here, by the window which overlooked the back garden and from there, when it was daylight, he could see parts of Peesdown park over his laurel hedge. It was a beautiful aspect with the trees beginning to change colour, an array of lime greens, gold and red. Now, it was pitch dark and he couldn't see a thing. He pulled down the blind and turned to look at the wall opposite. That was beautiful too. He had pinned up pictures of Miranda ... all of which he had taken without her knowledge. He studied them. She was in the park, laughing at the dogs. She was telling them off when they were naughty. She was sitting on a bench staring over the lake.

He put out a finger and stroked her cheek, wishing it was for real, wishing she was here with him now, about to go to bed and make passionate love. Because that was what it would be when they finally got together, passionate and real love. Not sordid sex.

He had that with other women but with Miranda ... that was going to be so very special. She was going to fall madly in love with him and they would get married ... at St. Edmunds .... and they would live happily ever after here at his lovely old Victorian house backing onto Peesdown park. He couldn't wait.

CHAPTER 4

The next day dawned and Miranda pulled herself out of her cosy bed and grimaced when she pulled back the curtains to reveal a grey sky with dark clouds in the distance, heading towards Leeds. It was going to rain for the third day running which meant taking spare clothes out with her again. Even though she owned good quality outdoor wear, she liked to change her trousers and jacket between walks after a soaking and her lovely clients made it so easy. All those who were out at work all day had extended an invitation for her to use their toilet or to make herself a drink when she picked up or dropped off their pets so she had plenty of opportunities to change and make herself comfortable for the next walk on a wet day.

As she pottered into the bathroom for a shower, her thoughts turned to Anna and the viewing of the shop in Peesdown this afternoon. It was lovely to know Anna valued her opinion and hearing her excitement on the phone last night was so nice. Miranda hoped the premises would be suitable for Anna to be able to start a new chapter in her life which, in turn, would help her over her deep grief for her husband.

Yes, she was looking forward to seeing what Anna had found … and then there was Belinda Stevens to see later that evening … a potential new dog walker. She looked really good on paper … experienced with dogs and free to walk a pack during the day but in the flesh, what would she be like? It seemed, from the few already interviewed, that the information candidates wrote on their application forms did not necessarily add up when they were standing in front of her. Two ladies, in particular, sounded perfect but in reality, they were pretty useless, not enough gumption or self-confidence to cope with walking a pack of six dogs in a public park.

Miranda often likened a group dog walk to an obstacle course. Even if all the dogs were good, which was a rarity she had to admit, it was what had to be faced; people who didn't like dogs, children who were a damned nuisance and didn't know how to behave with them or were scared witless if one approached, then there were blasted cyclists, joggers and then, of course, park keepers such as old Fart Features. Oh, then other

49

dogs felt threatened by a pack of boisterous dogs approaching them and went on the defensive.

Miranda grinned. So many people had commented on what a wonderful job she had. They had no idea! Professional dog walking was a nightmare at times but then there were the good bits. The fun she had with her pack, how they trusted and looked up to her with their bright, shiny eyes and waggy tails, waiting for her to make their day brighter before their parents came home; the walks when they didn't encounter obstacles and could just enjoy the environment, the sunshine, the cool winter days, the snow … most of the dogs loved that … and even the rain … and she met some fabulous people … people on her wavelength, true doggy people … and then there was Anna, a potential new best friend. Yes, she loved her job, even though another good soaking was on the cards today.

* * *

Anna was up as soon as it was light, made coffee and sat down at the kitchen table with her pad and pen, pouring over the notes she had made the night before. She then turned on her computer to search for wholesalers to check stock and prices. She made a list of other costs involved in running her business; insurance, stationery, postage … although exactly what she was going to post wasn't quite clear to her yet but there would doubtless be something. Then she thought about staff. She couldn't man the place on her own for six days every week. Gosh, there was a lot to think about. She had never employed anyone before. She would have to find out about PAYE, health and safety laws, etc., etc.

Her heart missed a beat. Was she biting off more than she could chew? Was this all a bit crazy … her … running her own business? She gritted her teeth and gave herself a good talking to.

"Anna … you are not stupid. You are not lazy. You have the money. You are fit and healthy and anything you don't know, you can learn. There are hundreds of books on how to run a business

... you can do courses; you can ask others ... Miranda and Donna ... and you'll have an accountant to advise you. You can do this.
You really can. You mustn't let nerves get in the way."

She thought about the alternative. She had felt so uplifted in the last few hours after seeing the shop with Jeremy. Not going ahead would lead to sinking back into depression. That wasn't a good choice. For the first time since Gerald died, she had something to look forward to, to get excited about, and could begin to feel positive about a future without him. She would always love him. He had been the best husband any woman could wish for but she was still reasonably young and could go on for many more years. She had to make the most of it, make a life for herself. Even though there was the second viewing with Miranda this afternoon, she already knew what she was going to do. She was going to buy the shop. She really was!

* * *

Desperate to see her, he had been trying to find Miranda all day. He had gone to the park this morning but she hadn't turned up, which was most unusual so he had limped home, taken off his disguise and driven around in his van, touring the remainder of the parks; Roundhay, Meanwood, Temple Newsam and finally, Golden Acre. She was there. He just arrived as she was pulling out, her car full of well-exercised dogs. He followed her at a discreet distance because there was every likelihood she would return home once she had dropped off the dogs and he wanted to find out more about her and where she lived.

Miranda did just that. Having deposited all five dogs back at their respective homes, she drove smartly to what was obviously her own house in Roundhay. It was a decent-sized terrace, two streets down from the main road, Street Lane. A nice place to live, he surmised, just a short stroll away from an array of shops, pubs and restaurants and easy access to Leeds city centre.

She parked outside the front door as he pulled up at the top of the street and watched as she opened the back door of the Volvo so Nellie could jump out. Miranda locked the car, walked up the path with Nellie, opened the front door and they disappeared inside.

With nothing else to do, he sat as a matter of habit, as he had with other women he had stalked, studying the street, checking out who was likely to be around at this time of day; if there were cars outside, lights on inside, indicating someone might be working at home but it was very quiet. Only two cars. Only one lounge light on. Obviously, most people who lived here were employed elsewhere during the day. He sat, motionless, checking anything and everything that moved but there was only a woman with a baby in a pram, a man with two small children skipping along, excitedly chatting and swinging school bags and an elderly lady who couldn't walk very well and leaned heavily on a walking stick.

He remained there for an hour and when his tummy began to rumble, he realised how hungry he was, not having eaten since breakfast. He had nothing in the van and nothing in his fridge either so would have to shop ... or buy a takeaway. He mulled it over. Fish and chips, pizza or Chinese? He didn't like Indian. He started the van, intending to cruise down to the parade of shops where all three of his favourite takeaways were situated, when he was surprised to see Miranda emerging from her house, jump back into her car and shoot off towards the ring road. She hadn't got Nellie so couldn't be going to the park. He forgot about being hungry. He followed her.

* * *

Miranda arrived at the shop at the same time as Anna. The door was wide open so Jeremy must already be there. Anna smiled at Miranda. "Thank you so much for coming. I do value your opinion
... although I have to warn you, I have already made up my mind
... I am going to buy it."

"Well, that's nice to know," Jeremy said.

Both women turned to look at him, leaning nonchalantly against the door frame with a big grin on his face.

Miranda nearly swooned. He was utterly gorgeous. The bestlooking man she had seen for quite a while. He was dressed in jeans and a dark blue sweater and those broad shoulders, those eyes, that mouth. Unusually for her, she was speechless.

Anna smiled at Jeremy, not noticing the look of sheer adoration on Miranda's face. "Hello. Yes, I think I have made up my mind, although I do need to see the place again so thank you for giving us the opportunity. This is Miranda, my friend I was telling you about. Miranda, this is Jeremy."

Miranda's face flushed as Jeremy put out a hand to shake hers. "Nice to meet you," he said, smiling widely.

Miranda shook his hand, unable to speak, just nodding and seemingly grinning like a Cheshire cat. She was touching his flesh. Oh, my God, it was good. His fabulous big hand totally covered hers. Oh, that his whole body was covering her too. She had never felt such intense sexual attraction before and was quite taken aback. The Beastly Bastard had never made her feel like this!

"As promised, ladies," he was saying, "I am going to leave you to it. I'm meeting a friend in Leeds for lunch, so, Anna, here are the keys. Please post them through the letterbox when you leave and I look forward to hearing from you."

"Thank you, Jeremy. That's very kind and yes, I'll be in touch later. Enjoy your lunch."

"Thanks," he said, nodding at her. His eyes twinkled at Miranda. "Perhaps we'll meet again someday."

"Um," was all she could utter, only just managing to smile back, unable to tear her eyes away from his retreating body as he stepped past them into the street and walked away. God, he was sooo gorgeous.

"Miranda?" prompted Anna, suddenly realising why her friend was virtually comatose.

"Oh goodness, Anna," Miranda gasped. "That man has quite bowled me over. You must never lose his telephone number." Anna laughed. "What excuse will you have for ringing him?"

"I simply have no idea but I shall certainly think of one. There's no way that man is walking out of my life ... now," she added, pulling herself together. "Let's have a look at what will be your future, as mine disappears into Leeds for lunch with a friend

… I do hope it's not a woman … and after we've looked around, you must tell me absolutely everything you know about him."

Anna grinned as they entered the shop, remembering Miranda's words that she never wanted another man in her life after the Beastly Bastard. She shut and locked the front door and they turned to look at the interior of the ground floor.

"This is perfect," announced Miranda firmly. "The location is really good, so near to the main shops and the park and with a huge built-up area surrounding it and as most people seem to have one kind of pet or another these days, a massive target audience … and this room is big enough to display an enormous number of items. Wow, Anna. You did well to find this … and so quickly."

"I know. I can't believe it either," replied Anna as they moved through the main room into the back. They didn't linger long in the stock room but on entering what Anna had decided was going to be called 'the garden room', she turned to Miranda. "It's so lovely in here and I don't quite know what to do with it."

"I do," Miranda said enthusiastically. "Have a little coffee shop … somewhere your customers can come with their dogs and relax for a while with like-minded people. Most of the cafes around here don't allow dogs so it would be a real draw."

"Oh, what a brilliant idea … I hadn't thought of that," Anna remarked, glancing around the room. Miranda was right. It would be perfect. She could just imagine lots of customers sitting at the tables and enjoying the view of the garden. "And I can put in French windows so in the summer people can go outside … perhaps have tables and chairs out there too … after all, there is enough room. Gosh, I shall need a few more staff for this side of it though."

Miranda poked her head into the kitchen and nodded with satisfaction. "This is a decent enough sized area to prepare snacks and drinks … and you have a downstairs loo too. It's ideal … although I think you will need permission."

They explored the rest of the building, Miranda cooing enthusiastically about everything. "What will you do with the accommodation?" she asked as they peered out over the garden from the lounge window. "Will you move in here   …   or let it out ... increase your income? It would have to be to someone utterly trustworthy with the shop downstairs."

"I'm not sure," Anna said with a thoughtful look on her face. "I love my house but I tend to rattle around in it now I'm on my own ... and if I'm going to work here all hours that God sends, it would make sense to live here too ... and I do like it ... and I love the garden."

"Yes, it's lovely," Miranda agreed, "In fact, darling Anna, the whole place is great ... and I can't wait to see you properly installed and busily tending to your customers downstairs."

Anna laughed. "I think you're more excited about this than I am."

Miranda giggled. "Yes, I might well be ... but is this what you honestly want, Anna? It's all so sudden. It was only yesterday morning that we first talked about it ... and now, here we are, with you virtually signing the papers. Don't you want to think about it a little longer ... I am sure the delicious Jeremy won't mind."

Anna bit her lip and looked out over the garden where she could see the street of neat, semi-detached houses stretching out far beyond. She could see the road, the cars zipping up and down, she could see people, walking, chatting. There were buses, delivery vehicles, an ambulance and a police car. It was busy, busy, busy. The house where she and Gerald had lived ever since they were married was tucked down a quiet cul-de-sac. Their neighbours were middle-aged professional people who were out at work all day and their children were either at university or had left home. Nothing moved much throughout the day, just the odd delivery driver with a parcel or two. She loved her home. She and Gerald had spent a lot of money on it over the years and it was exceedingly comfortable but now she wasn't working, it was becoming a prison ... a lonely prison and unless she got another job, she was going to wither up with depression ... and the thought of another office job wasn't appealing. It didn't excite her. It wasn't going to encourage her to get out of bed in the morning. But this

... her eyes flickered over the rooms as she and Miranda ventured back downstairs ... this was daunting and scary ... she had never run a business before ... she had no idea what owning a pet shop would be like … whether she would be any good at it even … but what she did know was that for the first time in a very long while she was deeply excited and didn't want that feeling to disappear. If she walked away now, the dark depression was going to hit hard. No, she had to do this and if it all went wrong, at least she would have tried … but if it went right … her tummy flipped over nervously.

They had reached the ground floor and stood in the middle of the room, Miranda staring at Anna questioningly. "I think it's perfect, Anna and I'll help you all I can, I promise … but are you one hundred per cent sure? I would hate to think I was encouraging you to do something that just wasn't right."

Anna stroked Miranda's arm. "You're not. You've pointed me in the right direction, that's all. I want this. I really want this and I am going to do my very best to make it work."

They left the shop, Anna locking it up carefully and pushing the keys through the letterbox as Jeremy had instructed.

"Right," said Miranda. "I better get off and interview this Belinda woman. If I don't get some assistance very soon to walk all the dogs in Peesdown, I shall be too exhausted to help you. Wish me luck and pass my regards on to that gorgeous hunk of a man when you inform him that you are going to buy his shop … and whatever you do, don't lose his telephone number," she instructed with a mischievous smile.

Anna grinned back as Miranda virtually danced down the road towards her car. "I'll ring you," she called, "and thank you."

"My pleasure," Miranda called back.

Anna crossed the road and stood looking at the shop. Her shop. Her very own business. What could she call it? She would have to think of something catchy. She pulled her phone out of her handbag and pressed Jeremy's number.

He answered on the second ring. "Hi, Anna. How did you get on?"

"Fabulous, thank you, Jeremy. I definitely want it so please can we set the wheels in motion as soon as possible."

"Of course … I'll ring my solicitors now … oh, and Anna,"
"Yes."

56

"Is Miranda ... is she attached at all ... boyfriend, fiancée, husband?"

Anna giggled. "No, Jeremy. She isn't."

* * *

William had followed Miranda to the shop but hadn't been able to hang around for long as Samantha had invited him to tea at the Vicarage. Since he had told her about his parents, she had taken a keen interest in him and was desperate to make him feel included. He didn't mind ... he liked it ... but if she knew the truth ... that it was him who had murdered his parents, her attitude would be somewhat different. He hadn't thought about them or what he had done very much until Samantha had brought it all back and as he drove home and put the van in the garage, carefully locking it behind him, went indoors and began getting ready to walk down to the Vicarage, he clearly remembered details of their demise, just a few weeks after his eighteenth birthday and a considerable amount of careful, meticulous planning.

The Two Towers had been released. He had driven to a cinema in Manchester, which he thought far enough away from Liverpool so as not to bump into anyone he knew, and sat through the whole three hours, loving every minute of it, although he had made sure to chuck his ticket in the wastepaper bin in the foyer when he left, not wanting the police to discover he had seen the film that day. He had just needed to see it all the way through so he could answer any questions about it they might throw at him.

The following evening, he went to his local cinema to see it again, carefully placing his ticket in his wallet for safekeeping, making sure he had a seat as near to the back as possible so he wouldn't be noticed by too many people, especially in his absence in the last half of the film. He had a carrier bag with him containing his black anorak, his mother's blonde wig, her spare pair of glasses, her dressing gown cord and a pair of rubber gloves. On top, he had placed a couple of cans of coke and a bar of chocolate. A few minutes prior to the interval, before the lights were switched on, he had slipped to the toilet before anyone else and exchanged his leather jacket for the anorak. The blonde wig was tight but served its purpose, as did the glasses. Luckily, his mother's eyesight wasn't too bad so he could see reasonably well out of them. He had looked in the mirror. The chap who stared back was nothing like him. Taking a deep breath, he had left the toilets, making sure the dressing gown cord and rubber gloves were secure in his anorak pocket and the carrier bag containing his leather jacket was tucked under his arm.

The interval had commenced; people rushed to the toilets and the foyer had been awash with long queues for hotdogs, sweets and drinks. He had hurried through, praying he wouldn't see anyone he knew and be recognised. He had been lucky. No-one did. Having pulled his hood over his head as soon as he stepped outside, he ran home swiftly, silently slipping into the house through the back door.

His father had been watching television in the lounge and had his back to him as William entered the room and donned the rubber gloves. His hand had reached in his pocket for the cord and in a flash, it was around his father's neck. Having taken him by surprise there wasn't much of a struggle and it was only a minute or two before the deed was done.

Breathless, his heart thudding loudly, William had turned to walk upstairs. His mother was banging cupboards so was putting away laundry. He had found her on the landing. She heard him and turned, opened her mouth to speak but screamed instead as she saw the look of grim determination on his face and the cord in his hand. He had silenced her, hitting her hard in the face. As she slumped to the ground, he had grabbed her, put the cord around her neck and pulled hard. Within a short space of time, she was as dead as her husband.

He had pulled the cord away and laid it by her side, sat back on his haunches and smiled. His troubles were finally over. Making it look as if someone had come in to rob the place, he had flown around the bedroom, rummaging through drawers, chucking the contents on the thick pile cream carpet. He had tipped up his mother's jewellery box and pushed the contents into his jacket pocket; all the good pieces were in the safe downstairs but there was a pearl necklace, earrings and a diamond bracelet. His father's gold Rolex watch had been on his bedside cabinet where he had left it before having a shower earlier. William grabbed it and pushed that into his pocket too. Skipping past his mother's body with a grin, he had shot downstairs, ignoring his father as he whipped around the lounge, pulling pictures off the wall as an intruder would do, looking for a safe. He knew where it was, of course, behind the small Canaletto his father had bought at Sotheby's a few years ago. He had removed it carefully. It was worth a bit and he hadn't wanted to damage it. It exposed the safe. He had whirled the knob a few times. He knew the code but an intruder wouldn't. He had grabbed his father's laptop on the sofa and took one last look around the room. It would appear as if the robber had been disturbed and hadn't been able to find the code for the safe.

He had left through the back door, not wanting to smash any glass as the police would want to know why his father hadn't heard and investigated. When he was interviewed later, William told them that the door was never locked until they all went to bed. He had left it ajar to add credence to his story. Along the path, near to the door, he had dropped the jewellery and the laptop, making it look as if the intruder was in such a hurry to get away, he had abandoned them.

Leaving by the back gate, he had flown back to his van in the cinema car park, changed his jacket, ripped off the blonde wig and glasses, shoved them back into the carrier bag with the rubber gloves and dumped it in the footwell.

The film had been due to finish in twenty minutes and he returned to the cinema entrance to make it look as if he was one of the first out and then leaned nonchalantly against one of the huge posters advertising The Twin Towers and lit up a cigarette.

Within minutes people had started to flood out of the cinema, some chattering excitedly about what they had seen, others yawning, glad to be able to go home after such a long viewing. He had puffed on his cigarette.

"Hello, William. Have you just been to see The Twin Towers too?" said a voice by his side.

He had turned to see Veronica, one of his mother's friends, with her son and his girlfriend. "Oh, hi, Veronica. Yes. It was good, wasn't it?"

"Well, not quite my cup of tea … but these two dragged me along … I think I would rather have stayed at home and watched Coronation Street," she had laughed.

William had smiled widely, letting her think he was enjoying her joke. Little did she know he had been delighted to have bumped into her. She would be a really good alibi for him … and her son and girlfriend.

"Would you like a lift home?" she had asked.

"No. No, thank you. I have my van in the car park. I just don't like to smoke in it so that's why I'm having one here … Mother doesn't like it either … indoors." He had smiled wryly. God, it had been a fantastic feeling, knowing he was finally free of all the bloody nagging.

"Okay. Tell your mother I'll give her a ring in the next day or two to have a chat. We haven't spoken for ages. I do hope she's well."

"Yes … very well … and yes, I'll tell her."

"Goodnight then," she had added, heading to the car park with her son and girlfriend trailing behind.

Delighted things were going so smoothly, William had finished his cigarette and walked smartly back to the van, wanting to get home and 'discover' his dead parents … and face the police and all their questions.

He had driven back, parked his car in his garage and holding onto the carrier bag, walked up the path to the back door.

"Hi, Mum. Hi, Dad. I'm home," he had called as he stepped into the kitchen.

The silence had been eerie. He had shivered and got to work. He restored the rubber gloves to where they were kept in the cupboard under the sink and the carrier bag to the receptacle where there were many more. With the wig and glasses in his hands, he had steeled himself to enter the lounge and grimaced at his father's body slumped on the sofa. He had dashed upstairs. His mother was laid prostrate on the landing, the pile of clothes she had been about to put away before he attacked her, scattered around her. He had grinned. She needn't have bothered to iron them.

He placed her wig and glasses in the top drawer of her dressing table, where he had taken them from earlier that day when she was at work, and then picked up the telephone by the bed and dialled 999.

"My parents," he had sobbed to the operator. "They're dead … someone has murdered them … please, please help me!"

CHAPTER 5

The next few weeks went by in a whirl of activity for Anna, right from the moment she rang Jeremy to say she definitely wanted to purchase the shop. Before she knew it, she was at the solicitor's signing all the necessary documentation and within four short weeks, had the keys in her hand.

Jeremy arranged a couple of days leave and on the day of the handover, made the journey up to Leeds and took Anna and Miranda out for a celebratory dinner, picking them up from Anna's house in his silver-grey Jaguar, much to Miranda's delight. She had been so thrilled when he had told Anna to invite her and had spent days agonising about what to wear and how to have her hair. She didn't dress up often, mainly living in casual clothes for dog walking so it was a real treat ... and a huge bonus to be seeing him again.

Anna and Miranda were fast becoming firm friends. Anna joined Miranda for her first walk most mornings and they spent hours discussing the shop and what Anna was going to stock it with, along with Miranda's plans for expanding Four Paws. She had interviewed Belinda, who had turned out to be a conscientious and reliable dog walker, at first taking on a couple of dogs and gradually increasing her pack as her confidence grew and was now up to six every day. She had been with Miranda for four weeks and so far, so good. She hadn't lost any dogs and all the owners seemed pleased with her efforts. However, Miranda still needed more dog walkers and people who were willing to board dogs for short periods in their own homes so was still busy interviewing in the evenings, as well as seeing clients who wanted to use her services. Anna sometimes wondered when Miranda had time to eat and sleep as she seemed constantly on the go. However, she had made time for dinner with Anna and Jeremy without hesitation and Anna had been highly amused at her reaction when she told her of Jeremy's invitation.

"Oh my God!" Miranda had gasped. "Oh, Anna. He invited me too? Oh, wow. I can't believe it. Oh, heavens, what am I am going to wear?"

Anna had laughed. "I am sure you will find something nice."

"Nice! It's going to have to be much nicer than nice ... I don't want him to ever forget me ... actually, that's a point. Now he's sold you the shop, he might not bother to come back to Leeds much anymore."

"Well, he does stay with his sister a couple of times a year apparently, so he won't completely lose touch with the place."

"Right ... so I have to make a good impression in the hope that he'll want to see us again. Anyway, I didn't look too scintillatingly sexy last time we met, wearing jeans and a leather jacket. Looked more like an old Rocker ... all I lacked was the motorbike and helmet."

Anna giggled. "Goodness, the Mods and Rockers were all in the sixties ... I doubt Jeremy would think you were that old."

"It must have been great to be around then," Miranda added wistfully.

"Um. Hippies, drugs and everyone all loved up."

"There ... you see. Sounds great ... not the drugs though. Can't be doing with them ... now, don't distract me. I have to think about what to wear for this celebratory dinner. I must say, it's extremely kind of Jeremy to take us out."

"Yes. He seems a very nice man indeed."

"Um ...," grinned Miranda. "Very, very nice indeed."

* * *

The evening was thoroughly enjoyable for all of them. Jeremy had turned up at Anna's bang on time. Miranda had nearly swooned when she saw him get out of his car and walk up Anna's drive with two bunches of flowers. "I'll get it," she called to Anna who was upstairs putting the finishing touches to her make-up. She sprinted to the front door, her heart thudding wildly.

"Hello," Jeremy smiled. "I'm so glad you could join us this evening. It was only right to have you with us as I know you were instrumental in helping Anna make up her mind about the shop."

"It was very nice of you to invite me," Miranda replied, feeling a blush sweeping over her carefully made-up face. It was rare she wore make-up and it felt a little strange, as if she had put a mask on. She hoped he liked women who wore it. So many men didn't. God, what if he disliked it too? Perhaps she should go and wash it off ... but no, she couldn't. It was too late now. Oh damn!

Anna came down the stairs, a big smile on her face when she saw Jeremy. She looked lovely in a green cashmere sweater and smart black trousers. Miranda sucked her tummy in. She didn't have such a lovely figure as Anna. More rotund. People told her she should be as thin as a rake with all the walking she did every day but they didn't know about all the naughty snacks she grabbed as she tore around from place to place, unable to eat meals at the proper times. As a result, she had rather a bigger bottom and tummy than she should have done for her height and hadn't enjoyed the shopping trip to find something suitable for tonight. However, she had finally decided on a peacock blue top and navy trousers, which was lucky as she already owned a nice pair of dark blue leather boots and handbag to match. She had also splurged out on a new coat as all those she owned, apart from her black leather jacket, were used for dog walking and certainly weren't suitable for a posh restaurant. She had seen a cream suede affair in Debenhams, costing the earth but she handed over her credit card with a gulp and smiled sweetly at the assistant, praying there would be enough funds to cover it. Luckily, the transaction went through without a hitch and she walked away, utterly thrilled with her purchase, relieved Jeremy wouldn't think she was a scruffy lump this evening.

"This is so lovely of you, Jeremy," Anna was saying as she reached up and pecked him on the cheek, making Miranda irritatingly envious. Why hadn't she thought of doing that, although she would have probably appeared gauche whereas Anna did it so naturally but then she didn't fancy the pants off him, did she?

"These are for both of you," Jeremy smiled, handing a bouquet to each of them.

"Oh," gasped Miranda. She couldn't remember the last time anyone had bought her flowers. The Beastly Bastard certainly never had. She stared at the array of white and yellow roses, gypsophila and greenery with pleasure. "Thank you so much, Jeremy. They are really lovely."

"Yes," agreed Anna. "They are ... thank you, Jeremy. You are spoiling us. I'll just put them in a bowl of water in the sink," holding out a hand to take Miranda's bouquet. Having deposited the flowers in the kitchen to keep fresh, Anna returned to the hall where Jeremy was helping Miranda on with her coat.

"Now," said Jeremy, holding up Anna's for her to slide into, "I believe our table awaits so are you both ready?"

They went out to the car. Jeremy, in his blue suit and overcoat, held open the doors for them. Anna sat in the front passenger seat and Miranda slid into the back, which she was pleased about as she could sit and admire Jeremy's head of thick blonde hair and watch his left-hand changing gear as he started the car and headed out of the cul-de-sac. It all made her feel a little peculiar.

None of the occupants of the car took any notice of the white van parked on the road, four houses down from Anna's.

* * *

William followed the Jaguar along the ring road, keeping a discreet distance on the main road, a couple of cars behind until it reached Horsforth and parked in the main street, just opposite a new restaurant which had only opened a couple of months earlier. He pulled in further along, able to see the little group clearly once they were inside, seated beside the window. He seethed with jealousy as he witnessed the man making the two women laugh.

They were a long time lingering over their meal and he had nearly nodded off in the van. It was a chilly night but it didn't affect him as he always kept the vehicle ready for his sorties. He had thick woollen blankets to cover himself, a woollen hat which came down over his ears, heavy-duty gloves, a thermos of coffee and a big tin of biscuits, along with crisps and chocolate. He

65

could remain there for a long time without too much discomfort, watching whatever he wanted.

* * *

The evening was over long before Miranda wanted it to be. The restaurant, which was new and none of them had been to before, proved to be extremely good. The food was exquisite, the service prompt and efficient and the decor, stunning, with white leather seating and glass tables. Jeremy was an excellent host, attentive to both his companions, making sure he gave both of them his full attention and making them laugh at some of his army stories. He didn't tell them about the gruesome bits.

"I can't tell you how pleased I am that you've bought the shop, Anna," he said as they were waiting for their puddings. "I have fond memories of that place from my childhood and my father loved it very much and made so many friends in the area. I would have hated it to go to just anyone, especially someone who didn't appreciate the garden and did something awful such as digging it up and turning it into a car park. I would like to think of it staying as it is now, with all father's plants and hard work not going to waste."

"It's such a pretty garden," agreed Anna. "I shall certainly look after it, you need to have to fear on that score … in fact, Miranda suggested the customers could sit out there in the summer." She had told him earlier of her plans to turn the garden room into a small cafe.

"That's a great idea," Jeremy said enthusiastically. "Father would have been tickled pink … other people enjoying the fruits of his labours."

"So … will you still be coming back to Leeds occasionally?" asked Miranda. She had been dying to ask him all evening, desperate that this would not be the last time she set eyes on him.

"Of course," he said, his eyes twinkling. "I shall still visit my sister … in fact, she has asked me to ask you something."

"Oh?"

"Yes. With your dog walking business … do you happen to cover Headingley?"

"Well, yes, I do. I usually take my second group who live over that way to Golden Acre Park as it's so near, following the first lot in Peesdown. Why?"

"Daphne has a couple of cream pugs ... about eight months old now ... totally out of control I hasten to add as she spoils them rotten. She needs some help with them. I don't know why she did it, even she admits that, but she bought them whilst on maternity leave, which was fine as she's been able to walk them herself, even managing after the twins were born but she's going back to work and won't be able to give them quite so much attention. Do you think you would be able to fit them in?"

Miranda gulped, unable to believe her luck. She wouldn't lose contact with him if she was walking his sister's dogs. She didn't hesitate.

"Of course. It will be a pleasure. I like to have them young and then I can train them up. I shall need to visit your sister and have a chat and fill in some forms ... here," she said, rummaging in her bag for the little wallet in which she kept her business cards. She handed him one. "Here are my details. Just ask your sister to give me a ring when she's ready."

"Thanks. I will," Jeremy said, eyeing up the information on her card. He slipped it into his jacket pocket and Miranda's heart skipped a beat. He had her number now.

As their puddings and coffee arrived, the conversation turned back to the shop and while Anna enthused about what she was going to do with it, Miranda's mind wandered as she surreptitiously watched Jeremy under her eyelashes. Had she made any impression on him tonight? He was terribly polite and treated them both the same but was there any hint of interest when he looked at her. She hadn't seen any ... but now she would have contact with his family, that might change in the future. Oh, get a grip, Miranda, she told herself. You're acting like a lovesick teenager and you know how you vowed never to have anything to do with another man after the Beastly Bastard.

* * *

It was 11.00 p.m. by the time the party left the restaurant. William felt the jealousy wave over him again as they strolled arm in arm, one woman on either side of the man, still laughing and talking, totally at ease in each other's company. Christ! He couldn't get one woman to remain with him. This bloke had two!!

For a brief moment he felt sorry for himself as he started the van and trundled down the road behind them. He had never had a proper girlfriend. There had been a couple of dates in his late teens when he had invited girls to the cinema but after some breathless fumbling in the back seats, which never amounted to much, they hadn't wanted to see him again and he found it easier to get what he wanted by force after that, rather than through the romantic route ... until he had met Miranda. He had fallen for her ... in a big way. He didn't want to hurt her. He wanted to love her ... he wanted her to love him. He wanted them to be together for eternity.

They reached the house where they had started from. Would Miranda go home now? Her Volvo was parked in the drive. William pulled up the van in the space he had used earlier, far enough away for them not to notice him but close enough for him to see what was going on.

* * *

Anna asked Jeremy if he would like coffee. He shook his head and declined.

"I better not. I've an early start in the morning as I need to get back to London before 9.00 a.m. Thank you both, ladies, for a lovely evening and I wish you all the success in the world with the shop, Anna. When I come home on leave next time, I shall pop in and say hello if that's okay as I would really like to see what you do with the place."

"And you'll be very welcome, Jeremy ... and thank you for the wonderful meal. It was very kind of you," said Anna, stepping out of the car as he opened the door for her. She kissed him lightly on the cheek and turned to walk to the front door.

Jeremy took Miranda's hand to help her out. As she stood up and they came face to face, his eyes twinkled.

"And I am sure I shall see you again ... in the company of

Daphne's lunatic puppies and maybe without them too. Will it be okay if I give you a ring sometime? I shan't be home again for a couple of months and when I do, perhaps you would like to come out to dinner with me again ... on our own ... I would love to hear more about your plans for expanding your business and how you're getting on ... there's nothing I admire more than an enterprising woman."

Miranda's heart flipped over and the butterflies in her stomach were doing somersaults. Her voice, when it eventually managed to work, was almost a squeal of delight. "Oh ... oh, of course. I should love too ... and yes, please do ring. I would love a chat now and again," she stammered.

He bent down and his lips brushed hers. "Good. I shall look forward to it. Goodnight, Miranda."

"Goodnight," she sang, her pulses racing. She threw him a cheeky grin as she followed Anna into the house and closed the door. Anna had taken her coat off and was making her way into the kitchen to make coffee. One look at Miranda's face as she followed her, told Anna exactly what was going on.

* * *

The rage in William was intense. He thumped the steering wheel, again and again. How dare that man kiss Miranda! How dare he! Never, in his whole life, had he hated anyone as much as he did that man.

Miranda had gone indoors. The man got back into his Jaguar and drove out of the cul-de-sac. William followed him. He wanted to know more about him now, especially where he lived.

It wasn't long before the Jaguar turned into the drive of a very smart residence in Headingly. William parked his van further down the road and walked silently towards the house and studied it from the road. The man had gone indoors, leaving his car parked next to a new sports car and a big Mercedes. So obviously there were a few people living here.

He didn't linger long in case anyone happened to notice his interest. He returned to his van and headed back to Peesdown, still seething, still jealous but there was nothing he could do

69

about it at the moment. He had to find out a lot more about the man first and whether or not he was a real threat to his relationship with Miranda.

He reached home, put the van away and went indoors. He was cold and tired. It had been a long day. He made himself a hot chocolate and went to bed but he couldn't sleep. For some reason his thoughts kept turning back to his past, to his parents, to what had happened afterwards. It was weird how he suddenly kept thinking about his parents. He hadn't during all those long years abroad after they died. It could only be telling Samantha which had brought it all back and how he had got away with it.

It had been hard. The hardest thing he had done in his life, convincing the police he had nothing to do with the murder of his parents. They hadn't believed him at first, even though they had found him cradling his mother closely, tears pouring down his cheeks. They had listened to him sobbing, they had taken his fingerprints, they had checked his cinema ticket, they had talked to Veronica and her son and girlfriend. It had gone on, for days and days. Relentless questions ... especially about his relationship with his parents ... then they discovered he had been cautioned after the peeping tom incident, that he had walked out of school, that he hadn't been able to hold down a job for very long ... that he was their sole heir. On searching his room and garage, they had insisted he unlock the cabinet. Their faces had been impassive as they sorted through the pornography. However, there was no real, concrete evidence that he had killed his parents and, in the end, they concluded that there really had been an intruder, who had been disturbed, probably by William arriving home.

It had all been in the papers of course, especially the pictures of the funeral, which had been a grim affair with a crowd of people turning up, wanting to pay their last respects. There had been the neighbours, people they knew from church and a good many of the staff from the restaurants, the bank manager, the accountant, the solicitor. No family, apart from his aunt and uncle, his mother's older sister and her husband, who hadn't been on friendly terms with the Brownlow's and left as soon as decently possible. William's maternal grandmother had been in a nursing home with dementia and was unable to attend and probably didn't even realise her daughter and husband were dead anyway. His father, like him, had been an only child and his parents were both dead so there was no-one from that side of the family.

The police turned up, sitting at the back of the church and later, at the crematorium, watching everyone, especially him but William put on a convincing show of grief, having smoothed on a bit of talcum powder on his face to make himself look paler than normal, took a handkerchief to keep dabbing at his eyes and constantly rubbed his brow as if he was in terrible pain.

He had hired caterers to put on a funeral tea at the house afterwards and most of the mourners came, offering their deepest sympathies and asking if there was anything they could do. They had been shocked by the loss of two such lovely, kind and generous people and feared William would find it very hard to cope with life without them. The police, the Detective Inspector and Sergeant who were investigating the case, also put in a brief appearance and pulled him aside for a quiet word.

"We wanted to let you know, William, that we're not going to investigate you any further. It's pretty obvious there must have been an intruder and we will do all we can to catch him but as far as you're concerned, that is that. We're very sorry for your loss and will be in touch if we discover anything further."

The overwhelming feeling of relief when they drove away was like a ton weight being removed from his shoulders. He had done it and once he had spoken to the family solicitor, everything his parents owned would be his.

The meeting with the solicitors had gone well. William had arrived at the offices of Benson and Benson in the centre of Liverpool at exactly ten o'clock as requested. Half an hour later he emerged, richer by a few million and the owner of a house worth even more. He owned five businesses, a brand-new Jaguar that his father had only purchased a month before his death and his mother's Audi TT, plus jewellery and paintings. He had gone home, opened a bottle of Krug and drank the lot.

A few months later he had sold the house, the businesses, the cars, including his own BMW, the paintings and the jewellery and had over ten million in the bank. The only thing he kept was his van and his personal effects.

71

He had changed his name by deed poll, from William Brownlow to William Pemworthy. It had been relatively easy and quick to do and then he notified the passport office so he could have a new one and the DVLA regarding his driving licence. He closed all his parents' bank accounts, along with his own and opened another in his new name at a different bank and deposited all his millions. The bank manager was delighted and invited him into his office for a sherry. William declined. He didn't want to make relationships with anyone in authority.

He put all the possessions he wanted to keep into storage and went abroad, travelling extensively in Europe; Italy, France, Switzerland, Germany, Spain. He dined in the best restaurants, he slept in fabulous hotels, he sunbathed on beautiful beaches ... and that was when it really started.

He ended up in Mataro in Spain, delighted to discover there was a nudist beach, where he began to spend a great deal of time, enjoying the sensation of the sun on parts of his skin which had never been exposed before while relaxing on recliners, watching women flaunting their bodies for all to see. He befriended two ... stupid, silly, giggly young females. They all ended up in bed together but it was like the last time ... with the prostitute in Liverpool ... he couldn't do anything. They sniggered and laughed and left his bedroom. He was utterly humiliated and distraught ... and angry.

He bought a dark brown wig and moustache, a rope, masking tape and gloves and stole a steak knife from the table at dinner and slipped it into his trousers pocket, which proved most uncomfortable walking back to his room. He took a day trip to Barcelona and paid a visit to a stationer. He bought glue and white card and black felt tip pens. He wandered around the back streets until he saw exactly what he wanted. A really old white van parked down a lane, all on its own and not overlooked by houses. He stole it. It had been easy. He had found out how to do it online before he left Liverpool and tried it a few times to see if it worked. He hadn't driven any of the cars away, just gained access.

Praying it didn't have anything wrong with it, he had driven it towards Mataro and stopped on a track off a remote forest road to sort out the number plates. He made up some numbers and

72

letters, printed them on two white cards and glued them over both registration plates. On arriving back in Mataro he had parked the van in the furthest position away from the road in a car park a few yards from his hotel.

Wearing the wig and moustache, he had followed the two women for three evenings in the van, trying to get an idea of their routine … and then he pounced. They always visited the Stardust nightclub about a mile from their hotel and didn't leave until it closed, usually accompanied by young men but on the third night, they emerged on their own, holding each other up as they staggered along the pavement, down a dim and lonely road towards their hotel.

He had pulled the van up just in front of them, opened the back doors, grabbed them both and shoved them in. Being so drunk and taken by surprise they hadn't put up a fight or even screamed. He jumped in with them, brandished the knife he had stolen from the hotel and made them lie down so he could tie them up securely and tape their mouths. He had then driven the van out of town, the girls moaning and crying and kicking the sides of it with their feet.

They hadn't recognised him but when he clambered into the back of the van with them half an hour later and removed the wig and moustache, the horror on their faces amused him highly. He had been slow and deliberate with them, raping them both, high up in the mountains on a lonely track off the main road. It had been a fantastic feeling, knowing he could do it at last … and given him such a boost of strength, of manhood … and they had deserved it. Laughing at him. Humiliating him. No woman was ever going to do that to him again. He was powerful … and they were the first to find out.

He hadn't dare let them go. He strangled them both with his bare hands, pulled them out of the van and chucked their bodies down a slope where they probably wouldn't be found for a very long time, if ever.

He had driven back to Barcelona, and stopped in a quiet road about a mile from where he had stolen the vehicle, to change his clothes, which he had concealed carefully in a carrier bag under the passenger seat and taped up so as not to be contaminated by any forensic evidence. He hid behind some bushes, ripped off those he had been wearing, donned the fresh ones and shoved the others into the carrier bag, which he chucked back into the van near the knife, the rope, the masking tape, the wig and moustache. He had set fire to them with his lighter and then slipped away into the night. There had been a massive bang a few minutes later as the vehicle exploded.

He dozed for a few hours on the beach. There had been a party in progress and some courting couples lay on the sand but none of them disturbed him. He had stretched out on the sand near the promenade and allowed the sounds of the waves to relax him and bring him down from the high he had been feeling earlier. He had wanted to get back to his hotel and relax in private but hadn't wanted to catch a train until he could blend in with the crowd and not stand out. By 8.30 a.m., people were moving around freely and he headed to the railway station and caught the next train to Mataro.

He showered and then lunched in the hotel restaurant, studying the local newspaper the waiter procured for him from the bar. Nothing had been mentioned about the girls and surmising it could be days, weeks or even months before they were found, he decided to remain in Mataro as long as he had originally intended and then move on. It wouldn't have done to make a hasty departure as it might be commented on even though, as far as he had been aware, there was nothing to link him to their disappearance. He had covered all eventualities but couldn't be too careful.

For a few more years he meandered around Europe, looking for opportunities to make more women suffer. There were a few … there was Ingrid in Amsterdam, Charlotte in Berlin, Michelle in France but although enjoying his wanderings and the lifestyle, he had a hankering to return to England. He had been away for a long time and was growing bored of foreigners … the heat, beaches, tourism and hotels and was surprised to discover he was craving countryside, rain and English accents and fancied putting down roots … perhaps purchasing a property of his own.

In the privacy of his hotel room, he opened a map and looked at England. Where should he go? Where should he finally settle? He hadn't wanted to return to Liverpool. The place names had jumped out at him; London, Birmingham, Coventry, Oxford,

74

Bournemouth. It was difficult to choose. In the end, he closed his eyes, circled the map with his index finger and then plonked it down ... on Peesdown, a suburb in the east of Leeds, near to a stately home called Temple Newsam. He had looked it up on the internet. It wasn't a large place, just a few rows of shops ... a sizable residential area ... and a park with a lot of acreage which didn't belong to the council but to the Pee family. Their mansion had burned down, killing most of them. The surviving members had moved away but opened the grounds for the public to use. How generous of them. Peesdown Park. He had liked the sound of it. He had looked forward to seeing it.

CHAPTER 6

Miranda stayed the night at Anna's. She had consumed too much champagne to safely drive her car home so Anna offered her one of the guest rooms. In the morning they breakfasted on cornflakes and coffee and then Miranda departed to feed cats for her clients who were on holiday and to collect Nellie from her parents' house in Seacroft, where she had deposited her before going out the previous evening. She didn't like leaving Nellie at home alone for long periods as even though she was an adult dog, she still had a tendency to chew things she shouldn't when there was no-one around to watch her … and she didn't take kindly to being put in a cage, howling the place down and upsetting the neighbours. Naughty Nellie!

Once she had waved Miranda off, sad she wouldn't have time for a walk with her for a while, Anna sat down at the dining room table with her pad, pen, telephone and a pile of brochures from various wholesalers and shop equipment and signage suppliers. First of all, she studied shelving, display units and counters, marvelling at the choice but determined not to become overwhelmed, although she would definitely need advice and help. She rang the company nearest to Peesdown and was delighted when an efficient young lady informed her that she would send a representative to the shop that very afternoon to discuss her requirements and to take measurements.

There was no point in ordering any actual stock until the shelving was in situ so she rang Alfie Johnson, the painter and decorator who had made such a lovely job of her house three years ago, and asked if he would be so good as to give the shop a lick of paint prior to the shelving being fitted. He was busy, he informed her, but would make time in the evenings and the coming weekend so it would be ready for the fixtures and fittings the following week. Turning her attention to the front door of the shop and the possibility of installing two sets of French windows in the garden room, she rang the local door and window fitter who was also happy to meet her there that afternoon.

She flicked through the signage brochure but as she still hadn't thought about what she was going to call the business, she had no choice but to leave it for a while longer while she mulled over names. She had made a list of possibles but nothing seemed quite right. It was either too fancy or too boring. Perhaps she should just call it the Peesdown Pet Shop. That was boring too but at least everyone would know where and what it was. She would think about it a little longer.

She thought hard and long about the cafe side of the business but that needed council permission and a lot more besides and as she had enough to contend with, just getting the shop up and running, that would have to be put on the back burner for a little longer, especially as she would need staff and that was another worry as she had never interviewed anyone for a job in her life. Gosh, there was so much to think about.

She had a quick lunch; a banana sandwich and a slice of lemon cake, washed down with a cup of Yorkshire tea, put a comb through her hair and set out for Peesdown to meet the two salesmen she had appointments with at the shop. Her shop! She still couldn't believe it.

* * *

Miranda fed the cats, collected Nellie, and shot home to change into her walking attire and arrange her fabulous bouquet from Jeremy in two cut-glass vases someone had given her for a wedding present when she had married the Beastly Bastard. They had never been used before. Adorning her mantelpiece, the vases and their beautiful blooms looked divine and Miranda hugged herself with delight at the memory of Jeremy and last night's kiss. She could still feel his lips on hers. Jeremy. Oh God, he was so gorgeous!

Bundling Nellie into the car, having picked up all the house keys she would need for the day for her two group dog walks, piles of poo bags, tissues, and handfuls of biscuits, she collected the first pack of dogs, which took nearly an hour as none of them lived close to each other, and drove straight to Peesdown Park. It was a fairly nice early November day. No rain and quite mild, which people who were only walking their family dog would think perfect for a walk in the park. However, as far as professional dog walkers were concerned, their hour meandering around the lake and through the woods could prove to be a nightmare if tons of people turned out with their dogs and kids.

As soon as the dogs were unloaded from Miranda's car, they bounded off towards the lake, all bar Pongo and Purdy who were on their extension leads. Miranda hurried them along, in hot pursuit of the remaining four before they started depositing their poo all over the grass. Luckily, they hadn't gone far and within seconds Miranda had scooped it all up and placed the bags in the bin provided on the lakeside path.

Surprisingly, as she cast her eyes over the park, there weren't many people about this morning. She could see old Fart Features and Mrs Smedley deep in conversation at the far side of the lake. She would have to skip up into the wood to avoid them. Suffering from a nagging headache, no doubt from the champagne last night, a confrontation with either of them wouldn't be a good idea today.

There were one or two other people dotted around the park, some with dogs, some without. She could just make out Mr Pemworthy coming towards her but he was okay. Quite a nice old gentleman. Always stopped for a chat. Always had something nice for the dogs in his pocket and they all loved him ... greedy things. It would take a while for them to meet as he walked very slowly, even with his stick. He had mentioned during one of their chats that some kind of accident had caused damage to his leg when he was young but he never explained exactly what and she had never liked to ask.

Miranda called the dogs and headed towards him. She never minded talking to him. He was always so interested in what she was up to and she could tell him all about Anna and the shop. He might well turn out to be a customer as he was always buying doggie treats.

With no-one else on this side of the lake, Miranda was able to relax and let the dogs wander at will, apart from little Pongo and Purdy on the extension leads, who plodded happily along, one on either side of her.

Her thoughts turned to last night. She still felt a warm glow every time she thought about Jeremy wanting to telephone her and even take her out next time he was in Leeds. She hoped it wouldn't be long as she couldn't wait to see him again. God, he was soooo perfect. He was a true gentleman with impeccable manners, he had interesting things to talk about but he listened as well, he was kind and thoughtful and most of all, he was damned good looking. However, that all added up to a man who was going to be terribly desirable to lots of women and she didn't want any competition. She would have to smarten herself up, lose some weight, get her hair done somewhere more sophisticated than the quick trims she had at the cheap and cheerful hairdresser down the road. Oh goodness, what a chore it was, finding a decent man and then trying to keep him interested. Could she be bothered? She thought of his eyes twinkling into hers. She thought of his kiss. She thought of that thick mop of hair which she wanted to run her hands through. Oh, yes. It was definitely worth it for him.

* * *

Not wanting to miss Miranda in the park, William headed out early and there she was, in the distance, the dogs darting hither and thither but never going too far away from her. She was the leader of the pack and they all knew it and respected her for it.

He felt a thrill rush through him. She was alone. That damned woman wasn't here for once. He could engage Miranda in conversation, keep up the trust she had for him … that was what was so important … the trust. He wondered if she would tell him about last night, about who she had been out with and why. She was an open person, never one to hold back with providing information, so it should be easy to let her chatter on and she would reveal all. He hobbled towards her, making out his leg was particularly painful today due to the damp weather. She smiled and he smiled back.

* * *

Freddie Fletcher stared across the lake. He could see Miranda and her blasted dogs talking to that elderly gentleman, William something … he was hopeless at remembering people's names … who had become a frequent park visitor in the last few months. Nice old boy. They had sat on a bench together in the summer and had quite a chinwag. As Freddie walked in their direction, having said goodbye to Mrs Smedley after listening to her usual complaints about professional dog walkers and how they should never be allowed to use public parks, and the fright she received yesterday, he shoved his hands into the pockets of his jacket as even though it was milder than usual for November, he felt chilly.

He hoped he hadn't a cold coming on but it wouldn't be surprising, having been holed up in the woods during the middle of the night for a week now, instructed to do so by Reginald Barrington, from Barrington & Barrington, solicitors in central Leeds, who looked after the affairs of the Pee family and who had employed him to manage the day-to-day care of the park. There had been reports of men turning up to bait badgers in their setts deep in the woods. He wasn't to confront anyone, of course, just keep an eye out and if they turned up, report them to the police. On the first night, he was accompanied by a police officer but as nothing happened, indeed it hadn't all week, a Chief Inspector decided it was a waste of resources so he was left to keep watch on his own. After a week of damned uncomfortable nights and then having to stay awake for a few hours during the day while he did his rounds, Barrington decided enough was enough and Freddie didn't have to be on duty at night again for a while.

He yawned and thought longingly of his bed. He was due to knock off after lunch and then he was going home to a decent meal and then bed and he wasn't going to get up until tomorrow morning if he could help it.

* * *

"Oh dear, here comes old Fart Features," said Miranda under her breath, casting her eyes around quickly to make sure all the dogs were behaving themselves.

William gave her a reproachful look. "I presume you mean Freddie Fletcher?"

"Well, yes, but Fart Features seems far more appropriate. He's such a miserable little man … and he's always moaning

80

about something. Why he was appointed as park keeper I have no idea. We need a person who is cheerful and fun, not someone as miserable as him."

"Morning," said Freddie, approaching smartly. He found walking quickly kept him awake. If he ambled along, he was quite likely to close his eyes and nod off and he didn't want to end up in the lake. It was pretty deep in places and he wasn't a strong swimmer.

"Morning," replied William and Miranda simultaneously.

"Mrs. Smedley ...," Freddie began, glaring at Miranda.

"Oh no," she groaned. "What's the woman complaining about now?"

"Well, the usual regarding you, young lady but she also informed me there was a flasher in the park yesterday afternoon. Gave her a right fright apparently ... he was standing over there, near to the trees at the far end of the lake," he pointed to where the woods were at their thickest, "and you know they have never caught the rapist from a few months ago. It could well have been him."

"Oh, heavens. Poor woman. I hope she reported him to the police."

"Yes, but even so, be careful. I know you have all these dogs," he grimaced as Nellie approached him and Pongo cocked his leg against the trunk of a weeping willow, "but you never know what these men will do ... carry poison meat or something. You can't rely on animals to protect you."

"No. You're right," Miranda said, astonished to discover she was agreeing with the horrid little man for once. "And I don't ... see, I have my rape alarm with me," she continued, pulling out the little black device from a pocket in the top of her jacket. "I never go walking without it."

"And I'll keep you company today, Miranda," William said quickly. "I know I'm not much use physically but at least I have another pair of eyes to see if there is anyone threatening about."

"Right. Good," Freddie muttered. "Well, just be careful anyway ... now I must be off. Goodbye ... and if I were you, I would keep well away from the woods for a while when you are on your own."

He marched off briskly in the direction of the car park where the toilets were situated. He needed a wee badly. Damned prostate. It didn't matter when he was up in the woods and could have a wee anywhere but when he was down here, in full sight of everyone, it was a flipping nuisance.

* * *

William was enjoying himself. Freddie had just given him a really good excuse for accompanying Miranda this morning and looking around the park, there were few people about who would stop to engage them in conversation so he would have her undivided attention, apart from the dogs of course.

"So, who is that lady who has been walking with you recently?" he asked as they continued along the lakeside path towards the woods at the far end, the dogs milling happily around them, although Nellie was eyeing up a lone swan who was a little near to the bank for her liking. She decided to give it a fright and launched herself with an almighty splash into the water beside it. The swan, startled out of its wits, hissed and flapped madly and then decided it was safer further down the lake and headed off hastily. Nellie swam back to the bank and hauled herself out, shaking her coat furiously and wagging her tail, looking thoroughly pleased with herself.

"Oh, Nellie," Miranda said sternly. "When will you learn? That swan could have really hurt you if it had wanted to. You are a very naughty, silly girl."

Nellie laughed with her eyes at her mistress and darted off across the grass to join the others, totally unconcerned by the warning.

Miranda looked at William, who was still waiting for her answer. "Oh, you mean Anna. She's only recently taken up walking ... not long lost her husband and is grieving badly. She has just bought that empty shop ... in Peesdown High Street. She's going to turn it into a pet shop."

"That's nice. It will be handy for you then ... you must buy a lot of items with your business," William said, pleased that this Anna person would be too busy to have time for walking in the park any longer.

"Yes, but I'm going to miss her company ... although it's very nice to have yours," Miranda added quickly.

William gave a queer smile. Miranda just caught it as she turned to look at him. It was almost a sneer. For a fleeting second, she felt a little alarmed but then told herself off for being silly. He was a harmless old man ... and a very pleasant one, come to that. She enjoyed their chats as he was quite happy for her to prattle on about what was happening in her life as he said very little about his. In fact, she thought, he never did give a straight answer to any question about his life. The only thing she knew about him was that he lived alone somewhere in Peesdown but exactly where, she had no idea. It couldn't be far as he didn't appear to own a vehicle and as he was elderly and couldn't walk very well, his home had to be nearby. Perhaps she should offer to give him a lift home and then she would find out.

As soon as they reached the car park at the end of the walk, William watched the dogs all jump into Miranda's Volvo, amused that they all knew exactly where and by whom they wanted to sit.

"Right, Miranda. Now you're safely back at your car, I'll leave you. Thank you for your company this morning. It's been a real pleasure," he said politely.

"And thank you for yours, William. Can I give you a lift home? I know the car smells a bit doggy but the passenger seat is quite clean."

William smiled. "No, thank you. I haven't far to go and I don't want to hold you up as I know how busy you are. Just be careful on your next walk."

He turned and headed off towards the park gates, waving his stick in the air as a goodbye. Miranda watched him go. What a lovely old gentleman, she thought. It had been so kind of him to turn back and keep her company all around the lake. It had added a whole hour to his walk and she hoped he wouldn't suffer badly with his leg as a result. She drove contentedly out of the car park. Being a professional dog walker could be a lonely job sometimes, apart from the dogs of course, so it was an added bonus when someone wanted to join her to walk and talk.

She passed William just outside of the park gates. She tooted her car horn and waved, a huge smile on her face. He smiled back and waved his stick again, watching her car head across Miller Lane and up the High Street. He had enjoyed her company too.

CHAPTER 7

Busier than she had been in a very long while, Anna really enjoyed her day, the first since Gerald had died that she hadn't wanted to dissolve into tears at some point.

The two salesmen had been exceedingly helpful, especially the one whose appointment was first and whose firm was going to install the shelving, counter and display units. As there was nowhere to sit in the shop, she and Jules, as he liked to be called, adjourned to the Red Lion at the end of the High Street, adjacent to Miller Lane and the Peesdown Park gates, took over the table nearest the window and ordered coffee. Jules spread out all the brochures and Anna studied them carefully as he advised her on the most suitable fittings for her business and how much it would all cost. It certainly wasn't going to be cheap but then she had expected that and anyway, once everything was firmly in place, she wasn't going to have to replace any of it for a very long time. An hour later she had made her choice, they went back to the shop so Jules could measure up, she paid a deposit, he promised delivery and fitting at the end of the following week and then left her with a copy of the order.

She had just said goodbye when there was a knock on the shop door and she opened it to find Alfie, dressed in his painting overalls, on the threshold.

"I've had a cancellation so I can start here tomorrow if you would like me to," he said. "I can have a look now and see exactly what you want and then I can buy the paint this afternoon and start first thing … around 7.00 a.m., that's if you have a spare set of keys."

"Oh, that's brilliant, Alfie," Anna smiled. "The fixtures and fittings are coming at the end of next week so if you're all done and dusted by then, that would be great … and yes, I do have a spare set of keys. Here …" she said, taking a set from the bottom of her handbag.

"The walls just need freshening up but I don't want white," Anna said. "It's too cold and stark. Cream is warm and more inviting … and I certainly don't want bright colours as that would be too distracting from what I have to sell."

"That's a very good point," Alfie agreed, nodding his head of thick, wavy red hair. "Right, Anna. I shall be here bright and early and with a bit of luck, can be finished in a couple of days. I must admit it will be handy having a pet shop in Peesdown ... and with a lot more choice than the local supermarkets. My little Andy ... he's my little Westie, he's a flippin' fussy eater so I have to keep changing the brand of wet food and as for biscuits ... it's a nightmare. I've taken to grating cheese on top to tempt him but
that doesn't always work and I get so worried about him."

Anna nodded. "Well, I'm going to offer a wide selection of food, wet and dry ... and if anybody asks me for anything in particular, I shall certainly order it for them. So, hopefully, we can find something your little Andy will like."

"That would be marvellous, Anna. If you're going to be that flexible and helpful, you'll have pet owners flocking to your door."

"I do hope so, Alfie. This is a whole new venture for me and to be honest, pretty daunting, so I hope I can make it work."

"I'm sure you will, Anna ... and I shall be one of your first customers and will certainly spread the word. You won't need to pay for advertising once I've told the whole of Leeds."

Alfie left to head down to the wholesalers to buy the paint and Anna removed the box of sandwiches and a flask of coffee she had brought with her from her car, along with couple of sun chairs, and took them through to the garden room. She placed the chairs by the window, sat down and ate her lunch. It had been a very productive morning and now she just had to wait for the salesman from Peesdown Windows who had an appointment at 2.00 p.m.

She finished her sandwiches and coffee, unlocked the back door and stepped outside into the garden. Even at the beginning of winter, it was lovely and she was so looking forward to seeing what it would look like in the summer. She walked all the way around, examining the apple tree in the middle of the lawn, now devoid of leaves but looking healthy. With a bit of luck, it could provide a good supply of apples next year. If so, she could use them in the cafe, make apple tarts or something similar to sell.

She would have to look at recipes at some point. She smiled. It was another thing to add to her to-do list.

She checked the flower beds on all four sides of the garden to see exactly what was growing there. Lots of shrubs; rhododendrons, roses, hydrangeas and heathers and Jeremy had mentioned there was a fabulous show of daffodils, tulips and crocuses in the spring so there must be a good number of bulbs deep down in the soil as well. There were also trellises attached to the walls with clematis and honeysuckle stems snaking along in gay abandon. Anna sighed. It was all going to look splendid once the winter was over and she was looking forward to sitting out here and enjoying it all, especially in the evenings when the traffic was quieter … which meant, of course, she would have to seriously think about selling the house. Steady on, she told herself.

One thing at a time. The shop had to come first.

She took one last look at the garden before going back inside. It would be so easy to place tables and chairs out here to extend the sitting area for the cafe. She began to feel excited, visualising all her patrons, with or without their dogs, chatting amongst themselves, drinking her beverages, eating her cakes and sandwiches. Gosh, it was going to be such an adventure … and damned hard work. She did hope she hadn't bitten off more than she could chew.

Mr Fleming from Peesdown Windows arrived promptly at 2.00 p.m. and showed her a brochure with the most secure front door he could provide, along with French doors for the garden room. He, like Jules before him, measured up, she signed the order form, paid her second deposit for the day and off he went with a promise that the fitter would be there at 8.30 a.m. in two days' time.

Tired, she decided enough was enough for now and she would go home but as she was passing the stairs, she looked up and decided to have another quick look at the accommodation on the second floor. If she was going to be here, working long hours, it would be more sensible to move in. It would certainly save a lot of travelling in the rush hour, which she didn't like the thought of, especially in the winter when the roads were icy and dangerous.

She went upstairs, poked her head around the bedroom door and then entered the lounge. She would have to change some of her furniture; sell some of her bigger items, especially the king-sized bed and the massive corner sofa she had picked with Gerald. Here, she could make do with a single bed in the bedroom and perhaps buy a couple of recliners and a two-seater sofa for the lounge. That would work and left room for a couple of bookcases, a coffee table and her television cabinet.

She didn't like the decor. Jeremy's father had chosen ice blue which made the upstairs rooms seem a little cold. That would have to be changed and maybe Alfie could decorate up here when he could fit it in. After all, there was no rush. If she put her house on the market, it could take weeks or even months to sell, especially at this time of year … and anyway, she had enough to contend with at the moment, just getting the shop up and running.

She went back downstairs, picked up her handbag, flask and sandwich box, took her keys from the pocket of her jacket, locked up and went out to her car, tired and content … and yes … happy.

* * *

Miranda made the telephone call, with her heart in her mouth. Speaking to someone, actually a member of his family, his nearest and dearest relative, was … well, she didn't know what it was really. Her nerves were all over the place. For goodness sake, Miranda, pull yourself together, she told herself, gripping her mobile with one hand and tapping her pen on her diary with the other.

She was in what she called her office, which was actually her dining room, although she couldn't remember the last time she had eaten a meal there. Probably when she had first married the Beastly Bastard. She had been a bit wifey then. She cringed, remembering how she had bought cookbook after cookbook to try and find delicious recipes to wow him with when he returned home at the end of the day … but it hadn't lasted long.

It had always been Barry's ambition to be his own boss after years of working as a mechanic for other outfits. Miranda had supported him and along with their savings, a business loan and help from his parents, two years into their marriage, Barry had bought premises in Meanwood and called it, very originally, Denton's Autos.

Unfortunately, being in total charge of his business went to his head and Barry began to throw money around recklessly, often entertaining prospective clients with fleets of cars needing regular maintenance. The bills for his expensive 'business' lunches began to mount, Miranda's attempts at satisfying his appetite came to an abrupt halt and she began to worry constantly about money instead. If she hadn't worked in the office at Miller Brothers, a high-class bathroom and kitchen specialist, they certainly wouldn't have been able to keep up with the mortgage payments on this house and even if she had wanted to, she couldn't afford to give up work to have children.

Miranda urged Barry to be more cautious as many of the clients he spent lavishly on took their business elsewhere and due to his focusing all his attention on them, his bread-and-butter clients began to use other garages in the locality but he threw her comments aside.

"Don't you worry, Miranda," he would say repeatedly, "things will soon turn around. You'll see."

With horror, she watched their bank balance dip more and more and even though she brandished statements under his nose, he still insisted on entertaining prospective clients as well as visiting the Granger's Arms, their local hostelry, at least twice a week. He always went on a Tuesday as it was darts night and he bought round after round for his so-called mates. Saturday nights, as far as he was concerned, was non-negotiable. They had to go out, come what may. Miranda would have liked to stay in, curl up in front of the television with a good DVD, a takeaway and a bottle of wine but no, down to the pub they had to go, where he would hang around at the bar with his mates, getting drunker by the second as they downed pint after pint while she had to sit with the wives, who all did the same, the only difference being they drank wine. They would all leave the pub at closing time, highly intoxicated and roll home to fall into bed. She had hated it and was pleased she didn't have to cope with all that any longer. Quite frankly, he had ended up doing her a huge favour, although she didn't think so at the time.

Tremendously good looking with dark hair, big expressive brown eyes (not unlike Nellie's, she giggled now), tall and slender, Barry was extremely attractive and it was a rare female who wasn't bowled over by his looks and charm. Miranda had put up with it, ignoring the silly girls who made cow eyes at him and came out with suggestive remarks but the crunch came when she returned early from work with a vicious migraine. As soon as she opened the front door, she had known she wasn't alone in the house. Barry's car keys were on the kitchen worktop, beside a bottle of expensive Chardonnay she had been given for her birthday. It was open and half empty. There was also a brown leather handbag on the floor, which looked vaguely familiar and it certainly wasn't hers. A whiff of perfume she recognised was in the air.

Then she heard it … the moans from upstairs … from their bedroom. She had nearly turned and walked out of the house, not wanting the confrontation that was probably going to end their marriage but curiosity got the better of her. She needed to clarify exactly who her husband was committing adultery with.

She took off her shoes and crept upstairs, the cries of the woman getting louder and louder as she neared orgasm. Well, her bubble was soon going to burst and that was no mistake.

She reached the bedroom and threw open the door. It crashed against the wall and the two naked figures on the bed shot away from each other.

Miranda had been aghast, unable to believe who was fornicating with her husband. The pain was unbearably intense that she had been so badly betrayed.

"No … no!" Miranda had cried. "Charlotte, how could you? Anybody … absolutely anybody but not you!"

"I'm sorry," Miranda's best friend since they had started secondary school together, gulped as she scrambled to cover herself with a sheet. "Miranda … please … let me explain."

"Explain! Christ! I don't think I need an explanation for this," Miranda shouted. "Get out of my house … both of you … and Barry … don't you ever come back. I want a divorce … and that's final. I've had it with you now … now, get out," she had screamed, throwing their clothes at them, her head splitting with the pain of the headache and the trauma of finding her husband in flagrante with the one woman she should have been able to trust, who had known all her secrets for more years than she cared to remember.

The divorce had been finalised six months later. With the help of a few thousand pounds inheritance from her maternal grandmother, she had been able to buy Barry out of the house and found living on her own was immensely satisfying. It was great to be able to do as she pleased, when she pleased ... Nellie permitting, of course, whose routine needed sticking to ... and then there was the business .... Four Paws, which she had set up two years ago, biting the bullet and jacking in her job. It had been a huge risk and she had many sleepless nights to begin with but she needn't have worried, she was good at her job and quickly gained the respect of the few clients that came her way. Word of mouth did the rest and before she knew it, she was well and truly busy and was now expanding rapidly.

"Hello, Daphne Roberts," came a pleasant voice at the other end of the phone.

"Oh," Miranda said, dragging herself back to the present. "Hello, Mrs Roberts. This is Miranda Denton, from Four Paws ... your brother ... Jeremy ... he said you were interested in my services."

"Ah, yes. Miranda. Thank you so much for calling. I bought my two young pugs, Fred and Merry, while I've been at home on maternity leave but I have to go back to work in a couple of weeks so need someone reliable to walk them every day. I have a childminder but she hasn't the time to see to the dogs as well so I thought the best thing to do was to find a professional dog walker. I happened to mention it to Jeremy and he said he had just met you, so there we are. So, is there any chance you could fit my little darlings in, Miranda? They're very sociable and just want to play with other dogs so you shouldn't have too much of a problem with them."

Miranda thought quickly. It was lucky Pongo and Purdy were away with their parents for a month's holiday. That meant she could fit Fred and Merry in their places while she advertised for another dog walker before they returned. She had interviewed a few over the past few weeks but they were all hopeless and she didn't want to risk taking on anyone who wasn't going to be fully committed to doing a good job. Belinda had turned out to be conscientious and reliable, and all the dogs loved her but she didn't want to take on more than the six she was already walking. Another advert would have to go into the Yorkshire Evening Post as soon as possible. Daphne's dogs couldn't be turned away. It was too precious a link with Jeremy.

"Yes ... yes, I could. Obviously, I need to meet you ... and Fred and Merry ... and there is some paperwork to complete. Are you free this evening at all?" she asked.

* * *

Daphne's house turned out to be a splendid detached red-brick affair in Headingley, not far from the renowned cricket ground. It had massive windows, a solid oak front door, an enormous, beautifully manicured wrap-around garden and a tarmacked drive with room to park a good number of cars directly in front of the house. There was also a double garage to the right of the property with what appeared to be a flat or office above.

Miranda parked her mud-splattered Volvo, kicking herself for not stopping off at a car wash on the way, beside a shiny and spotless royal blue Mercedes sports car. With a rising, bitterly cold wind hitting her full in the face as she got out of her car, she tightly clutched her handbag and her leather organiser which held her insurance documents, her police check, the dog walking signup form and information on all the services Four Paws could offer. She made her way to the front door and banged the heavy brass door knocker.

The door opened to reveal a female version of Jeremy. Miranda had no idea if she were younger or older than him but she looked amazing with expensively cut and highlighted fair hair shaped around her face, a perfect hourglass figure even though it hadn't been long since the birth of her twins, and her clothes were definitely designer; flowing leisure trousers and a pretty blue and yellow top. Large gold earrings, a solid band of gold on her wedding finger and an enormous amber dress ring on the middle finger of her right hand finished the picture.

92

"Hello, Miranda. I'm Daphne," she said. "Please ... do come in ... and let me take your coat," she continued, moving aside to allow Miranda room to enter the spacious hallway of the house, which was big enough to be a room on its own. "Would you like tea or coffee?"

"Coffee, please. Milk and two sugars," Miranda replied.

Daphne ushered Miranda through to the capacious kitchen which looked like something from a magazine, with a great deal of chrome, glass, gleaming white units and worktops and a black and white tiled floor.

"Have a seat," said Daphne, nodding at the breakfast bar as she prepared the coffee. "I'm so pleased to meet you. Jeremy did nothing but sing your praises before he left for London. He was most impressed by what you're trying to achieve with your business."

"Thank you," Miranda said. Hearing Jeremy had voiced his approval of her to his sister gave her a real thrill and added to the fleeting kiss and a request to call her and see her again, things were definitely looking up.

"Now, I must warn you, Fred and Merry aren't too well trained. I have tried but with two new babies, it's been difficult to give them as much attention as they need ... and my husband, Nigel ... he's a barrister ... as am I   ...   well, he works long hours and although he's good with them, he really hasn't the interest."

"I see ... well, I can help you with training. They need to be able to sit and stay, walk reasonably well on the lead and most importantly, are good on recall. Taking six dogs out at a time is a little more complicated than just taking your own dog so they all have to be reasonably well behaved ... and sociable of course."

Daphne smiled as she handed Miranda her coffee and sat down beside her. "You will find Fred is very keen to be a good boy but Merry ... she does tend to be a bit slower on the uptake and you will have to be firm with her otherwise she will walk all over you.
She's a proper little madam."

"Oh, don't worry, I can be very firm when I have to be ... firm *and* kind," said Miranda hastily, in case Daphne thought she was going to be too strict.

"Well, I suppose you should meet them," laughed Daphne, showing beautifully formed white teeth, making Miranda jealous. Her teeth had never been white, however much she brushed and used numerous products, advertising how brilliantly they worked. Consideration had been given to having the procedure done properly at the dentist but she could never afford it so put up with being envious of people such as Daphne and hoped no-one would notice how her own were more off white than pearly white.

Daphne stood up and moved to a door to the far side of the kitchen and opened it. Two cream balls of sheer energy hurtled in, dashed up to Miranda and sniffed her legs madly, checking her out. 'Who are you? Who have you been with? Do we like you?'

Miranda let them sniff her, then stood up and fished in the pockets of her jeans for two biscuits. "I presume you don't mind me giving them a treat?" she asked Daphne.

Daphne shook her head. "No, go ahead."

"Sit," Miranda commanded firmly to the dogs. Their bottoms touched the tiled floor instantly. They stared at her adoringly, licking their lips in anticipation. They loved her already if she was going to bring them treats.

"Right, that's enough, you two," ordered Daphne once they had devoured a little marrowbone biscuit each. "Beds ... while Miranda and I complete the paperwork."

Reluctant to leave their new friend, they walked despondently to their baskets in the corner of the kitchen and settled down, looking hopefully at Miranda in case she countermanded their mistress.

"I think we shall get along very well," said Miranda, smiling at them, pleased to see they knew how to behave even if they didn't want to do as they were told. "How often would you like me to walk them?"

"Monday to Friday, please, Miranda. I had hoped to go back part-time but it's just not possible I'm afraid. Although I can bring work home sometimes so there may be days when we don't need you. Will that be a problem?"

"No. I'm very flexible. I text all my clients at the weekend to check which days they require for the week ahead. Quite a number work different shifts, being in the medical profession or police force, so their needs are variable. I'll put you on the list to contact too."

They completed the dog walking form, Miranda showed Daphne the insurance and police check documents and gave her the sheet listing details of all the services Four Paws could offer. Daphne gave her a key for the back door which led into the utility room, and the alarm code.

"They will be in the utility room when you come ... and they can stay there after their walks. They have beds in there as well as in here," said Daphne "and all their things are in there too, i.e. their leads, towels and if they're extra dirty, you have access to the sink to wash them down ... and we always bring them in and out that way so they don't make a mess in the rest of the house ... or destroy anything."

Half an hour later, with all her questions answered and Daphne satisfied that her precious pooches would be in safe hands, Miranda departed, pleased as punch to think she was going to be on the fringes of Jeremy's life while walking his sister's dogs.

However, she was going to be in a pickle if she didn't get another dog walker pretty soon and the first thing she would have to do in the morning was to place another advert in the paper. It was a pity Anna's shop wasn't up and running yet as she could have put an advert in there too.

* * *

Anna was spending the evening thinking hard and was pleased with what she had decided to call the shop ... Pampered Pets. It sounded good and covered exactly what she was going to try and do as she would provide everything for domestic animals she could think of to make them physically comfortable. She would have an array of beds and mattresses, blankets, harnesses, leads, collars, toys and medical items which didn't need a vet's prescription. Then there would be a considerable amount of food, wet and dry, which would take up a lot of space. The main room in the shop was a really good size and she could squeeze lots of the smaller items in there. The larger ones, which people couldn't slip into their pockets, could be in the room at the back and she could place the counter at an angle so she or her assistants could see exactly what was going on in there at all times. She could get CCTV of course but didn't consider it essential at the outset but it might well be later on, especially when the cafe was up and running and more people were milling about.

She sent Miranda a text. "How did you get on with Jeremy's sister and her dogs? I've decided to call the shop, 'Pampered Pets'. What do you think?"

"Yes, she was lovely and so were the dogs," came the reply. "Pampered Pets is absolutely brill. Love it!"

Anna beamed, delighted to have Miranda's approval.

CHAPTER 8

As Belinda Dobbs set out to collect the pack of dogs which she was going to walk that morning, she sighed with satisfaction. She loved her new job. She liked her new boss, Miranda, she liked being with all the dogs and she liked walking them in Peesdown Park. She had always wanted to work with animals but had somehow, after leaving school at sixteen, ended up in offices instead … and endured four years of boredom in administration. It had been so frustrating, looking out of the window every day, wanting to be outdoors and not stuck in, hour after hour, in a stuffy office with stuffy people. She wanted freedom, to be outside, surrounding herself with nature and animals and here she was, doing exactly that, although the circumstances in which it had come about had been traumatic, to say the least.

Belinda lived alone with her mother, Angela Dobbs. Her father had left the family home when Belinda was three and she could barely remember him. She had no other siblings and as her parents had moved to Leeds from Brighton in search of work before she was born, she barely knew her grandparents and her aunts and uncles, who rarely visited Leeds and vice versa. She hadn't minded. She and her mother were great friends, although they had to be careful with money, especially when her mother lost her job as a hairdresser when the salon she was working in closed down. Finding it difficult to obtain a position elsewhere, she debated on whether or not to go mobile and many of the women whose hair she had been caring for, urged her to. So, she did. She bought a little Fiat, all the hairdressing paraphernalia she would need and set it up. It took a few months for her new business to take off properly but within a year she was doing well and managed to finish paying off the mortgage on the little terraced ex-Council house she had bought in Crossgates, not far from Peesdown Park and the Temple Newsam estate.

Then, two years ago, Angela suffered a catastrophic stroke when driving home from a client's house. Luckily, she had been stationary at traffic lights at the time and hadn't crashed the car, even though she caused a massive tailback and the fury of drivers behind her who couldn't understand why her car didn't move when the lights turned green. A pedestrian went to investigate, found Angela slumped over the steering wheel whereupon the aggravated motorists calmed down, rang for an ambulance and pushed her car to the side of the road.

A nurse from the hospital rang Belinda and from then on life changed dramatically for both mother and daughter. Belinda had wanted to reduce her hours to help look after her mother, especially as the state benefit Angela was entitled to was fairly generous and with no mortgage to worry about, money wasn't a big issue and they could manage if they were careful. However, Belinda's boss wouldn't consider it so she gave in her notice and stayed at home. Her mother improved slightly and became a little more mobile as the months progressed and Belinda eventually decided she wanted to return to some kind of work, not full time but something that would get her out of the house for part of the day. Carers would be able to pop in to help Angela dress and prepare her meals so there was no reason not to look for something suitable. Angela urged her on, desperately worried Belinda was becoming isolated and lonely as all her old friends either moved away or settled down to married life and children and rarely had time to socialise.

Belinda started to look for part-time positions, seeing nothing she wanted to do and then, a few weeks ago, Miranda had advertised for a dog walker to join Four Paws. Belinda was intrigued. She had seen one or two professional dog walkers in the parks when she was walking Bailey, her daft, soppy six-year-old Golden Retriever and had often wondered about setting up her own business but felt the time wasn't right with her mother the way she was … but she could certainly work for someone else. She rang Miranda and arranged an interview.

Belinda took to Miranda instantly and was thrilled to be offered a job. Miranda was willing to pay a certain amount for each dog walked, which added up to a nice little sum if she walked five dogs, with Bailey, from Monday to Friday. It was a drop in salary from what she had been earning in an office but far better than the carer's allowance the government paid and doing just one walk every day only took around three hours, which included picking up and dropping off the dogs as well as walking them, so it was well worth it … and it was so much nicer than being stuck in an office. She loved being outside, whatever the weather, having the freedom to go where she wanted, walking miles, keeping the dogs under control and amused ... and being allowed to include Bailey was such a bonus. He loved being with a pack of other dogs and was livelier than he had been for a long time now he had lots of new friends and could have fun with them every day.

The only thing Belinda didn't like about her new job was the odd creepy man she came across. There had been two she had seen so far. When walking Bailey on her own, she had steered well away from wooded areas and kept in sight of families or other women but now she had no choice when the parks were busy. Miranda had warned her that on a sunny day, of which there hadn't been too many this October and November, it was a bit of a nightmare with cyclists, joggers and people with children or unruly dogs in the main part of the parks so it was wise to keep out of their way. Belinda had soon found out how right Miranda was when clashing with a temperamental jogger and a week later, a woman with a child in a pushchair who screamed and screamed at Bailey when he ventured a little too near, accompanied by Mindy and Puff, two black Labradors, who were part of her pack.

She began to venture into the woods, enjoying the solitude, watching the wildlife; the birds and the squirrels; studying and testing herself on her knowledge of species of trees, being able to recognise them just by the bark. It was spectacularly beautiful too now the leaves were all different colours and sometimes, if there was a bit of a breeze, they fell silently and gently around her, reminding her of how snow did the same but this was a fabulous colourful autumnal display settling on the ground; a glorious carpet of red, gold and lime green.

As the trees shed more and more, it also became far easier to see if anyone was lurking around ... and she felt reasonably safe with a pack of dogs. Bailey idolised her but quite frankly, she didn't expect him to do much to look after her as he was too soft and gentle. However, Mindy and Puff, who were the long-legged working variety of Labrador with masses of energy and very loud barks, were enough to put a lot of people off coming too close to her. Then there was Sasha, a pretty little ginger and white mongrel who adored the two Labs and would back them up in anything they did and finally, Tara, a massive no-nonsense Dalmatian and Luca, a funny little Pomeranian who charged around after the bigger dogs, yapping his head off. It was a good crew and with four big, energetic dogs and the two noisy smaller ones, pretty daunting to anyone who wasn't happy and relaxed in their company. So, Belinda began to enjoy exploring the pathways she had never dared venture down before.

Then, only two days into her new job, an encounter with a young bloke attempting to hide behind a tree gave her the willies and she called the dogs and hurried back to the safety of the lakeside path. Then there was an older man, short and tubby with glasses, who seemed to be following her, grinning innately every time she looked around at him. Again, she gathered up her band of dogs and headed back to the main part of the park.

However, even though the men had given her a bit of a scare, it didn't put her off her job. After all, they hadn't actually done anything to her, or even got close, so she mustn't make a mountain out of a molehill and anyway, there were some nice people around too. Some had dogs and some didn't but most people exchanged the odd pleasantry or even stopped for a chat, like that old boy, William Pemworthy, he said his name was. Nice old man, keen to get friendly with the dogs, carrying biscuits in his pockets and doling them out. The dogs liked him immensely and as soon as they saw him coming, would make a determined beeline for him. He was always keen to have a chat, probably because he was lonely, and as Belinda liked to talk, she found it easy to communicate with him for ten minutes or so until they went their separate ways. He always asked about Miranda too, which was nice. Yes, he was a really friendly old boy; so polite, with lovely manners and keen to make sure they were all safe and well during their time in the park. It was so good to have people about like him, instead of those nasty creepy chaps up in the woods.

* * *

Miranda was frantically busy that morning and deep in thought as she drove her first set of dogs to Peesdown Park. She had visited four sets of cats first thing which took up nearly two hours including driving time as none of them lived close to each other, given Nellie a quick wee and poo walk as she called it, dashed to Tesco to do some urgent shopping as she had nearly run out of dog food and milk, hung out a load of washing, threw a hoover around her lounge as Nellie had managed to shed a good deal of brown dog hairs last night and then, finally, set out to do the first group walk of the day.

Now the domestic side of her day was dealt with, her thoughts turned to her business. Four Paws had received two new enquiries last night, which meant going out this evening to visit them both. One was a lady who had four guinea pigs which needed looking after while she was on a Caribbean cruise in January, and another with a six-month-old chocolate Labrador who required walks four days every week. Goodness knows what he would be like if he was let loose with Nellie. She would certainly lead him astray.

There was also another advert for dog walkers going out today as although she had appointed Belinda three weeks ago and was very happy with her, more and more enquiries for the services Four Paws could provide were mounting by the day and she needed more walkers, although getting them was a real challenge.

She had used her home phone as the contact number, not wanting to be disturbed on her mobile by applicants when she was working so there would probably be plenty of messages waiting to be answered when she arrived home later. Whenever she advertised, half the population of Leeds contacted her, thinking the job sounded easy and the money would be good. She grimaced as she reached Peesdown Park and drove into the car park. If they only knew ... but then they soon did!

A year ago, Miranda had tried looking for dog walkers to help her and it had been a disaster, although an excellent learning curve for her so she was a lot more careful now. The first girl she had tried out, Veronica, lasted all of two days. She had informed Miranda she was well experienced with her own and her mother's dogs but all hell had been let loose on her very first day. Miranda had asked Veronica to walk her normal five; Pongo and Purdy, Sammy, Roger and Polly so she could stay at home and catch up with paperwork, Nellie having been taken out earlier. However, none of the dogs responded to Veronica and totally ignored her commands. She completely lost control and rang Miranda on her mobile in floods of tears saying she couldn't cope. Luckily, Veronica wasn't far away from Miranda's home, having insisted on walking in Roundhay Park as she knew it well. Miranda and Nellie had jumped into the Volvo and within minutes were in the small lakeside car park. She found Veronica, still crying, trying to round up the dogs who were causing havoc, chasing ducks and swans in and out of the water, much to the dismay of other dog walkers who were muttering under their breath about professional dog walkers and how they should be banned from the parks as they had no control.

Miranda strode down to the lake, let out one almighty yell and all five dogs stopped what they were doing instantly and charged up to her, desperate to let her know how much they were enjoying being in charge of their new dog walker! Miranda tried very hard to control her fury and to be professional with Veronica, who had made Four Paws look totally incompetent as well as letting Pongo and Purdy off the lead when she had been instructed not to. They were both soaking wet and bedraggled and their mother would be furious.

Veronica only lasted another day. Miranda just gave her two to walk. Easy dogs who were always obedient and could be let off the lead quite safely as their recall was brilliant. However, nervous after the previous day's debacle, Veronica decided to keep them on extension leads. One of them, a lively whippet who wanted to be tearing after everything he encountered, saw something in the distance that was too exciting to ignore and headed off, dragging Veronica and the other little Shih Tzu with it. Veronica tripped over a tree root, went crashing into the bushes and banged her head on another tree. The whippet disappeared into the distance, extension lead trailing behind, and when it did return a few minutes later, came back with a limp and a cut on his leg. Yet again, a tearful Veronica rang Miranda, who was walking her group in Peesdown. She was not overjoyed to have to interrupt her walk, persuade all the dogs to jump back into her Volvo, much to their disgust as they were all well aware their fun was being curtailed, and drive over to see what was occurring.

Needless to say, Veronica's services were dispensed with and Miranda was a lot more careful when recruiting. She had spent nearly a week out with Belinda, making sure she was competent to be in charge of a pack of dogs and they responded to her ... and it was all working out very well. Belinda was proving to be a good find, the dogs loved her, she gave them good walks and Miranda's clients were delighted. Hopefully, Belinda would stay with Four Paws for a long time.

Miranda reached the car park in Peesdown Park, jumped out of her car and started unloading the dogs. She could see Belinda and her crew in the distance, standing on the lakeside path talking to, of all people, Mrs Smedley. Miranda groaned. Please, God, the damned woman wasn't complaining again. She was such a pain.

Nellie shot out of the car. She wanted the grass under her feet, needed a poo, and she could also smell Belinda and her pack ... and yes, there was that old lady with her silly little Poodle. Nellie was off.

* * *

Janet Wrigglesthorpe from Woofs and Waggles, further along the lakeside path, was watching Miranda trying to prevent her wayward chocolate Labrador from teasing that nice elderly woman's lovely little white poodle. Janet smirked, seeing the lady having words with her. It was good to see Miranda getting a telling off. That damned dog of hers was so naughty.

Smugly, Janet called her pack to her, three Cockapoos and a Springer Spaniel. Walking four at a time was her limit as, in her opinion, it was ludicrous to take a larger number as they were far more difficult to control. It just proved her point, with Miranda engaged in heated conversation because of the behaviour of one dog while the others were merrily pooping everywhere and she hadn't noticed. If Mr Fletcher, the park keeper, happened to appear, he would have a field day. He had often stopped to chat to Janet, praising her on the way she kept her dogs under strict

103

control, 'unlike other *professional* dog walkers,' he would say with a sniff of disdain. They both knew to whom he alluded.

Janet turned and headed away from the lake. With only four, who were all very well behaved and sociable, she could walk anywhere in the park without worrying about the people and dogs they met. Unlike Miranda, who had to head for the woods more often than not … and with a rapist still at large and the odd creepy chap hanging about, even with a pack of dogs, that was something Janet certainly didn't want to do.

She sighed with satisfaction. She was going to enjoy her walk. She had a feeling Miranda might not.

* * *

"I've managed to find the address of the Pee family in Ireland and I fully intend to write to them about this terrible trend in walking packs of unruly dogs in public spaces," Mrs Smedley stated adamantly. "It shouldn't be allowed and I am going to do the best I can to have it stopped, my girl … I am extremely tired of your dogs, in particular, bothering my poor Precious." She glared at Nellie, who was on the lead but crying and struggling to get loose so she could get to the poodle, who was hiding behind his mother and staring out over the lake to avoid Nellie's eye.

"And just look, you haven't noticed your dogs are all over the place, soiling the grass."

"Well, no, Mrs Smedley. I thought it was more important to make Nellie leave you and Precious alone. I shall collect it now."

"You better, young lady. I am going to watch until you have collected every bit."

"Yes, Mrs Smedley … and I am so sorry about Nellie. I will keep her on the lead if I see you approaching from now on."

"That is a very good idea … the dog should never be allowed off at all in my opinion. Totally unruly."

"Yes, she does have a mind of her own," Miranda agreed, fascinated by the way in which the heavily made-up woman, with far too much blusher on her cheeks, pursed her lips which showed up all the wrinkles around her mouth, making her look even older.

"But she doesn't mean any real harm. She's just playful and greedy. That's her main fault. She's very loving and wouldn't hurt

anyone ... and certainly not another dog."

"That's as maybe but I am thoroughly fed up with it ... our visits to the park become a somewhat daunting experience as one or other of your dogs make a beeline for us ... unlike dear Janet," she nodded her head in the direction of the owner of Woofs and Waggles. "She never allows her animals to put a foot wrong." "Yes, Mrs Smedley ... I am truly sorry," said Miranda, throwing a dark look at the grinning Janet and the four dogs trotting by her side. Trust Miss Goody Two Shoes to be around while she was being castigated by Mrs Smedley. Hauling Nellie after her, along with Pongo and Purdy, she pulled out her poo bags and started the collecting process, fully aware of Mrs Smedley watching her every move.

"There," Miranda said, proudly waving three bags of poo in the air before depositing them in a nearby bin. "All collected ... now, good day, Mrs Smedley. I hope you enjoy the rest of your walk."

Mrs Smedley gave her a withering look, not sure whether Miranda was being deliberately sarcastic. She decided she would give her the benefit of the doubt for once, turned on her heel and walked towards the car park, glad it was time to go home and have a nice warming cup of soup.

Miranda sighed with relief once the woman was out of sight. She hadn't needed that as soon as they had reached the park ... and have it all witnessed by flaming Janet Wrigglesthorpe. Janet had only started up her dog walking business a couple of months ago and had been a proverbial pain ever since, assuming that she knew it all and using a particularly irritating pompous air when they engaged in conversation. Miranda hoped they wouldn't bump into each other further into the park. She headed for the woods. Janet didn't like going up there.

Miranda strode along, desperately missing Anna's company but she was busy at the shop now the decorating was finished, the fixtures and fittings secured and from today, the stock was arriving. The opening day was a week on Saturday and Miranda was looking forward to going in to help. Hopefully, a lot of people would turn up after all the advertising she and Anna had done. Between them, they had handed out hundreds of leaflets and pinned up notices everywhere it was allowed. Anna had contacted the Yorkshire Evening Post, where an advert was going in every night up until the big day and they had sent out a reporter to interview her, which was going to be broadcast next Thursday, two days before the actual opening. After all that, if there was anyone in Leeds who wasn't aware there was going to be a new and animal-free pet shop in the vicinity, Miranda would be very surprised. She did hope it would turn out to be a huge success. It was so good to see Anna excited about her project. She had been so despondent and a bundle of sheer misery when they had met and now look at her; completely revitalised and desperate to get stuck into her new venture. Anna was a lovely person and deserved all the luck she could get and Miranda was determined to help in any way she could. However, there was a walk to do now and another after this. She would ring Anna later and see how her day had gone.

* * *

Anna was having a ball. Her shop was beginning to take shape now the fixtures and fittings were all in place and it hadn't been long after she arrived that morning when deliveries started turning up. Boxes were beginning to pile up on the floor and it was becoming a struggle to get in and out of the door.

She locked the shop and set to, wishing she had thought to ask the delivery men to take the heavier stuff straight through to the rear room where it was going to be displayed; all the cat and dog beds and baskets and the big sacks of dried food, along with the tins. Two hours later, she looked around the room with pleasure. It was all taking shape. All the sacks of food were lined up beautifully, providing a good choice, including some which were wheat, gluten and grain-free. Hopefully what she had to offer would satisfy the majority of her customers … and as she had told Alfie before he commenced the decorating, if anyone required something specific, then she would be more than happy to order it for them.

The wet food, all the tins and sachets, were lined up on the shelves; again, a wide choice which should tempt the most discerning of feline and canine palates and the beds, baskets and blankets looked lovely, in an array of colours and textures in which their future owners would no doubt curl up in complete comfort and luxury.

Yes, the display looked good but she was quite exhausted, starving hungry and needed to sit down and have lunch in the garden room, then she would tackle the front of the shop, which would need a lot more thought as it was going to be the first place customers saw as they came through the door.

Just as she had bitten into her cheese and tomato sandwich, the bell rang. Thinking it was the last delivery she was waiting for, she got up readily and opened the shop door. She was wrong. It was Mr Pemworthy, standing smiling on the threshold.

"Hello, Mr Pemworthy. I'm afraid we're not open until a week on Saturday."

"I know, Anna ... I do hope I can call you Anna?" Anna nodded.

"I just wondered ... I have the afternoon spare. I wondered if you would like a little help. I see you're arranging your stock. I could always open things for you while you decide where they should go ... that's if you would like me to. I wouldn't want to get in your way."

"No, not at all. That's so kind of you," Anna said, realising he was probably a bit lonely and would like the company ... and it would be nice to have some help. "Please, come in. I'm just having my lunch in the back room before I get started again. Would you like a sandwich and a cup of coffee?"

"A cup of coffee would be most welcome but I don't want to interrupt your lunch. Just show me what you need doing and I'll crack on," William smiled, entering the shop. He locked the door behind him.

CHAPTER 9

The phone, which sat on the counter next to the till and had only been connected yesterday, began to ring, making Anna jump. She grinned at William.

"Gosh, that's the first time it's rung ... frightened me to death."

William smiled and continued what he was doing, slicing open boxes of rawhide chews with the sharp blade of his penknife.

Anna picked up the phone. "Pampered Pets," she stated clearly, having to think what to say for a second. It was going to take a while to get used to the name of her business.

"Hi, Anna," Miranda said on the other end of the line. "Just wondering how you're getting on today with all your deliveries."

Anna smiled. "Really well. William ... Mr Pemworthy ... has given me a hand. He popped in earlier and offered. I managed to sort the back room this morning and between us, we've found a home for everything in the front this afternoon. It's looking good and I'm quite overwhelmed with it all. I can't wait to open and welcome my first customers."

"Oh, that's great ... and how nice of him to help you. He's a lovely old boy. I can't pop in today," Miranda continued, talking quickly as she was in a rush. "I'm up to my eyes with cats and dogs and I have more interviews for dog walkers this evening. Belinda is absolutely great but she only has time to do one walk every day as she needs to get home to her mother ... and I'm receiving so many enquiries from dog owners and don't want to turn anyone away if I can help it ... and I don't think I'm going to be able to sit down at all over Christmas. It's going quite potty with bookings as so many people are going away and want their cats fed and watered. I already have seven booked in, with two visits per day, and I have a sneaky suspicion there are going to be a lot more enquiries before the big day."

"Well, that's good. It just shows you're trusted and good at your job ... and I certainly shan't be working over Christmas, so if you need to pop in, just for lunch or something, you must ... I would love it if you did, as I shall be alone ... although, sorry, Miranda. I wasn't thinking, you'll probably want to drop in to see your parents in your free time."

"Not necessarily … we have a bit of a get together a couple of weeks before as I'm so busy … and that's very kind of you, Anna.

I may well take you up on that … even if it's only for a turkey sandwich or something. Anyway, must go, loads to do. I might pop in for a few minutes tomorrow and have a look at what you've done. I'm so looking forward to the grand opening. I think just about everyone who uses Peesdown Park knows about it and are going to turn up … even Mrs Smedley expressed interest when I mentioned it the other day. Perhaps she will accompany old Fart Features," Miranda giggled.

"Behave yourself," Anna grinned. "Good luck with the interviews. I hope you find someone good. See you tomorrow, hopefully."

Anna put down the phone and turned to see William placing the last rawhide chew into the special containers beneath the counter.

"There," he said, standing back to admire the display. "I think that all looks good, Anna. You've done an excellent job."

"With a lot of help from you, William. Now, would you like a cup of tea? You can take the weight off your feet for a little while in the garden room before we shut up and go home. I'm going to turn it into a little cafe before the summer. I've had two sets of French windows put in so when the weather is nice, customers can walk out and sit outside if they want to as there is such a lovely garden. Come and have a look and see what you think."

William accompanied her through to the rear of the building, glanced around the garden room, fresh and clean with its new coat of cream paint, and then admired the view from the French windows.

"This is lovely, Anna, and will make an excellent little cafe. You could get quite a few chairs and tables in here and make it cosy … and as you say, people could spill out onto the lawn in the summer. It's very nice, very nice indeed."

William sat down on one of the sun chairs while Anna made tea in the kitchen. She had one sandwich left from her lunch.. She cut it in two and handed William one half on a plate, along with a mug of tea.

"I'm sorry but that's all I can offer you at the moment for all your hard work."

"It's been a pleasure. I've thoroughly enjoyed myself and if you ever want a hand in the future, you know you can call on me," he said pleasantly, realising that everything he said was true. He had enjoyed himself and he wouldn't mind coming back. Anna was extremely pleasant and he could see why Miranda had become her friend … and if he was pally with Anna, that was another way to curry favour with Miranda.

They sat in mutual harmony for half an hour, finishing their snack and discussing what needed to be done to get the cafe up and running before William stood up. He had been wearing his bald wig for most of the day and it was beginning to irritate him and he needed to get home to take it off.

"I think I've taken up enough of your time, Anna and there's a programme on television I always watch in half an hour and I don't want to miss it."

Anna stood up, walked back into the front of the shop and unlocked the door for him. "Thank you so much, William, for all your help this afternoon. I really appreciate it."

"You're most welcome, Anna. Good day."

She watched him walk away, leaning heavily on his stick. What a really nice man, she thought. A really, really nice man.

* * *

William walked slowly along the High Street towards the gates for Peesdown Park at the far end, in the centre of Miller Lane. It was growing dark but with the street lights and car headlights, it was still possible for others to see him clearly and he didn't want to create attention if he moved too quickly.

He undid the chain around his gate and did it up again once he was standing on the gravel drive. The security light came on and then clicked off again as he entered the house. He locked the door and, with a sigh of relief, ripped off his glasses and moustache and then the wig. He didn't usually wear the blasted thing for so many hours at a time. Usually, it was just for a walk in the park and sometimes a couple of hours at the Vicarage or church but he'd been to the park this morning and then spent the

110

whole afternoon with Anna. Christ, his head itched madly. It was driving him crazy. He needed to have a shower and wash his hair. He headed for the stairs and the bathroom.

His scalp felt immediately better once the hot water gushed over it and he stood for a while, allowing it to ease the irritation, feeling pleased with the way his day had gone. His acquaintance with that Belinda woman who worked for Miranda was coming along nicely following this morning's walk and then, this afternoon, he had become friendly with Anna. All satellites who surrounded his darling Miranda ... and they all trusted him ... just as she did ... but then he didn't mean her any harm.

He entered his bedroom, sat on his bed and picked up the gold framed photograph of Miranda which stood on his bedside cabinet. He had snapped her a few weeks ago when she was laughingly chastising Nellie for trying to forage in one of the litter bins in the park. He ran a finger down her cheek. God she was so beautiful. His Miranda. He laid down on the bed, closed his eyes and cuddled the picture frame.

* * *

Anna left the shop, locking both back and front doors carefully and turning on the burglar alarm. It was dark now, even though it was only just turning five o'clock. She did her coat up, hurried to her car and got inside. She pressed the heater button. It was turning cold in the evenings ... and it would soon be Christmas ... only a few weeks to go.

As she sat in the rush hour traffic jams, she thought about how much she had always loved Christmas, firstly with her parents, who had died many years ago in a dreadful car crash on the M1 when returning from a weekend down in London, and then with Gerald, who had made it such fun and always spoiled her rotten, insisting she didn't cook and that it didn't matter how much it cost, they would go to a posh hotel and splurge out. That was in the early years of their marriage. Once they were more financially stable, he booked fabulous two-week cruises in the Mediterranean and once they had even gone to the Bahamas. She had to smile, just thinking about how much they had enjoyed themselves. Being away for two weeks in the sunshine had made a real dent in the winter and set them up until the spring.

Last year had been perfectly awful. Totally alone, she had cried nearly all of Christmas Day, pouring over old photographs of their wonderful holidays and the precious memories of her parents. By Boxing Day, she was utterly exhausted and slept for hours, glad when it was time to go back to work at the builder's yard the next morning.

This year would be different, she told herself. She wasn't going to wallow in misery. She was going to go to church and then, if Miranda couldn't pop in for a spot of lunch, she would do some charity work … perhaps she could go to the local animal sanctuary and walk dogs or help clean, or something. Anything that would keep her occupied, be with other people and do something useful.

Thinking about the animal sanctuary, she toyed again with the idea of having a dog but if she moved into the flat above the shop, it wouldn't be ideal if it wanted to go out during the night. Perhaps she should get a cat instead of a dog … and fit a cat flap in the back door. A cat would be easier. She wouldn't have to worry about walking it in all weathers … but then, if she did get a dog, there was always Miranda who would be able to include it on a group walk if it proved difficult to take it herself. Not all the time though. There wasn't much point in owning a dog and not taking it out. That would be part of the enjoyment of having one.

She finally reached her cul-de-sac and pulled up her car in front of the house. She needed a decent meal and a good rest. It had been a busy day and tomorrow she had to get organised for the opening next week. Lots to do, so little time.

* * *

Miranda was having a fruitful evening. She interviewed two girls, who had both turned up at her home bang on time; one at 7.00 pm and the other at 8.00 pm and decided both of them would be suitable. They were in their mid-twenties, fit and healthy and had experience of working with dogs.

Julie had been employed at Happylands, the local animal sanctuary, for four years before leaving to have her little boy, who was now in school and she wanted to work while he was there. Kate was employed as a veterinary assistant but wanted to work outside. She was single and quite happy to be available whenever needed.

Miranda decided to offer them both a job, explaining to Julie that she could start immediately as she could walk some of her dogs which would free her up to do other things. Kate had to give a month's notice, which would provide time to advertise for more dogs for her to walk. It was a balancing act in no mistake but one Miranda was up for.

She went to bed like Anna and William, totally satisfied with what she had achieved that day.

* * *

Freddie Fletcher wasn't so happy. He'd received instructions from Barrington and Barrington's that he had to spend yet another cold night keeping watch in the woods as they had received a tipoff that the badger hunters would be back this week. They had requested police back up for him but being short-staffed due to sickness and two of their officers tied up on a murder case, it was down to him to gather evidence.

At 8.00 pm., his lovely wife, Beryl, packed him a flask of coffee, three sausage sandwiches with thick white bread and a slice of her home-made fruit cake while he wrapped up as best he could in his thermal attire and thick coat. He kissed Beryl on the cheek, wishing he could stay at home with her, donned gloves and a hat and set off with his torch to go back to the hide he had made last week. He was utterly fed up with the prospect of spending another night out in the cold. If he ended up with pneumonia, he was going to sue Barrington and Barrington's … although that was probably a stupid idea, taking solicitors to court. God, he was cheesed off!

CHAPTER 10

The next day, Miranda managed to find a spare half hour before commencing her dog walking to pop to the shop and see for herself just what Anna had achieved. She brought Nellie with her, not wanting to leave her in the van in case she was stolen. She had been informed by an extremely good source that over 4,000 dogs went missing every year in the United Kingdom and she was determined Nellie wasn't going to be one of them. Although if anyone else bought her, they would probably dump her pretty quickly once they found out exactly what she did get up to, Miranda chuckled as she knocked on the door of Pampered Pets.

Anna was in the office upstairs. She leaned out of the window and smiled. "Oh, hi. I was hoping you'd have time to come and have a look. I desperately need your approval. I'll be down in a second."

While she was waiting, Miranda looked up and down the street. It was only 9.30 a.m. on a Wednesday morning but it was already busy with plenty of footfall, especially ladies out doing their shopping. It was certainly a good spot for a pet shop with the gates for the park at the end of the road, with dog walkers either coming out or going in. Pampered Pets was sited perfectly for them to pick up bits and pieces as they walked past. Anna should do very well. Very well indeed.

The door opened and Anna stood on the threshold, looking tired but happy to welcome Miranda and Nellie into her domain. They both laughed as Nellie strained at the lead, scenting food and treats. She wasn't interested in the toys or dog beds. Her belly ruled her.

"Can she have a little something?" asked Anna, pointing at the chew bones and doggie chocolates near the counter.

"If she does, she'll always want something every time she comes and will make a complete pest of herself," warned Miranda.

"I don't mind, if you don't," replied Anna. She had a real soft spot for Nellie with her lovely thick, gleaming chestnut coloured coat, her sparkly, mischievous eyes and waggy tail.

Miranda sighed. "Ok, then. You'll live to regret it, or I will as it will cost me a fortune."

Anna looked at the treats. "Here, Nellie. Sit and you can have a nice crunchy chew."

Nellie duly sat, her tail going nineteen to the dozen as she watched Anna unwrap it and hand it to her. She took it daintily, devoured it in a split second and then sat patiently staring at Anna, pleading for another.

"There. I told you," Miranda grinned. "The damned dog is incorrigible and so greedy."

Anna smiled at Nellie. "That's all you're getting this time, young lady. You'll have to wait until your next visit before you get another. So, what do you think?" she looked at Miranda and waved her arm around the room.

"Brilliant," Miranda nodded, staring at the neatly arranged display units. "It looks great."

"And there's the back room of course, with the large sacks of food and the dog beds. Come through."

"Wow. I love those," Miranda said, eyeing up the different dog and cat baskets in all different sizes and textures. "If I bought Nellie one of them," she pointed at the doggie sofa covered in red velvet, "I might keep her off my sofa and have it all to myself again, just as I did before she came to join my household. Perhaps I'll treat her to one for Christmas. What do you think, Nellie?
Would you like one?"

Nellie ignored her. Those huge bags of food were far more interesting and anyway, she liked to curl up with her mistress in the evenings. What did she need with a velvet sofa?

"Have you time for a coffee?" Anna asked, pointing at the garden room.

Miranda looked at her watch. "Just a quick one and then I shall have to get going. Can't have all my furry friends desperate to get to the park for a wee."

Anna made the coffee as Miranda sat down, Nellie at her side, staring out of the French windows at the garden. It was a gloomy day. There had been a heavy fog during the night and it was only just lifting.

Anna brought in two mugs, placed them on the table and patted Nellie on the head as she sat down.

"Have you thought any more about having a dog of your own?" Miranda asked.

"A bit ... but I don't want to do anything about it for a little while as I have so much going on here ... and I'm seriously considering selling my house and moving in here ... and am not sure if having a flat upstairs is such a good idea for a dog. What do you think?"

Miranda frowned. "Well, you have a fabulous garden, you're two minutes from the park, you'll be at home with it all day ... you could make a bed up for it in the back room while you're open ... if it's a lively one, you could have a big cage so it doesn't bother people. I don't see a problem. In fact, it's ideal really."

"But what about when it gets old and can't manage the stairs?"

Miranda giggled. "You'll have to get a doggy stairlift."

Anna raised her eyebrows. "Do they make such things?"

"I'm not honestly sure, but I would sincerely think so. As you are finding out, the pet market is huge so someone, somewhere, will have thought of it."

"It's certainly a good idea and will put my mind at rest over that problem."

"I think we should pay a visit to Happylands ... you need to meet Sonia, she's the owner. It's a wonderful place and she tries so hard not to turn anything away that needs her. She has horses, goats, pigs, sheep, alpacas, chickens, geese, rabbits, guinea pigs, as well as dogs and cats. She does an amazing job, helped a lot by the patronage of Gary Saunders, you know the film star who was in 'The Big Sky', that war film that was so popular a couple of years ago. He's in another which is due to be released next month.

God, he's gorgeous and has such a big heart. He's helped Sonia enormously."

"Oh, yes ... I remember. He switched on the Christmas lights in Peesdown last year."

"Yes, he did. Actually, you and Sonia could help each other, you know. Perhaps you could display pictures of the animals she needs to rehome and I know she would recommend you as you don't sell animals."

"What a lovely idea … creating a display for her. Yes, I can certainly do that," Anna enthused.

"Do you have time to pop over there later … when I've finished walking the dogs? We don't need to stay long. Just say hello and invite her to your opening. I'm sure she'll come … and she knows a lot of people in the animal world … who might well come too."

"Yes, I'd love to … this afternoon. I've a desk, chair and a filing cabinet being delivered this morning for the office, as well as tables and chairs for in here. I'm offering lots of free snacks and drinks on opening day and people will want to have somewhere to sit. I must admit, I'm cheating a bit … caterers are seeing to all of that."

"That's a very sensible thing to do. Right, Nellie and I will pick you up around 3.00 p.m. and we'll trot over to see Sonia. You never know, you might just see a dog you'd like too," Miranda grinned.

"No. Not yet," Anna said firmly. "It's too soon but once I've sold the house and moved in here   ...   that will be the right time."

Miranda and Nellie got up and moved through to the front of the shop, Nellie sniffing hopefully at the doggie treats.

"Come on, you greedy girl," Miranda urged, tugging on Nellie's lead.

Nellie went … reluctantly, throwing a last pleading look at Anna. Anna smiled and locked the shop behind them.

* * *

The sanctuary was out on the Wetherby Road, between Shadwell and Scarcroft. It was accessed by turning off the main road and down a tiny, windy lane with ploughed fields on either side, and then they drove around a bend and there was a five-bar gate in front of them with a big sign indicating they had reached Happylands. The opening times were from 10.00 a.m. until 6.00 p.m. seven days per week. Volunteers and good homes for pets were always needed and to enquire at the office. There was an added poster giving details of their Christmas fayre.

"I shall be coming to that," Miranda stated. "I always do ... I help out, usually on a stall or with the refreshments. It's always packed. Sonia's very popular and gets tremendous support."

The fayre was on a Sunday. Pampered Pets would be closed. Anna had decided that even if other shops were open seven days a week, she was still going to close on a Sunday. She liked to go to church when she could and if she was busy all week, she had to have at least one day when she could relax a bit and do other things.

"I'll help," she said, liking the idea of assisting the unknown Sonia to fundraise for her very worthwhile cause. "I can always bake some cakes as no doubt there will be a cake stall ... and give something from the shop for the raffle ... perhaps a dog bed ... what do you think?"

Miranda nodded with approval. "I'm sure Sonia will be delighted," she said, changing into second gear and heading up the drive towards the big farmhouse in the distance. The fields on either side were now occupied by horses of all shapes and sizes, two little dark brown Shetland ponies, and some sheep.

"As I told you, Sonia rescues anything and everything," Miranda said, "not just domestic pets. She receives calls from all over the place for help. She even took in some Dartmoor ponies once which had been cruelly treated. She's a very special woman, believe me."

They had reached the farmhouse, a huge rambling old building, covered with ivy. There were obviously kennels at the rear as they could hear a pack of dogs howling and barking, and then two big mongrels and a little Jack Russell came ambling out of the front door of the farmhouse to see what was going on.

"That's Bramble and Rosie. Tallulah is the smaller one," Miranda informed Anna. "All dumped at some point or another and Sonia kept them for herself. Couldn't bear to part with them."

Nellie shifted in the rear of the Volvo, desperate to jump out and greet her friends.

Anna and Miranda got out of the car and Nellie dashed after them, rushing up to rub noses with the three dogs who were just as pleased to see Nellie and her mistress, wagging their tails and licking Miranda's hand as she fished in her pocket for four biscuits. She made all the dogs sit in a line and gave them one each.

"Oh, hello," said a voice behind them. "I'm so glad you could come over. Hi, you must be Anna ... the lady who is setting up the new pet shop in Peesdown ... and won't be selling animals, thank goodness. I get so fed up with those damned places who have kittens and rabbits and as for those who have exotics, they want shooting in my opinion. Damned people. The sooner the law changes and prevents shops selling animals, the better. So many are bought on a whim and then end up in places such as mine. It's damned infuriating and so unnecessary. People want educating badly in my opinion."

Anna looked at the determined fifty-something slender woman who had appeared from around the corner of the house. Sonia's face was weather-beaten and contained lots of lines and wrinkles and her corn-coloured hair was tied up in a loose bun at the back of her head with wisps of hair having slipped out. She wore well-worn jeans and wellies, a green tatty sweater and an old black anorak which could certainly do with a wash.

"Yes, that's me," Anna said, holding out a hand to shake Sonia's. "I'm very pleased to meet you ... I'm certainly looking forward to having a look around if that's okay."

"Anna is after a dog at some point," Miranda said with a grin. "Not for a little while as she's terribly busy setting up the business at the moment and has to sell her house and move into the flat above the shop but when she's ready ... perhaps in a few months." "Oh, that's just fabulous," enthused Sonia, shoving her hands into her pockets. She had become hot cleaning out the kennels but now she was standing still, she was becoming a little chilly. "We need all the adoptees we can get, especially at this time of year.
We're inundated with dogs ... and cats ... before and after Christmas. Such a lot of people go away and don't want to fork out for petsitters, kennels or catteries and just dump their poor animals. Then after Christmas, we get all the puppies stupid people have bought at such a stressful time, find they can't cope with all the weeing and chewing and dump them. I hate it ...

Christmas. All goodwill towards men but bugger the animals in a lot of cases. It's the same in the school holidays, especially in August when people book holidays and find all the petsitters and kennels have been booked up for months so instead of cancelling their blasted holidays, they dump their poor dogs. Bloody people … the misery they cause … want shooting! Anyway, you don't want to listen to me pontificating … come in and have a coffee before you look around … or tea, if you prefer."

They duly followed Sonia as she marched indoors, flung her wellies into the utility room on their left and walked straight into a massive country kitchen with a range, oak cupboards and a big table at the side of the room by the window.

"Sit yourselves down. This won't take long … would you like biscuits or cake?"

The dogs, who had all followed the humans into the kitchen, looked at Sonia lovingly. Biscuit was a magic word.

"I didn't mean any of you little buggers," she grinned, washing her hands at the sink and then putting the kettle on.

Miranda and Anna sat down at the table in the warm, inviting room. Anna looked around with pleasure. The kitchen had a real homely feel with dog baskets in the corner containing thick blankets, a smeary old television on a table in the corner, which was littered with papers and books and a sofa next to it with enormous cushions, upon which lay a tortoiseshell cat and two smaller black ones, all fast asleep.

"That's Marmaduke, along with Tiddles and Poo," Sonia said, noticing Anna's interest. "All rescued. Marmaduke was dumped here one morning in a cat carrier, just outside the gate, before we opened. One of the staff found him, meowing his head off and the other two were dumped as tiny kittens in a skip somewhere in Leeds. Luckily, the chap from the skip company who discovered them knew about us and brought them here. They were too tiny to have left their mother so I had to bottle feed them for a week or so and anyway, we bonded and now I can't part with them. Marmaduke made such a racket in our cattery, unsettling all the others, I brought him in with us. He decided he liked living here and has just stayed, knowing damned well he is king of the castle.

Even the dogs respect him and do as they are told."

120

She deposited mugs adorned with Dalmatians and filled with steaming hot coffee in front of Anna and Miranda, with three side plates and an enormous chocolate cake. She cut them all a piece, deftly ignoring the dogs who once they realised they weren't going to get anything, ambled back outside, all apart from Nellie, who was never, never, never going to leave the table until every crumb of cake had been consumed.

"So, how many animals do you look after?" Anna asked.

"Well, there are two donkeys and twenty-six ponies and horses at the moment. We did have thirty-one but I managed to rehome five in the last month. Then there are three sheep, a potbellied pig, nineteen rabbits, twelve guinea pigs and two hamsters ... which drive me mad at night running around on their blasted wheels so they have the spare room upstairs, well away from my room. Then there are forty-three dogs and twenty-nine cats."

"Oh, my goodness," Anna gasped. "It must cost a fortune to look after all of them."

Sonia nodded grimly. "You're telling me. It's not just food but it's the vet fees. We have a marvellous vet, Jemma, who runs the surgery near Wetherby. She's so good. She never charges for her time, just the medicines and operations but even so, it can get damned expensive, especially as some new arrivals are in a pretty dire state and need instant attention and then, of course, if they're not neutered or spayed, I always get that done before they are rehomed. So, yes, Anna. You can see we need all the help we can get ... but I must say, I have some fabulous support across Leeds and beyond. Our events are always well attended and people are so good and fundraise all year through and donate food and blankets and beds. We really are very lucky."

"Wow. Well, you can always count on me to help in any way I can," Anna said enthusiastically. She was so impressed with Sonia, giving up her life to helping all these animals in need. What a truly remarkable woman. "Miranda suggested I put up details of the animals you want to rehome in my shop and I can certainly do that ... and have a charity box too ... and I can help at your
Christmas fayre."

"That's very kind. Thank you. Advertising the animals will be a huge help," Sonia smiled, sipping her coffee, her eyes sparkling at Anna. She liked her too … even more now that she was offering her assistance. "But of course, one of the best ways to help is to adopt a dog. The more I can suitably rehome, the more space I have for others who turn up."

Anna nodded. "And I will take a dog at some point, I promise. However, I really must get the shop up and running first. I simply don't have time at the moment. Perhaps after Christmas."

"That would be an excellent time as, like I said, we will be inundated with new dumpees so you will have a big number to choose from. What sort did you have in mind? I have such a lot of pedigrees turn up. People always think that they won't be dumped as they cost such exorbitant, silly prices … God, I do hate breeders with a passion … and it's just not true. We get tons of working type dogs, Labradors, Spaniels, German Shepherds, Border Collies, etc, etc. Stupid people get them as pets and think they're just going to look pretty in front of the fire and not need much stimulation and exercise. Then, when the poor animals wreck the house because they are desperately frustrated and bored, they get rid. Oh, don't get me started on that one. I get so damned angry … but there again, you won't have time for a working dog unless you intend Miranda to give it plenty of exercise."

"That's another reason I don't want one just yet … until I hire staff so that I can leave the shop to walk it … after all, that's half the pleasure of having a dog, being able to get out and about with it … although it will be handy, having Miranda to turn to if I can't get out for some reason." Anna grinned at her friend. "And to be honest, I don't know what sort I would like. Just something that will fit into my lifestyle, young enough to be able to spend a good, long time together, although I wouldn't want a very young puppy, something a little older perhaps. I don't know, Sonia … but I'm sure that when the time is right, the right dog will turn up … and by the way, your chocolate cake is delicious."

Miranda nodded in agreement, having just eaten her last mouthful, much to Nellie's disgust. "I second that."

"Well, actually, I didn't bake it. It was Josh ... he's become such a good cook ... he's my son," Sonia informed Anna proudly. "He's at catering college in Leeds, training to be a chef. I shall certainly miss him when he finally leaves home ... he's hoping to get a job in a top hotel or restaurant in London when he passes his exams."

"Good for him," Anna said. "If his chocolate cake is anything to go by, he will be very much in demand."

"Right, let's show Anna around ... I promise I won't try to persuade you to have a dog today," Sonia grinned, finishing her coffee.

Anna smiled. "Yes, I would like to see everything, then I can tell my customers all about you, if they don't know already ... and if you can prepare some photographs with a few details of any of the animals you would like me to display in the shop before next Saturday, when we have the opening, I can get them up. I've been advertising the event quite widely so hopefully lots of people will come, if only for a sandwich and a cup of something and, with a bit of luck, we might be able to find some suitable homes."

"Thank you so much, Anna. I'll put something together this evening. I have to come into Leeds tomorrow so I'll drop them off with you and if you're not around, I'll put them through your letterbox. I presume there is one at the shop."

Anna nodded. "Yes. I should be there though ... and if you have time, come and have coffee with me too."

They all stood up and went outside to where Sonia's dogs were sprawled out on rugs just outside the front door, watching anything and everything that moved. Miranda put Nellie on the lead and looped it over a post near to them so she couldn't misbehave.

Sonia led the way, Miranda and Anna following behind. There were several buildings behind the farmhouse, including a big stable block where two horses had their heads over the doors and neighed greetings to their visitors. Sonia produced a couple of carrots from her pocket and gave them one each.

"This is Ned," she said, nodding at the bay "and this is Tilly," smoothing the nose of the smaller dappled grey. "Their owners couldn't afford to keep them any longer so asked us to take them.

They're in at the moment as we're waiting for the farrier to turn up later as they both need their feet trimming … and over here," she pointed to the next block, "is the cattery and beyond that, the dog kennels."

They entered the cattery first, a huge barn-sized building filled with thirty-five large covered runs and little rooms in each with soft beds and toys, along with litter trays and water and feeding bowls. All the cats looked relatively content. They had ample space to move about, plenty of company and the whole place smelled fresh and clean and was nice and airy with floor to ceiling windows all along one side so the cats could see out.

"This is as nice as I can make it for them but it's not ideal. Tigger," Sonia said, pointing to a tabby cat at the end, "he's been here for nearly three months now and I dearly want to find him new owners. He seems happy enough but needs to be in his forever home … well, they all do, bless them … but it's hard, trying to rehome them with suitable people … I always vet potential owners first … go to their homes and check them out as I certainly don't want any of my rescues to end up as house cats. I simply abide that idea. Cats aren't meant to live their lives shut up indoors. They need to be out and about. It's so damned cruel keeping them in, not allowing them to go hunting, explore, sit in the sun … to enjoy a natural, free life. Those people who keep them coped up need shooting too," Sonia spat. "The poor animals must go stir crazy."

Anna nodded. She hadn't given it any thought before but Sonia was definitely right. It was cruel.

"I hate visiting house cats," Miranda remarked. "I did it for the first year or so while I was getting established but now I refuse to do it. Like you, I can't bear seeing them stuck indoors, especially on a nice day."

"Right," Sonia said, "now for the dogs," leaving Anna and Miranda to follow her to the kennels across the yard.

The sound was almost deafening as they entered another enormous brick building, housing spacious individual runs which led to covered outside runs. All the dogs had hard plastic beds, obviously easier to keep clean than fabric ones, with plenty of duvets and thick blankets to make them comfortable. There were also lots of toys and half-eaten chew bones in their runs. None of the dogs looked particularly stressed out. They were all wagging their tails as their visitors grew nearer. Some barked, especially the little ones but some of the bigger dogs just stood watching with smiling eyes, eager for any attention they could get. Two kennel maids were busily collecting feeding bowls and taking them through into an adjoining room.

"That's the feed room," explained Sonia, "which is why the dogs are excited. They know it won't be long before they're fed and just after that, they go out for some fun. We let those who are sociable into the big field at the back so they can play and stretch their legs," said Sonia. "Those who aren't or have some kind of issue which means it's not safe to let them out with the others, are walked on extension leads around the next field. We do that in the morning, after lunch and again in the late afternoon so they have plenty of exercise, which means they stay relatively calm, don't make too much mess in their kennels, and are reasonably tired and tend to sleep a lot."

"That's nice," Anna remarked. The more she heard from Sonia, the more she admired her. She was doing everything she could to make the lives of these unwanted animals as pleasant as possible.

"We have an isolation unit next door too in case any of them are ill or recovering from an operation or having puppies. It's empty at the moment as they are all pretty fit and healthy apart from a bit of arthritis here and there on the older ones … and they're all on medication."

Anna was watching two young mongrels in the end kennel. They were both vying with each other for her attention, pushing each other out so one or the other could get a better look at her.

"They're cute," she said, smiling at their antics.

"Yes, aren't they? I love mongrels … usually far healthier than inbred pedigrees. I have no idea if they are related. A woman brought them in who found them in her garden one morning. She asked all around the street and put notices up in the local shops, and reported them to the police and anywhere else she could think of, but no-one claimed them and after a couple of weeks she brought them here. She couldn't keep them as she worked full time and they were wrecking her house. It was such a shame as she had grown fond of them and they of her but it wasn't working for any of them. I felt quite sorry for her. She had tried her best. She rings up every day to see if I've found a nice home for them but so far nothing. Not so many people want to take on two in one go, especially young ones ... which, in my opinion, is easier as they amuse each other and lots of play means they become tired much quicker, which is a real bonus."

Anna knelt down by their kennel. "Hello, you two. Aren't you cute?"

"I would imagine they have a bit of Labrador in them somewhere but apart from that I haven't a clue," Sonia said.

"Oh, you still have Charlie," Miranda cried, moving towards a kennel at the far end, towards a handsome black and tan dog with enormous brown, expressive eyes. He cried when he saw Miranda and pushed his paw through the kennel bars to touch her.

"Yes. Someone did want him but then it all fell through, poor boy. He's so lovely. He's been here quite a while now so I think I'll include his picture and details with those I'm going to give Anna to display in the shop."

"There's no need," Miranda said quickly. "I'll have him. I've had my eye on him ever since he arrived here and he likes Nellie. Remember, he hung around her when we joined you in the field last week ... and you know he'll have a great life with me. What do you think, Charlie? Would you like to come home with me and
Nellie?"

Charlie whimpered and licked Miranda's hand as she held his paw.

"I think that's a yes," Miranda laughed.

"Are you absolutely sure, Miranda? You're so busy." Sonia said.

"Positive ... he can stay with me for most of the day, as Nellie does. I have Belinda working for me now and one more walker starting on Monday and another in a month, which will ease the pressure and I intend only doing one big walk a day from now so I can concentrate on paperwork and expanding my empire," she grinned. "So, including Charlie in our little family won't be a problem and he will be company for Nellie too. Yes, Sonia. I'll have him and as he's part Labrador and Rottweiler, he will guard me too. He certainly looks more like a Rotti then a Lab anyway."

Anna stared at the big dog. He wasn't as tall and heavy as a male Rottweiler but even so, he was large and would probably look formidable if his eyes weren't twinkling at Miranda.

"I can collect him in the morning, if that's okay. I'm busy this evening with cats and it will give me time to get him some food and a nice bed. In fact, Anna, I will have one of those large velvet sofas for him, if I may … and while I'm at it, Nellie better have one too. Her bed is beginning to fall apart, not that she uses it much, but I don't want her to feel left out."

Miranda entered Charlie's kennel and gave him a big cuddle. "Don't you worry, darling," she whispered. "I'll be back for you in the morning and you're going to be so happy with me and Nellie."

They left Happylands half an hour later to drive straight back to the shop, Sonia waving them off with her dogs standing beside her. "See you in the morning," she grinned at Miranda, "and you in the afternoon," she smiled at Anna.

"I need a nice new bowl for Charlie, a big bag of food, some wet food and those sofas," Miranda said when they entered Pampered Pets a while later.

"And you're only paying cost price for them," said Anna, as they stuffed the sofas into the back of Miranda's Volvo next to Nellie and much to her chagrin, put the food on the front seat where she couldn't get at it.

"No. You'll never make a profit if you do that."

"Think of it as my donation towards helping a dog in distress and anyway, I have a lot to thank you for. It's a present … to you and the dogs."

Miranda hugged her. "Thank you. That's so kind. I'm so glad we met, Anna. I think this friendship is going to last a very long time."

"I do hope so," Anna said.

"Are you going to give those little mongrels a home? I know you were very taken with them."

"By the time I'm in a position to do so, they'll probably have been rehomed. However, if they are still there, I might. They were very cute, although I hadn't anticipated having two."

127

"Well, as Sonia said, they will keep each other amused."

"Um. Well, we'll see."

Miranda grinned, hopped back into the Volvo and headed off in the direction of the first cat she had to feed that evening. It had been a successful day all round and she was really looking forward to picking up Charlie in the morning ... then there was the shop opening next week ... all she needed now was to see Jeremy. He still hadn't called her, although she had received a text

from him to say he was going to try to get home for Anna's opening but he couldn't guarantee it. She did hope he would turn up. She desperately wanted to see him again.

CHAPTER 11

Charlie settled down in his new home with Miranda and Nellie very quickly. He loved his red velvet sofa once Miranda made it clear it was his and as soon as his busy day was over, accompanying his new family around the parks with his new friends and stopping off at houses where his mistress went in and out in the early mornings and evenings and always came back to the car smelling of *cats*, he gobbled his tea and then headed for the comfort of his lovely bed.

Miranda was delighted he seemed to be enjoying his new life and Nellie had accepted him readily, relieved he didn't try to usurp her position on the sofa with Miranda in the evenings and not even minding when he wandered around the house with her soft bunny rabbit, her favourite toy.

"I'm so happy you've decided to take him," Sonia said when Miranda and Nellie had picked Charlie up from Happylands. "Not many people want a dog with Rottie in it ... frightened to death, some of them ... but he's such a lovely, kind boy and I just know he'll have a wonderful life with you and Nellie. Thank you so much, Miranda."

Miranda had hugged Sonia and driven off, Charlie and Nellie sitting up and watching out of the windows, Nellie no doubt telling him all about what to expect, as he was now part of a petsitting business.

That first morning, she only had four dogs to walk and had no qualms about Charlie becoming integrated into the pack quickly. He was great with other dogs, proved on Sonia's field when they were all let out together and the pack that morning was all small and well socialised so he wouldn't feel threatened on his first proper walk with them all.

She had headed straight up into the woods so Charlie wouldn't intimidate others in the park, especially Mrs Smedley and her darling 'Precious''. Miranda couldn't have dealt with it that morning and since then she had kept a sharp eye out for her nemesis and if she saw her in the distance, made a quick detour to steer clear of her. So far, avoidance tactics had worked but Miranda had no doubt Mrs Smedley would probably throw a fit when she did see Charlie and they would have a few choice words, probably about the Dangerous Dogs Act, until the silly woman realised the laid-back animal was no threat to man or beast.

That first walk with Charlie had been lovely. He was a hit with the others, who all decided they liked him, having sniffed him all over and licked his face. He licked them all back, wagged his tail, smiled at Miranda and then ambled off to find out what was so interesting in the woods. Nellie followed him. Miranda just hoped her darling dog wouldn't teach him any naughty habits.

Their walk was nearly over and they were just moving along the path in the direction of the car park when William Pemworthy startled them all by suddenly appearing on a parallel path a few feet away from them.

"Oh, hello," Miranda gasped. He had made her jump and the dogs bark. "Gosh, you gave me a fright … I didn't realise you were in the woods too."

"Hello, Miranda," he replied. "Sorry … I didn't mean to startle you. Have you got a new dog?" he asked, eyeing up Charlie who had followed Nellie to the lakeside. She threw herself in and swam about happily in the cold water, much to Miranda's annoyance. She didn't like Nellie going in when it was really cold but the naughty girl was tremendously good at sneaking off when Miranda was distracted, the draw of the water nearly as strong as food and not to be ignored.

Charlie, who was obviously not a keen swimmer, stood at the water's edge, watching Nellie but sensibly not joining her, much to Miranda's relief. It was bad enough drying one dog with a thick coat.

"Yes … he's called Charlie. He's mine. I just took him from Happylands. This is his first walk with us."

"He's a handsome animal. What is he … Rottweiler?"

"Well, Rottie cross Labrador, we think. He's not quite big enough for a male Rottie."

"Umm. He's still quite large … will be a good protector for you, Miranda, especially when you're up in the woods … or at home."

William's expression was strange. Miranda looked at him with surprise. He didn't look scared of Charlie but there was something ... as if he was weighing up the dog in some way.

"Does he like biscuits?" William asked, leaning on his walking stick with one hand and delving into his pocket with the other.

"Oh, yes," smiled Miranda, noticing how quickly Nellie saw what was going on and dashed out of the water to get to William's side, not even stopping to shake off the water clinging to her coat. Charlie ran behind, desperate to know what was suddenly so urgent. The remaining four dogs, having met William before, all sat at his feet expectantly. He gave them all a biscuit, leaving
Charlie to last. He gave him his and then patted his silky head.
"Charlie," he said. "Nice to meet you. I do hope we'll be great friends." Charlie wagged his tail. If this man was going to give him biscuits every time they met, they would be.

"How is Anna getting on?" William asked, showing the dogs his empty hands so they wouldn't expect any more treats. "I'm looking forward to the opening. I said I would help out if she needed me."

"That's kind of you. I'm helping too ... Belinda, and the other two girls I have just taken on to dog walk for me, are also popping in for an hour or two to lend a hand."

"More staff ... goodness, Miranda, you must be doing well if you're taking on more dog walkers to help you ... will they be walking in Peesdown ... and won't we be seeing as much of you?"

"They will be using all of the parks in and around Leeds as we're having enquiries from all over now but Belinda will always walk here as she lives not far away and can easily collect local dogs. I shall still come ... I want to do at least one walk every day but as I'm going to expand the business, I need to be free to concentrate on that."

"You mean more dog walking?"

"Well, yes ... but I want to set up a home boarding side too ... find some suitable people who are willing to look after dogs for a week or so while their owners are on holiday. Not so many people want to use kennels these days and are looking for an alternative for their precious pets."

"That's a good idea … and I wish you luck with it … but make sure you still come to Peesdown Park, Miranda. You will certainly be missed if you don't."

Again, a strange look passed over his face and Miranda felt a sense of unease. She resisted the urge to shudder. Whatever was the matter with her? He was a harmless old man with a bad leg.

* * *

The first week of owning Charlie shot by and Miranda's acquaintances in the parks of Leeds, all bar Mrs Smedley, whom she managed to avoid, began to feel at ease with him and it was only those she didn't know who did a nervous detour when they saw her approaching with him in the pack.

It was now Thursday and Pampered Pets opening day was only hours away. Miranda hadn't managed to pop in to see Anna since their visit to Happylands but they spoke regularly on the telephone and it seemed everything was going according to plan. Miranda had promised to be there at 9.00 a.m. sharp to lend a hand. She had a few cats to feed but intended to get up early to do the visits, even if it meant zooming around the outskirts of Leeds in the dark

… but then that was the best time. There was very little traffic at 5.00 a.m. on a Saturday so it was possible to fly from one client to another in record time. Nellie and Charlie were going to spend the day with her parents so she would be free to help Anna before visiting the cats again and picking up her dogs in the evening.

She was deep in thought about Anna and the shop when she arrived at Peesdown Park, unloaded the dogs and walked quicker than usual down the path towards the lake. Nellie, Charlie, Roger, Sammy and Polly kept up with her, eager to get to the woods. The wind was biting this morning, although the forecast had said it was going to be a reasonably mild day. She pulled her woolly hat down over her ears and pushed her gloved hands into her jacket pockets, glad she didn't have any dogs on extension leads today. Two of Belinda's pack were away so Pongo and Purdy had gone with her..

It was less windy on the far side of the lake, which had only taken them twenty minutes to get to as their pace was fast. Miranda slowed down. A weak sun was beginning to show through the clouds so perhaps the forecasters were right after all.

There weren't many people about this morning and those that were hurried past, too cold to want to stop and chat, even though the temperature was a degree or so higher than it had been on arriving at the park.

Miranda had her thermals on and was warming up nicely. She had intended to walk through the woods but it was much more pleasant on the lakeside path which, if it wasn't for the damned clouds which kept scudding past, would be bathed in continuous sunshine. The dogs were enjoying themselves, chasing each other up and down the bank to the woods. Nellie had wanted to go in the water but Miranda let out a yell and she decided it was more prudent not to. Charlie thought that was funny and his big brown eyes laughed at his mistress.

"Hello, Miranda. How are you today?"

Miranda jumped. She hadn't seen William Pemworthy standing on the path on the bank above her. That was the second time in a week he had startled her.

"Oh, hello. I'm fine. How are you?" she asked, watching his slow progress down the path towards her.

"Chilly," he said. "I do wish I could walk faster in this weather. Don't ever become old, Miranda. When I think about what I could do when I was younger," he sighed despondently.

He stepped onto the path beside her. He had a cap on this morning, covering his bald head, and a thick full-length coat rather than the jacket he usually wore but even so, he was hunched up and didn't look at all warm.

"Perhaps you shouldn't walk so far now we're heading fast and furiously into winter," she suggested. "Perhaps it would be better to stay indoors."

"Perhaps ... but I need to get out, Miranda. Get fresh air into my lungs ... and after all, I have nothing much to do all day. If I didn't spend time here ... and enjoy the odd chat ... it's the highlight of my day, you know."

Miranda felt a pang of sadness for him. How dreadful it must be to be getting on in years and lonely.

Having offered all the dogs a biscuit, making a particular fuss of Charlie, William wandered along beside Miranda, chatting about Anna and the shop and they had nearly reached the car park when they were interrupted by an exhausted-looking Freddie Fletcher hurrying towards them. He grimaced at Miranda and nodded to William.

"Morning," he muttered.

"You look tired this morning, Freddie," remarked William.

"Yes, I damned well am. I was up there until the early hours...," he pointed high up in the trees above the lake. "There are badger baiters about and I'm expected to try and catch them ... single-handed might I add ... the police haven't any officers spare to do surveillance and will only come out if I witness something."

"Goodness, that must be pretty awful, sitting in the cold all night, waiting for something that might not happen and then if it does, hoping the police turn up in time," Miranda said, appalled at what he was expected to do all on his own. She didn't have much time for the man but this was a bit much and she could sympathise. She certainly wouldn't want to do it. What if those awful men saw him? What would they do to him?

"Um. Well, it can be interesting too. I didn't think anyone would want a walk in the middle of the night in November but that's not strictly true," Freddie stated mysteriously.

"Oh?" William looked intrigued.

"Well, there's the odd courting couple about of course but they remain in their cars in the car park at this time of the year but I've also discovered there's a very strange woman who likes to walk around the lake at midnight. I've seen her a few times now ... and once during the day. I recognised her and asked her why she took such a risk, especially as she doesn't even have a dog for protection. She said she prefers it ... likes to commune with nocturnal nature, said she wasn't frightened as no-one was about at that time. I told her she was putting herself in peril but she just laughed." He shook his head. "Some people ... very silly ... and naive. I told her there was a rape here a few months ago

134

and noone caught for it but she just shrugged and walked off. Stupid woman."

"Quite," agreed Miranda. She wouldn't want to venture into the park during the night, even with all her dogs. It was bad enough in the day, keeping an eye on who was about.

"Anyway, I must be off. As none of these so-called badger baiters turned up, I've been told I needn't keep watch for a while … at least until we're alerted again I suppose … and in lieu, once I've finished checking everything this morning, I have a couple of days off, so, while I'm not about young lady, keep your dogs under control," he growled at Miranda, unwilling to disappear without getting in a dig at her.

Miranda smiled sweetly. "Of course. By the way, Mr Fletcher, are you going to the opening of Anna's new pet shop on Saturday?"

"I might pop in with my Beryl … she's my wife. We have a cat and if Anna sells the food she likes to eat, we might well buy it from there as the only shop that stocks it is over in Headingley and it would be handy to be able to buy it closer to home … and she's a nice woman is Anna. Very nice indeed. Yes, we'll pop in and support her new venture."

He marched off along the lakeside path, leaving Miranda grinning at his back. "Do you know, I think he might just have a crush on our Anna."

William was looking vacantly across the lake with a strange expression on his face. Miranda had no idea if he had even heard her. She looked at her watch. Time was getting on, she had to get all the dogs home and then visit some new clients. She clipped her pack onto their leads, said goodbye to William and headed off to the car park, still thinking about that stupid woman, walking around here in the middle of the night on her own. Crazy or what?

* * *

William was intrigued. A woman, absolutely asking for it, risking being on her own in the dark of night, miles away from anyone who could hear her if she screamed. He licked his lips. He might have a wander over tonight and see if she was around.

He'd never thought to come to the park at that time to look for women, naturally assuming they wouldn't take such an enormous risk.

Obviously, he was wrong. He could feel the itch.

* * *

Anna was exhausted. The opening was only hours away and everything was in place but goodness, it had been hard work. She would make sure to have a couple of early nights or otherwise she wouldn't be able to keep her eyes open on Saturday, when it was imperative to be completely alert and chatty. Such a lot of people had told her they were coming so hopefully she had ordered enough nibbles and drinks from the caterers, although they said they could always supply more if things were running out.

A row of tables, covered with white damask tablecloths, had been placed in a line along one wall of the garden room, awaiting the refreshments which would arrive first thing on Saturday morning. Other tables, also covered with cloths, along with a dainty cut-glass vase in the middle, were dotted around the room, with four chairs at each. Anna had ordered flowers and on Saturday there would be a red rose for each table. A bouquet of red and white roses would be displayed on the oak dresser in the corner. Leaflets had been printed, which would be dotted around the room for customers to take with them. They contained information on all the different kinds of cat and dog food and care products she would be stocking and an invitation to enquire if there were any other items customers would like her to supply.

She looked around the room with satisfaction, trying not to let her nerves get the better of her. Just a few short months ago she had been in the throes of despair, with no idea of what she was going to do with the rest of her life. Now, here she was, in her very own shop, fully stocked and ready for opening. How on earth had she got here and so quickly? It was all down to Miranda of course. What a brilliant friend she was and how she had quietly chivvied her along, keeping her spirits up, keeping her focused on the shop and a future ... and there was the dog thing too. A furry companion would certainly join her at some point but at the moment she had to concentrate on this, her business, her very own business. Goodness, the butterflies in her stomach were going crazy. She needed to get home and have a brandy. That would steady her for now.

* * *

Miranda arrived home later than expected, fed the dogs and collapsed at the kitchen table with a cup of tea. She felt too tired to cook and anyway there was very little in her fridge and nothing much in the freezer. She really would have to find time to do a shop otherwise she would whittle away to nothing.

Her mobile rang. She nearly didn't answer it, lacking the energy to talk to anyone but curiosity made her look to see who was calling. She squealed with delight and pressed the answer button immediately.

"Jeremy! Hello. Are you coming to Anna's opening? I know you said you wanted to."

"Hello, Miranda, I'm in Leeds already ... at Daphne's. I came up today and yes, I'm going to the opening and if Anna needs any help, I shall be delighted to assist. Now, I don't know about you but I'm starving. Would you like to join me for dinner ... we can go into town if you like or if you're tired, I could pick up a takeaway and bring it over to you ... unless, of course, you've eaten or you're just not hungry."

"Oh please ... I'm famished," Miranda smiled. "I haven't stopped all day and now I'm home with a virtually empty fridge and freezer so your suggestion has come just at the right time."

"Good. So, which is it, dinner in a fancy restaurant or fish and chips at your kitchen table?"

"Oh, fish and chips, please. I'm bushed, to be honest, and the thought of going out is appealing but ..."

"That's it then. Fish and chips it is. I'll bring some plonk too and see if I can rustle up a fancy pudding. Daphne always keeps delicious things in her freezer ... she won't mind if I take something. Any preference as to where I should buy our supper?" "Yes. Go to Donna's ... the one in Market Street in Moortown, just around the corner from Anna's. You won't be far from it, coming from Headingley. Donna cooks everything the traditional way. The fish is huge and the chips are chunky, juicy and delicious."

"Right, Donna's it is. I'll see you in about an hour. Is that okay? You won't wilt away by then, will you?" Jeremy laughed.

Miranda grinned. "I don't think so. See you soon."

She turned off her mobile and dashed upstairs. Suddenly she didn't feel tired anymore. Jeremy was home for the weekend and she was having a meal with him ... in her own home ... all alone. Eeeeek. She reeked of cats and dogs. She needed a shower pretty damn quickly and what the hell was she going to wear?

* * *

William spent the evening impatiently waiting for midnight. He flicked the television on but it was all rubbish and nothing could hold his attention. He turned it off. He was too hyped up. He wanted to see this woman who so casually threw caution to the winds in the park late at night.

He nibbled at a cheese and pickle sandwich, even though he wasn't hungry, and downed a mug of tea. He didn't want his stomach to start rumbling at a crucial moment and give his presence away before he wanted this woman to know he was near. Not that he intended to hide. In his disguise, he didn't look at all threatening. All the women he had encountered when he wore it obviously considered him harmless as they easily engaged in conversation with him and made no effort to hurry away. So, he could amble around the lake, pretending he couldn't sleep, sit on a bench watching the stars. It would be damned cold though and perhaps she wouldn't come, this stupid, silly woman. How long should he hang about? An hour should do it and then, if she didn't turn up, he would come home and go to bed. He put the electric blanket on and turned it up high. He hated chilly sheets. They would be beautifully warm when he came home, hopefully with his needs satiated. He looked at Miranda's photo in the picture frame. He didn't want to think about her now. He picked it up and placed it carefully in the drawer of his bedside cabinet.

* * *

Tanya pulled on her duffle coat, wrapped a scarf around her neck and pulled on her wellingtons. Sometimes there were big, muddy puddles on the lakeside path in the park and if her feet became damp, it set off the athlete's foot she had suffered from for months.

She shut the front door of her smart little mid-terraced house, locked it and walked along Wimpole Lane until she reached Peesdown High Street. There was no-one about and she sighed with pleasure. During the day, with the shops open, it was teeming with pedestrians and cars but now it was peaceful.

She liked to walk along the street and window-shop before she made her way into the park. The jewellers, the vets, the post office and the bank all had shutters, which was understandable, but the others were brightly lit, displaying their wares. She idled away a good twenty minutes, studying the latest offers. With Christmas only a few weeks away, there were many. So much off this and so much off that, in an effort to get people to part with their money.

Thank goodness she didn't have anyone to buy for. She had never married so hadn't had children. Her parents had died long ago and her only living relative, her older sister, lived in India and they hadn't been in contact for years, let alone sent each other Christmas presents. There were no real friends either. Lots of acquaintances but no-one she was close to. So, as usual, instead of spending money on others, she would treat herself to a present. Last year it had been a new bed, the year before it had been an expensive washing machine. This year … she wasn't sure. A new cooker maybe or a sofa. She'd have to give it some thought as whichever it was, she would have to order it soon otherwise it wouldn't be delivered before Christmas.

She came to the new pet shop, Pampered Pets, on the corner with Baker Lane. Tanya had seen the woman who had bought it, going in and out over the last few weeks. They had stopped to chat this morning when Anna, she had said her name was, had dropped some papers out of a folder and Tanya had picked them up for her. Anna had told her about the opening and she said she would go. Anna had smiled and told her there would be refreshments and that in a while she was hoping to open the back room as a little cafe and would have to hire some staff to help her.

Tanya's heart had leapt at her words. Last year, she retired from her job as a cook in the Windmill Nursing Home, where she had worked for most of her life, and not having something to get up for every day was depressing. She was still fit and healthy and needed something more to do than sit and read and watch television all day.

"I've catering experience ... and I need a job," she had chirped up.

"Right," Anna had said. "I haven't time now but pop in sometime in the next week or two and we'll have a chat about it."

Tanya had every intention of doing so. It would be handy, having a little job only yards away from where she lived ... and there was Marmite too ... the cat she had rehomed from Happylands two years ago. She could buy all his paraphernalia from Pampered Pets. Anna might even give her a staff discount and then she could really spoil him. Bless him. She did love him. He was the only living thing she did.

She moved on, crossed Baker Lane and headed up the road towards the park. The three houses on her left and the five on her right were all in darkness. The Red Lion, on the corner with Miller Lane, had a light on upstairs so Chris and Jane Perkins were obviously in the process of going to bed. As she crossed Miller Lane, towards the park gates, she looked to her left and right. It appeared everyone else had retired for the night as nothing stirred, no lights shone in any of the houses, nor the vicarage. The church, however, was floodlit. Some people would find it eerie but Tanya loved it. The old medieval architecture looked utterly beautiful.

She wandered into the park and onto the path which led down to the lake. The moon was out and the stars were bright. She breathed deeply. She loved the fresh night air and the sheer peace of the park ... only her and the creatures of the night up and about. It was the best time to come; no people, dogs or even worse, children. She disliked the park during the day as people wanted to stop and chat and she didn't want to. That's why she loved her nocturnal walks. She could be totally alone, to think, to dream, to ponder ... and just enjoy the sounds of the night; the gentle lapping of the water in the lake, the cries of the owls, the rustle of foxes or badgers in the undergrowth. It was best in the winter, of course, as any courting couples tended to stick in their cars in the car park. In the summer it could be quite different. Lovers would be found all over the place, especially in the woods and as it didn't get dark until around 11.00 p.m. and the temperature was warm, they would hang about, being a damned nuisance with their drinking, singing, barbecues and lovemaking. No, it was much nicer in the winter.

* * *

William was standing behind the thick trunk of an ancient oak tree only feet from the lakeside path when he saw her. She was heading towards him. He licked his lips. He couldn't see her features, even in the moonlight, but he was delighted to see she was wearing a skirt. Perfect. It would have been a damned nuisance if it had been trousers. He was wearing his jogging bottoms, which he always wore on his sorties. So much quicker to pull down than blasted zips on ordinary trousers. He felt in his pocket ... for the cord ... to pull around her neck. He smiled as she drew nearer.

CHAPTER 12

The event was going well, Anna decided, having tossed and turned all night, wondering what she would do if no-one turned up or alternatively, if too many arrived and the shop wasn't big enough to hold them all, causing a health and safety issue.

But it hadn't turned out either way. She arrived bang on the dot at 7.30 a.m., followed by the caterers and florists. By the time they had finished, an hour later, the garden room looked stunning and the aroma from the freshly made finger buffet and the coffee was enough to tempt the most hardened of appetites.

At nine o'clock, Anna opened up, her heart in her mouth, almost terrified about what the coming day would bring and if she could cope. However, Miranda was on the doorstep, with a big grin on her face and waving a bottle of champagne.

"Congratulations, my darling," she said, giving Anna a big hug. "See, you did it. I knew you would and it all looks amazing," she continued, gazing around the shop and following her nose through to the garden room.

"Oh, my goodness, just look at this. It's brilliant. It all looks so pretty. ... oh, and I see Sonia brought you something to put up," she said, striding up to the end wall where Anna had attached the Happylands details and photographs of six of the dogs, two cats, three ponies, two rabbits and the hamsters on a big chalkboard, which should catch the eye of everyone entering the room. "I do hope she receives some enquiries from this."

"So do I," said Anna, pleased Miranda thought all the hard work had been worth it. "Would you like a coffee?"

"I would prefer champagne but we better leave it until later," Miranda giggled. "But no, I had a coffee before I left home."

"You look positively glowing this morning, by the way. What have you been up to?" Anna asked curiously.

"Oh, nothing much ... Jeremy turned up last night with fish and chips ... but that's all."

Anna snorted. "That's all, is it? By the look of you, you're the cat who got the cream."

"Well, he is pretty amazing ... he'll be along later this morning

… his car is playing up and he's paying a visit to his garage to see if they can fix it before he goes back to London on Tuesday. If not, he'll have to take the train."

"That's nice … that he's going to join us. I do like him."

"Yes … so do I," grinned Miranda.

"Coooeee," came from the front of the shop. "Anyone home?"

Anna stepped out of the garden room, pleased to see Sonia with a young man in tow.

"Hi, Anna. I must say this all looks marvellous. This is my son, Josh," Sonia said, waving a hand at the tall, gangly youth with thick, wavy blonde hair and a nice smile.

Anna shook his hand. "Hello, Josh. It's lovely to meet you."

"Did you manage to find somewhere to display all our details?" asked Sonia.

"Oh, yes. Miranda was just admiring them. Go through to the garden room and help yourself to coffee and nibbles and you'll see them up on the wall."

The rest of the morning was crazy. All of Miranda's dog walkers; Belinda, Julie and Kate, turned up and helped out behind the till while Anna and Miranda chatted to the steadily increasing flow of people who entered the shop, making sure they were taken through to the garden room, had refreshments, saw the information on the chalkboard and took the information leaflets.

Sales were steady and welcome. Anna noticed quite a few of the luxury cat and dog beds disappearing out of the front door, along with numerous packs of food, toys and treats. Leaflets were also being handed in with details of items customers would be interested in buying.

Then, just before lunch, when Anna had already changed her shoes twice as her feet were hurting from standing for so many hours, the door opened and in walked Mrs Smedley, accompanied by Precious, who unused to a room full of people, stood and shook with fear.

Miranda grimaced behind her hand, Belinda grinned, Anna smiled widely, walking forward to shake Mrs Smedley's hand.

"Good morning, Mrs Smedley. It's so nice of you to pop in. Would you like some refreshments once you've had a chance to look around?"

143

"Yes, Anna. I would. Thank you ... but I was wondering ... have you heard the news ... from the park?"

"What news?" Anna asked, well aware that Miranda and Belinda behind the counter had their ears pricked.

"They've found a woman ... in the lake this morning ... she's dead ... been sexually assaulted and strangled."

Anna gasped, putting her hand to her mouth. "No."

Miranda and Belinda stood with their mouths open and their eyes wide.

"Who?" Miranda asked. "Do we know her?"

"I'm not sure. Poor Mr Fletcher is in a bad way. He found her. Had to call the police, who sent divers to fish her out. The whole area, by the top of the lake, near the woods, is cordoned off."

"Poor Mr Fletcher," Anna said, sitting down in the chair beside the counter.

"Indeed, Anna. He could hardly talk to me when I bumped into him in the car park. He was as white as a sheet and looked thoroughly shaken up."

"Does he know who it is?" asked Miranda.

"He said something about warning her, telling her not to visit the park at night. All seemed very strange to me. What woman would want to ... on her own? Seems utterly ridiculous."

Miranda looked astonished. "Oh, my goodness. He was only telling William ... you know the old gentleman with the walking stick, and me, about her yesterday. He told us he had warned her not to do it. What a silly woman ... but who the hell is the murderer? I wonder if it's the same man who raped that other woman a few months ago? If so, he's now gone a whole awful step further. Poor woman. How awful for her. Goodness," she looked at her Four Paws staff, "we will have to rethink our walking routes. Whoever he is, he's obviously becoming far, far bolder and exceedingly dangerous."

With her dramatic news imparted, Mrs Smedley had a quick look around, picked daintily at a cupcake and drank a cup of tea in the garden room, where she eagerly dispensed her 'news' to three other ladies. She then bought a packet of soft chews for her 'little darling' and left the shop with the warning to Miranda 'to be careful in the park'.

"That's strange," Miranda said, with a puzzled expression on her face.

"What is?" asked Belinda, still digesting the information about the dead woman. She was seriously beginning to wonder if being a dog walker was the right occupation for her. Anna required an assistant in the shop. That might be a much safer bet. Perhaps she should apply. The thought of taking another load of dogs into Peesdown Park was not as attractive as it had been.

"William," Miranda replied with a worried frown. "He said he was going to come in and help today. He hasn't turned up yet and he's always about in the mornings so I would have thought he would have come in by now. I do hope he's okay."

* * *

William was in bed. He would have liked to have gone along to Pampered Pets for the opening but he was tired from last night's exertions and he was also sporting a nasty scratch all down the left side of his face, which was bloody sore and stinging like mad. He could hardly go out in public with that. It would cause a lot of questions and he simply hadn't an excuse. He would have to stay in for a few days until it healed and wasn't so noticeable and then he could cover it with make-up. If anyone asked why he hadn't been out and about, he could say he had come down with a bad cold or a stomach bug. Luckily, he had plenty of food in the kitchen so could manage for a few days … and there was the television, a couple of books from the library to read and his scrapbook to get up to date. He licked his lips and grinned. He had a nice gold earring now, which had belonged to that woman last night … which would make its way into his trophy box … he already had a pearl earring and a silver one, along with a gold watch and a charm bracelet and several chunks of hair from his victims who hadn't been wearing jewellery.

He rolled out of bed and drew back the curtains. It was another grey day. He tried to imagine what was going on in the park.
Someone would have found her by now … floating in the lake. He wondered who. A dog walker, a jogger, a cyclist? All of

145

those kinds of people turned up early for their morning exercise. It would be one of them. Probably gave them a hell of a fright.

He grinned and touched the deep scratch on his cheek. He had given her a hell of a fright too. He remembered how she had jumped as he had walked towards her and grabbed her arm. She had struggled, which was when she had raked at his face but she hadn't screamed. Probably too shocked and scared. He had propelled her to nearby bushes and flung her to the ground. She had tried desperately hard to push him off and then finally opened her mouth to yell. He had smashed his fist into her mouth and the force of it had knocked her out, giving him time to finish raping her at his leisure, making sure he used a condom and carefully removing it and placing it in a plastic bag to avoid leaving any evidence. He would dispose of it, along with his clothes later. Then he had pulled out the cord and finished her off. Mercifully for her, she hadn't regained consciousness, which was a shame really, as he liked them to suffer ... but he hadn't done it out in the open before and even though it was the middle of the night, it was possible they could be discovered so it was good she was out for the count and wouldn't make a fuss.

Checking there was no-one around, he had ripped out her earring and then pulled her body out of the bushes and rolled it into the lake. He had read once that any DNA was ruined if it came into contact with water. How true it was, he had no idea but it wouldn't hurt to try.

He had made his way home, keeping under cover of the trees until he reached the park gates. He had walked slowly down Miller Lane towards his house, making sure to limp, just in case anyone happened to glance out of a window and see him. His gate had tended to creak badly since he bought the house but he had oiled the hinges so they wouldn't make a sound when he returned in the night. They opened silently. He had wanted to chain and padlock them but decided not to as it would be impossible to do it without making a bit of noise. He had looked up at the sky as he skirted the gravel, onto the grass, and made his way to the front door. The stars had appeared brighter than when he had left the house earlier. He had smiled. The itch had gone.

But now he was cross with himself and went to his special little room, next to the two massive bedrooms on the second floor of his house. It overlooked the back garden and the park. He could see the lake glistening in the weak November sunshine, although he couldn't see the spot where he had attacked that woman last night. It was sheltered by trees and shrubbery.

He pulled down the blind. He didn't want to see the park now. He had to pray for his sins. He turned to the opposite side of the room where there was a large gold crucifix on the wall above a white clothed table on which stood two large cream altar candles standing on clear glass plates. He picked up a matchbox from an adjacent table and lit the candles, blew out the match and chucked it in the bin in the corner of the room. He looked at the bible with its black leather cover which lay between the candles … the one his parents had bought him when he had been confirmed. It went everywhere with him.

He opened it, sank to his knees, clasped his hands together and said the Lord's Prayer. Then he chanted the ten commandments, pausing for a moment before he spoke the words 'I shalt not kill'.

"I'm so sorry, God," he whispered. "but you know I can't help myself when the desire comes."

He knelt for a few more minutes, thinking about all those he had sent to heaven. They were in a better place and God would look after them. He had done them a huge favour and shouldn't really feel sorry. He should be proud of himself.

He stood up, closed the bible and left the room, making his way to the kitchen on the ground floor. He needed a strong coffee and then he had to get outside and burn the clothes he was wearing last night … and the condom. He could do a spot of garden clearing. No-one would think anything of it at this time of year. There were masses of dead leaves and fallen branches which needed tidying … in fact, that would provide a good excuse for his face … he could say a branch caught him if anyone asked.

He drank his coffee slowly, deep in thought. He felt better now he had spoken to God about what he had done. He always did. It was as if his apology absolved him of his sins and he could move on without feeling guilty about it … just proud he had put people out of their earthly misery and sent them to a better place. It was as if he was one of God's disciples … and he enjoyed his job.

However, as he finished his coffee and washed up the mug, he began to wish he hadn't succumbed last night. It was going to mess up his plans to marry Miranda as he would have to leave Peesdown for a while … until the dust settled and then there was that man to worry about … the one that had kissed her. William clenched his hands and gritted his teeth. Damn. What if Miranda started a relationship with him? He suddenly relaxed. It wouldn't matter, would it? He would lure the man into some kind of trap and then despatch him too. He could think about it while he was away. No. It wouldn't be too much of a problem.

He considered where to go. It was coming up to the three worst months of the year in England; December, January and February, and it would be good to remove himself from the cold and damp for sunnier climes. He could head off to Spain, or Majorca, Italy … or the Caribbean. Perhaps a cruise. Now that would be a good idea. He could indulge himself as there would be plenty of lone women, seeking romance and if the odd one fell overboard, well so be it. It happened … and it was rare they found a body to tell the tale. He rubbed his chin and grinned. Yes, a long Caribbean cruise, three months should do it, and then he could return here in March, just in time for spring and rekindle his relationship with Miranda. If he could persuade her to marry him then, they could have a summer wedding … a beautiful service at St. Edmunds, a reception at some fancy hotel or stately home and then a honeymoon … perhaps Miranda would like to go on a cruise. He would have to ask her.

He walked through to the lounge and picked up the phone. He would have to ring the Vicar to let him know he wouldn't be around to help with the Christmas events … he looked forward to the time he could ring him to book the wedding.

* * *

The opening day was turning out to be a huge success, business-wise for Anna and romantically for Miranda as Jeremy had turned up just after lunch with a bottle of champagne and a huge bouquet for Anna and a smaller one for Miranda. Belinda, Julie and Kate left not long after Jeremy arrived and he then spent the afternoon showering everyone with his charm, enticing customers to buy things they probably wouldn't have thought of, his sales pitch absolutely perfect. The women were bowled over, the men respectful and friendly.

Anna and Miranda had been able to leave him to it as they entertained their guests with refreshments and extolled the virtues of Happylands. That had been a huge bonus too. Four people had expressed the wish to take in a rescue dog or cat and two were interested in having a pony. Anna hoped Sonia would be receiving visits from them all in the coming days and some of the animals would be going to their forever homes very soon. In addition, she had placed a charity box on the counter before opening this morning which most people contributed to and by late afternoon it was full. She would take it to Sonia tomorrow and exchange it for another. It would be interesting to see how much was in this one.

All three of them were exhausted by the time Anna shut the shop at 6.00 p.m. and they sank into the chairs in the garden room and demolished what was left of the finger buffet, washed down with the champagne.

"I think I'm going to have to soak my feet for hours this evening," Anna said ruefully, easing her shoes off and wiggling her toes.

"That was probably an unwise thing to do," Jeremy said knowledgeably. "Your feet are going to hurt even more when you put them back on."

"Yes, I know you're right but they're killing me ... and I've already changed my shoes twice. I won't put these back on ... I'll wear another pair to drive home."

"You're going to have to stock up again pretty soon," Miranda commented. "Some of your shelves are virtually bare ... I can't believe how many of those dog beds you sold."

Anna smiled. "I'm looking forward to seeing how much I've taken today but I'm too tired to count it tonight. I'll take it home with me and do it in the morning. Thank goodness it's Sunday. I think I need a whole day to recover after today. What are you two doing tomorrow ... anything nice?"

149

Miranda and Jeremy exchanged a look. "We're taking Nellie and Charlie to the seaside ... Filey, probably. I know I don't like Nellie swimming in the winter but she's not so keen on going very far into the sea ... she's a bit wary of the waves and I think Charlie will just paddle. He's doesn't seem keen on swimming but it will be interesting to see what he thinks of the beach ... would you like to come?"

Anna shook her head. She wanted to spend the day letting all that had happened today sink in and prepare for Monday morning ... and she had to do something about getting an assistant. She had placed an advert in the Yorkshire Evening Post and received a few replies but so far hadn't found the time to look at them properly. Tomorrow would be a good opportunity ... and there was that lady, Tanya something, who had spoken to her the other day ... she might be suitable ... anyway, she didn't want to play gooseberry. Miranda and Jeremy would have a much better time without her tagging along.

"No, thank you very much. I have things I need to do ... you just have a lovely time and take lots of photos to show me in the week."

Miranda took their dirty plates and glasses through to the kitchen and washed them up, along with a few used by their customers who had turned up later in the afternoon. Between Anna and her helpers, they had managed to keep up with washing and tidying away the dirty cutlery and crockery reasonably well all day, popping into the kitchen with it every half hour or so to do it. The dishes the caterers had brought were all clean and ready to be collected on Monday

"Right," Miranda said. "I think it's high time we all went home. Thanks to Julie, I haven't any cats to feed this evening as she's doing them for me but I do need to pick up Nellie and Charlie."

"I wish I could join you," Jeremy remarked. "But Daphne and Nigel have been invited to dinner this evening by friends of theirs whose son is about to enter Sandhurst and I've been asked too so I can give them the lowdown of what he might expect," he rolled his eyes, "and as my darling sister provides me with free board and lodging whenever I need it, I ought to oblige and keep her friends happy. She rarely asks me for anything."

Miranda stifled a yawn. She was suddenly feeling exhausted. "It doesn't matter. I think I'm just going to do what I have to do with the dogs and then flake out."

Anna stood up and tried on her shoes. Jeremy had been right. Goodness, it was painful. She took them straight off again and went in search of her comfy loafers.

Duly dressed for a cold winter's evening, they left the shop, Anna switching on the alarm and locking the door carefully. She was laden down with her handbag and some gifts she had been given, Miranda carried Jeremy's bouquet and some more gifts and Jeremy had an enormous carrier bag with the day's takings. They reached Anna's car and placed everything on the back seat.

Miranda hugged Anna. "Congratulations honeybunch. You've made a real success of today and I do hope it takes off for you now. Well done."

As Miranda moved away, Jeremy threw his arms around Anna too. "Yes, I agree. I'm so pleased you bought the shop and brought the old place back to life, Anna. My Dad would be thrilled for you."

He kissed her on the cheek, held open the car door for her and stepped aside, putting his arm around Miranda as Anna drove out of the car park, happy but near to tears at their words. It was so good to have everyone's approval and she was so excited for the future now. It was such a shame Gerald couldn't be here to see what she was achieving but there was nothing she could do about that. She was on her own but there was to be no more moping ... no more self-pity. From now on it was onwards and upwards.

* * *

Anna reached home, dumped all her belongings in the kitchen, poured a large glass of Merlot and carried it into the bathroom. She was aching all over with tiredness and her feet were terribly sore. She needed a long hot bath and then an early night.

The bath filled rapidly, smelling divine with the liberal amount of lavender oil and bubble bath she had thrown in. She was just about to step into it when the phone in her bedroom began to ring.

She had no desire to talk to anyone but if she didn't answer it, whoever it was might ring again later when she was even less inclined to talk. She wrapped herself in her red velvet dressing gown and made for the phone by her bed.

"Anna Stapleton," she said tiredly.

"Anna ... it's Sonia. I know you must be shattered but I just wanted to tell you what a brilliant idea it was of yours to put up our details for rehoming. I've had loads of enquiries and have high hopes I can move a few animals on in the next few days, all thanks to you."

"Oh, Sonia. I'm so very pleased I could help. That's fantastic news."

"Yes. I really can't thank you enough ... and as for the shop, I think you've done a grand job with it and I'm certainly going to recommend you to everyone who comes my way."

Anna smiled. "That's really kind of you, Sonia. Thank you ... oh, and the charity box is full so I'll pop over with it tomorrow and then you can empty it and I'll bring it back again."

"That's great, Anna. Every penny we can get our hands on is needed so that's a bonus too. Oh, and by the way, I presume you heard about that poor woman who was found in Peesdown Park this morning?"

"Yes ... dreadful. We couldn't believe it. Apparently, poor Freddie Fletcher, the park keeper who found her, is in a terrible state."

"Poor man. Must have been an awful shock for him. Anyway, I have the woman's cat ... the Police turned up this afternoon with it. They found out who she was, went to her house ... which is just around the corner from your shop ... in Wimpole Street. Anyway, she had rehomed a cat from me a couple of years ago ... poor Marmite ... so he's back again."

"Marmite?" Anna gasped, remembering the conversation with that woman outside of Pampered Pets a few days ago. She had mentioned she owned a cat called Marmite and how many other pets could there be with such an unusual name?

"Yes ... why ... do you know her ... the woman?"

Anna sat down on the bed, her heart heavy with dread. "If it's who I think it is, yes ... I believe I've met her ... outside my

shop the other day … she was going to pop in and see me about a job
… what was her name?"

"Tanya … Tanya Philips."

Anna sucked in her breath. "Oh, no! It is her. Oh, goodness, Sonia. How absolutely awful. It's bad enough when you hear someone has been attacked in such a brutal way but when you've met them   … ."

"I know. From what I remember of her, she was a kindly lady and by the looks of it doted on Marmite. He arrived in beautiful condition and with a suitcase of possessions. She obviously idolised him. I'm so sorry to be the bearer of bad news, Anna. Try not to dwell on it. Go and relax and put your feet up for the rest of the evening. You certainly deserve it."

"Yes, Sonia. I will. I'll see you tomorrow." Anna
put the phone down and burst into tears.

* * *

Freddie Fletcher was feeling deeply miserable. Beryl had tried to make him feel better, baking his favourite steak pie for tea, followed by rhubarb crumble but it hadn't worked. He had been morose all day, sick to the stomach from what he had found earlier that morning. The image of that woman wouldn't leave his mind, floating face down in the water at the deepest end of the lake, her bottom half completely naked. They had found her skirt and knickers in the bushes. He would never be able to walk past that area again without feeling sick. Why the hell hadn't the silly female listened to him? Stupid, stupid woman.

"Do try and eat something," urged Beryl from the opposite side of the table. "You haven't had anything all day."

"I can't," he said hoarsely. "And I don't know if I can go back to my job, Beryl. What with having to stake out the place for badger baiters and now this. It's always been a nice cushy little number, patrolling the park during the day and making sure noone is misbehaving and giving out information to those who want it but now … all this violence … I don't think I can cope with it." "Freddie, you've always loved it and you've been there years

... you'll feel better in the morning, after a good night's sleep ... and something to eat."

"I don't know if I will, Beryl," he replied sorrowfully. "I sincerely don't know if I will."

CHAPTER 13

A week later and the police were no closer to finding out who had raped and killed Tanya Philips in Peesdown Park. Their enquiries were drawing a complete blank. With no-one apparently in the park at the time, not even courting couples, there were no witnesses and very little forensic evidence. Tanya's skirt and knickers had been found in the bushes where it was apparent that the attack had taken place and she was missing a gold earring from her right ear. The perpetrator had more than likely taken it as a trophy as there was no sign of it during the extensive search of the area.

Freddie Fletcher was interviewed and informed the detectives investigating the case that he had spoken to Tanya only days before and warned her not to walk alone at night. He was distraught to think if he had been there watching for badger baiters, he might well have been able to prevent what had occurred.

"From what you've told us, Mr Fletcher, it would seem Miss Philips was in the habit of visiting the park at night regularly so don't feel guilty. You did your best, warning her of the danger and she unwisely chose to ignore it," one of the detectives remarked.

His words did nothing to dispel Freddie's sense of gloom. His walks around the park became sombre and miserable. He gritted his teeth and clenched his hands when he had to go past where Tanya had been found, avoiding looking in the water at that point as the memories of seeing her in the lake were still so vivid. He watched men suspiciously, especially if they were alone and didn't have a dog, wondering if the attacker would be blasé enough to wander nonchalantly about the park during daylight hours, gloating over what he had done.

He began to dread going to work, feeling nauseous as soon as he entered the park gates. He badly wanted to pull himself together, get back to how he had felt about his job before having to sit up all night waiting for badger baiters and then that dreadful morning when he had found Tanya. He had enjoyed being in charge of the park with the little bit of power it gave him, but now he didn't. He couldn't even find his usual pleasure in chiding Miranda and as much as he disliked dogs, patted Charlie on the head on one occasion.

"You make sure this animal looks after you, Miranda," he said. "I don't want to find you dead in the lake."

"You won't," she had reassured him. "I'm a bit savvier than that poor woman. She was deluded if she thought it was safer here at night."

"Yes, she was. It's strange though," he said, rubbing his chin. "How it happened the very night after I told you and William about her. I'm not sure who else had any idea of what she got up to. I presume you didn't tell anyone."

"No, only Anna ... and she was too busy with the shop opening to worry about a woman's nocturnal wanderings." "Have you seen William since? I was going to see if he had mentioned it to anyone but he doesn't seem to have been in the park."

Miranda frowned. "No, which is strange as he's here most days. He didn't turn up to Anna's opening either, as he said he was going to. I do hope he's okay. Have you any idea where he lives?" she asked anxiously. "I know it's Peesdown but am not sure exactly where. I can always pop round and make sure he's not ill or something."

"I think he lives along Miller Lane, the road running parallel to the park, just outside the gates. He did mention it to me once ... I'm sure he said it was the house right down the end on your right, as you leave the park. I know it was up for sale a few months ago so I presume it's that one. He must be pretty wealthy. Those houses are worth a bob or two."

"Right. I'll drop by when I've finished walking all the dogs. Just to see if he needs anything because it's strange we haven't seen him ... and if he lives alone, anything could have happened and no-one would know."

"That's very kind of you, Miranda. Very kind indeed," Freddie muttered and went on his way. He would be glad when today was over and he could get home to Beryl. He still didn't know what to do about his job. He wanted to hand in his notice now but what else was out there for a man of his years? He only had twelve months more to do before he officially retired and should stick it until then. He sighed, pulled the collar of his coat

156

up around his ears and headed for the car park to check the toilets and litter.

* * *

With the dogs settled in the Volvo after their walk, Miranda drove out of Peesdown Park through the wrought iron gates. She turned right down Miller Lane and looked at all the houses with envy. They were huge Victorian residences, all detached, with beautiful gardens, massive gates and fancy cars outside. She wouldn't mind owning one of them but the chances of that were pretty slim. As Fart Features had said, they were certainly worth a bob or two and however big she grew her empire, it was doubtful she would ever have enough money to buy one.

She drove along slowly until she reached the very end house, which was difficult to see from the road with the massive hedge around it. She stopped the Volvo in front of the gates, got out and looked up the gravelled drive. It all looked sad; the house and the gardens. That was the only way she could describe it. Sad and unloved. Unlike the others, which were all done up, painted nicely and possessed well cared for gardens. This one looked like it hadn't seen a fresh coat of paint on the doors and windows since the place had been built, the drive was full of weeds popping up and rambling through the gravel, the shrubbery was like a jungle and the grass hadn't seen a mower all summer by the look of it.

With growing dread at what she might find, Miranda pushed open the rusty gates. She had expected them to creak and groan but strangely enough, there were traces of oil around the hinges and they moved easily and silently. How odd. William had oiled the gates but neglected the rest of the garden. She wondered why. If what Freddie said was true, and William was reasonably wealthy, why hadn't he hired a decorator and a gardener if he couldn't do the work himself? Anyhow, that didn't matter for now. What did was whether or not he was okay.

Trying to pretend a courage she didn't feel, she walked up the path, her feet crunching sharply on the gravel. She stared at the windows. All the downstairs curtains were drawn, which didn't bode well. She coughed nervously as she walked up the steps to the front door and banged on it loudly. No answer, no twitching of curtains. Had William popped out or gone away? Was he ill or dead inside? Her imagination began to go into overdrive. What if he was listening to her, unable to come to the door? He might have had a stroke or a heart attack. She began to wish she hadn't come alone. Anna was only down the road in the shop. She should have asked her to come up. Anyway, she was here now and better get on with it.

She moved around the vast building. The enormous sash windows on the side and around the back didn't appear to have curtains but were too high up for her to see inside anyway. She reached another flight of steps at the rear, which led up to the back door. She banged on it while staring at yet another jungle of a garden which must have been at least a hundred feet long and probably the same in width. It had probably been fabulous in its heyday as there was evidence of flower beds along the sides and in the centre, which were now full of dead and dying weeds. The laurel hedge at the front of the house continued to the far end at the rear, separating William from his nearest neighbour. It also ran the full length of the garden at the far end, the other side being Peesdown Park, and then disappeared behind a brick-built garage.

She went back down the flight of steps and looked up at the windows. Nothing moved. It was as if the house was dead. She prayed William wasn't too.

She looked at the garage. The doors were shut but William might be inside. She walked across to it but the black painted wooden doors were secured by one of the largest padlocks she had ever seen. William definitely wasn't inside. She wondered what he kept in there to warrant such a large lock. As far as she knew he didn't have a car, at least he had never mentioned it if he had and she hadn't seen him driving one.

Getting colder by the minute, with the wind whipping up and rain threatening, she was conscious of the dogs in the car who needed to go home. She would give it one more try and then she would ring the police and advise them of her concerns. Then it would be up to them to deal with it. She hurried back to the steps to the front door, ran up and banged loudly on it again. She peered through the letterbox into a long passageway with doors leading off to the left and the rear, along with a flight of stairs to the upper floors.

"William ... it's me, Miranda. Are you ok? Can you come to the door?" she yelled.

* * *

William had been asleep on the sofa in the lounge. Although he had wanted to make the excuse that his absence from the park was because of an illness, he really had felt extremely ropey. It must have been sitting about in the park waiting for that woman. He had caught a chill. He hadn't been able to leave his bed since the day after the attack on Tanya and it was only yesterday that he had started feeling a little better and could get up for a while. He had existed on soup since feeling poorly but this morning he had risen and fancied a proper cooked breakfast; bacon, eggs, fried bread and tomatoes. It had gone down well with two cups of coffee. He had then intended getting on with building a bonfire. His clothes and the condom were still in the utility room and needed to be destroyed ... and he would have to chain up the gates while he was doing it. They were still unlocked from when he had returned from the park that night which had nearly caused him to have a heart attack when a young police officer had walked up to the front door a few days ago. William had hidden in the bedroom, relief flooding over him when the man went away. He wanted to go down the drive and chain up the gates afterwards but if the police officer came back, it might look suspicious. As uncomfortable as it made him feel, he had decided to leave the gates as they were but while destroying evidence, he needed the security of knowing he wouldn't be disturbed.

However, the cooked breakfast and coffee made him drowsy and instead of doing what he intended, William fell promptly asleep on the sofa. Miranda had woken him up with her banging.

His heart had leapt when he heard her voice calling his name. He badly wanted to let her in, to have her all to himself but he couldn't risk her seeing the scratch on his face.

He listened to her banging on the doors and calling him. There was an element of panic in her voice. What if she decided to call the police to break the door down? Heaven forbid. That was the last thing he wanted. He had no choice. He had to talk to her. He grabbed his wig and pulled it on, praying it was straight. The mirror was in his bedroom and to get to it he would have to go past the front door to the stairs and Miranda would see him through the frosted glass. He attached his moustache, hoping that was aligned correctly too. He went to the front door and opened it, keeping the chain on and only showing the good side of his face.

"Oh, William," Miranda gasped. "I was becoming so worried about you as we haven't seen you in the park for days. Are you okay? Are you ill? Do you need anything?"

"No … thank you, Miranda. That's very kind," he said as weakly as he could. "I've just had a bad cold and didn't feel like going out and anyway, I don't want to give my germs to anyone." "No, of course not … well, is there anything you need … food
… medicines?"

"No. I'm well stocked up. I just want to sleep and get over it."

"Yes, of course. Well," she said, handing him one of her business cards. "Here's my number if you need anything. Don't hesitate to call me if you do. Promise."

He nodded. "Promise. Thank you, Miranda. Very much."

"That's okay. Now go and get better and I hope we'll see you in the park soon."

"Well, actually," he added, thinking it was best to tell her so no-one else would come snooping. "I'm thinking of taking a holiday … in the sun … for the winter … get myself really fit again."

"Oh … that's a really good idea. Where are you planning on going?"

"I'm not sure yet … Spain, Italy … or a cruise maybe … the Caribbean perhaps."

"Well, you make sure you have a lovely time and get yourself fit and well."

"Thanks, Miranda … and thanks for coming to see if I'm okay. I appreciate it."

Miranda waved and walked back up the path to her car. He watched her go reluctantly. She was so lovely, both in nature and appearance. She might be dressed in grubby walking clothes but it didn't matter. Her beautiful face bloomed with good health, her long, wavy hair shone, her eyes sparkled and her skin, with a rosy glow, was clear ... and she was so kind. She had been concerned about him, so much so that she had made it her business to find out where he lived and call to see if he was okay.

His heart turned over with love for her. It would have been so good to invite her in, spend quality time with her in his own home, the home which he would share with her one day soon. He couldn't wait ... and if hadn't have been for that crazy woman visiting the park in the middle of the night, he wouldn't have had to go away. He could have remained here, talking to Miranda every day. Bloody woman, this Tanya. He knew her name now from all the local news coverage. Bloody, bloody woman!

If only ... he hated that expression ... but he used it now. If only he had hadn't let his desire get the better of him that night with so little thought of the consequences. He had learned many years ago, with the demise of his parents, that everything had to be planned carefully beforehand. To do things on impulse was crazy as so many things could go wrong ... and he had been taking a real risk with Tanya Philips. He prayed he hadn't left any clues behind. The police had requested his DNA samples when his parents had died but once he was cleared of any wrongdoing, they were supposed to have been destroyed. If they hadn't, he could be in real trouble as Tanya would probably have his skin under her fingernails, if it hadn't floated away or been too damaged in the water for an accurate analysis. Anyway, if he headed abroad as soon as he could, he could keep an eye on the situation from afar and would soon know whether they had matched up the samples to him. Then he wouldn't return. He would change his name and live permanently overseas somewhere. It would break his heart, having to leave Miranda behind but he might not have any choice.

Damn, damn, damn!

Miranda drove happily away from Miller Lane, relieved to know that her fears of finding William either seriously ill or worse, dead, had been knocked on the head. He looked a bit peaky but at least he had her number now if he should need anything and it was good to hear he was planning a holiday to somewhere nice and warm for the winter. Lucky devil. She wished she could.

She drove out of Peesdown, deposited her client's dogs at their respective homes and then headed for her own with a tired and contented Nellie and Charlie on the backseat, snoring their heads off. She thought about having a little holiday with them. She could take them somewhere ... a cottage on the coast. Both dogs had enjoyed that wonderful day out with Jeremy at Filey. They had had such fun, splashing in the sea, chasing each other on the sand, Nellie rolling in it, trying to pretend she was a yellow Labrador and not a chocolate one. They had walked for miles and then ended up at one of the stalls on the promenade eating sausage and chips, the dogs having more sausages than chips. It was dusk when they finally left Filey for the journey home, having spent the last hour, with the dogs asleep in the back, sitting and watching the sea from their vantage point high up on the cliffs in the huge car park, which had emptied slowly during the evening. By the time they left, there were only three other cars still there.

They had journeyed home, Jeremy driving, while Miranda nodded off, trying hard not to so she wouldn't miss a moment of her time with him but a combination of sea air and plenty of food and exercise put paid to her desires and she slept most of the way home, only waking when they reached the outskirts of Leeds and pulled up at traffic lights.

They had driven back to her house where Jeremy had left his car. He declined to come in as he needed an early night, having to return to London early the next morning. It had been disappointing but they were both tired and Miranda knew if he had come in, it was doubtful they would have been able to control their feelings and as they hadn't known each other very long, she didn't want him to think she was easy, as much as she wanted him. So, as hard as it had been to pull herself out of his arms as they kissed goodnight, she knew it was the right thing to do. She still had a sneaky suspicion that there would be plenty of women in the army who worked with him who would be vying for his attention and she didn't want to be one of the hordes. She wanted to be special ... and jumping into bed with him on the first opportunity certainly wouldn't prove she was.

"I'll ring you," Jeremy said huskily, as he pulled away from her. He was reluctant to leave her too but he didn't want her to think he was only after her for one thing. He liked her too much and respected her. She was funny, outspoken and had guts, starting up her own business and making a success of it as she expanded. He liked women like that, was used to them. His mother had run her own catering business, his sister was a successful barrister and then there were the women he worked with, although they were slightly different. They had to be, in the army, risking their lives as much as the men. He had tried not to get involved with any of them, which had been difficult at times when one or two had formed a crush on him, Karen Watkins in particular, who was a real pain, and his only real, long-term relationship had been with Geraldine, the daughter of his Brigadier. They had been together for a year but for some reason, he couldn't bring himself to ask her to marry him. They got along well, had a lot of laughs and banter but he had never been able to see himself living with her for the rest of his life. In the end, they had drifted apart, she to a London financier who swept her off her feet and married her within six months of their meeting. Jeremy had been happy for her, attended the wedding with a couple of fellow officers from his platoon, and then concentrated hard on his career, until Miranda entered his life. He had been intrigued by her right from that first meeting at Anna's shop and had wanted to know more about her ... and what he was finding out, he liked ... and although he was due back at Barracks in the morning, he knew he was going to count the days until he could get back to Leeds to be with her again. Even Daphne was beginning to realise something was going on as he was heading home more frequently now than he had done for years.

He gave Miranda one more swift kiss on the cheek and left her.

"I'll ring you tomorrow evening ... and for goodness sake be careful in the park. I don't like to think of you putting yourself in danger with this damned murderer still out there."

"I will ... be careful," she said, smiling confidently. "I've got my alarm, Charlie, Nellie and all the other dogs and we won't go deep into the woods until this chap is caught. It doesn't matter too much at this time of the year anyway, now the weather is cooling down there aren't so many people in the parks and the children are all at school so we can stay out in the open parts without worrying about bumping into too many people."

"Good. Well, make sure you do. The last thing I want to hear is that you've been attacked in some way. You're becoming rather precious to me, Miranda," he said, hugging her close.

Miranda's heart skipped a beat and she wanted to shout for joy at those words.

"And you, me," she whispered as their lips met again.

He had rung her every night since then and was planning on coming home next weekend. Miranda's smile was wide as she thought about seeing him again. She couldn't wait.

* * *

The shop had been quite busy since opening day with a steady trickle of customers coming through the doors and Anna was loving it, meeting new people and greeting those she had met in the park with Miranda, along with their dogs, hearing their stories, exchanging gossip.

There was a lot of speculation about poor Tanya Philips as few people realised she was in the habit of taking nocturnal walks in the park. It was of the general opinion that she had been very stupid but even so, rape and murder literally on their doorstep? Who could have done such a thing? Would they be caught? Would they strike again? Most of the women were terrified of going to the park on their own during daylight hours now and husbands and friends were roped in to accompany them. Hardly anyone walked alone and once dusk descended, the park was deserted. No-one wanted to be there after dark.

Two young police officers were instructed to carry out house to house enquiries in the streets near the park. One was diligent, the other wasn't and if he didn't receive any answer from a particular house, he didn't bother to return. William's house was one of them.

The police also commenced evening patrols to reassure people but everyone knew they were stretched to the limit and there was only so much they could do and couldn't be relied upon to be there immediately they might be needed.

Anna had been questioned, like everyone else, but she had nothing of value to impart which could be of assistance. Her customers were the same. No-one had known Tanya very well as she was a bit of a loner, and was happy to remain so, living with her poor cat, Marmite, whom Sonia had rehomed.

Sonia had popped into the shop earlier this morning with the latest photos and details of animals seeking their forever home but Anna had been too busy to look at them until late afternoon, when she was alone and could treat herself to a cup of tea. She sat by the till, flicking through what Sonia had given her to display, her heart flipping over when she saw the two dogs she had made friends with, when the door opened and in walked a burly police officer with three white stripes on the arm of his uniform. His deep blue eyes smiled widely as he approached her and took off his cap, revealing a head of dark hair.

"Good afternoon," he said. "Sergeant Wilkinson from Peesdown police station. I just thought I'd pop in and make my acquaintance. You must be Anna Stapleton?"

Anna nodded and held out her hand for him to shake. "Yes. Pleased to meet you, Sergeant. Is there anything I can help you with?"

"No, not really. I'm just been patrolling the park, trying to reassure people that we're doing all we can to find the murderer of Tanya Philips but it's certainly an uphill struggle trying to find any evidence. I don't suppose you have anything you could tell me? Anything you've overheard in here. It's surprising what people think is of no consequence which could be something significant."

Anna shook her head. "No. I haven't a clue who could have done it and I certainly haven't heard anything which could be helpful. I'm really sorry."

165

"Don't be. By the way, the place is looking good. It was a shame old Michael Cross died. He was a nice old boy ... have known him for years ... and his son ... Jeremy. I believe he's in the army."

"Yes ... he's stationed in London. He's been here to help with the opening on Saturday but is now back at his barracks, much to the dismay of my friend, Miranda, who is going out with him at the moment," Anna smiled, having had to listen to her chuntering on about how much she was missing Jeremy.

"Ah, Miranda ... from Four Paws ... I see you have her business cards," he said, picking one up from the pile by the till. "I use her ... for my two Labs. She used to walk them but they can't manage a full hour any longer as they're too old and riddled with arthritis as it was impossible to keep them out of water when they were younger. Miranda visits them when I can't get home during a shift, and lets them out in the garden for a wee and feeds them. I don't know what I would do without her. She's so reliable and so kind. They both adore her."

Further conversation was interrupted by an elderly couple with a small black poodle entering the shop and smiling at Anna.

Sergeant Wilkinson placed his cap back on his head and turned to go. "Nice meeting you, Anna. I'll pop in again as I'm passing and if you do hear anything ...,"

Anna smiled. "Yes. I know what to do. Bye, Sergeant. It was nice meeting you too."

And it was, she thought, amazed to find she suddenly felt bereft as he disappeared out of the door. He was the sort of man you could sit and talk to and he would listen. She hoped he would do as he said and pop in again.

* * *

Andrew Wilkinson, better known as Andy to his friends and family, was thinking the same about Anna. He had warmed to her instantly. She seemed kind and genuine and he wondered if she was married. Probably. A woman like her would have been snapped up long ago.

He was divorced. It had been amicable, that was one thing. He and Maggie had married too young and then the constraints

166

of his job had interfered with married life. Then, four years ago, Maggie had attended French evening classes, had fallen madly in love with the tutor and left their family home. He had understood. Most of his colleagues were divorced and he knew it had been on the cards for a long time before it actually happened. Maggie wanted a man who would be home every day, safe and sound. She hated having to spend hour upon hour worrying about what was happening when he was at work, especially at night.

His only regret was that it was hard on their two children, Mark and Veronica, who now lived with Maggie and her new husband in York. Andy missed them terribly and tried to see them as often as he could but it wasn't always possible if the job got in the way.

It led to some frightful scenes, especially since the children had reached their teens.

Anyhow, since the divorce he had remained single, even though he had enjoyed the odd dalliance with a female police constable and a secretary but that was all they were, mere dalliances. Nothing deep. Nothing he wanted to continue over a longer term.

His thoughts turned back to Anna as he returned to his police car. Now there was someone he could converse with … would want to spend more time with. He glanced back at the shop.

Perhaps he would pay her another visit tomorrow … see if he could find out if she was married. Her left hand had remained under the counter while they were talking. He wanted to find out whether or not she was wearing a wedding ring.

CHAPTER 14

William was busy packing. He had found his passport and booked onto a ship leaving Rome in four weeks for a three-month cruise of the Caribbean. He would have liked to have joined one which was sailing from Southampton as soon as possible but if the police did decide to come after him, he didn't want to be in a vulnerable position on board with no chance to make a getaway. He had to leave it for a while, to make sure the coast was clear. So, he was going to Portsmouth by train in two hours, catching the overnight ferry to France and then a train to Paris, where he would go to ground for a few weeks in a nondescript hotel, keeping his head down and an eye on what was happening in Peesdown via the internet.

He would soon know if they had matched DNA samples and were after him. If so, he would disappear in Europe or maybe even further away. If not, he would head for Rome and join his cruise. The ship was going to stop at just about every major island in the Caribbean as well as spending quite a few days at sea, which would be good. It would be much easier if he did find a victim, to dispose of a body when they were miles out and it wasn't likely to be washed up on some island or other.

However, before he went anywhere, he had to finish tidying up from his attack on Tanya Philips. He had sorted the bonfire yesterday, clearing up debris from the garden, piling it up at the rear and then waiting until it was dark before bringing out his clothes and the condom and setting it all alight. He had checked it again this morning and not a shred of evidence remained. The fire had done its work.

That just left the garage, which had to be sorted in case something happened while he was away, such as a fire or some other catastrophe and someone entered the premises and poked around.

Months ago, he had dug a big hole at the rear, boarded it all out, fixed a wooden cover over the top and then placed a chest freezer over it. He now shut himself in the garage, turned on the light, pulled out the chest freezer and the wood beneath. He then placed all the magnetic van signs indicating he was either Terence Higgs, Plumber; Joe Masterson, Carpenter or Michael

Gough, Electrician inside the hole, along with the three sets of false number plates, plus his scrapbook and box of trophies, covered them up with a blanket, closed it all up again and replaced the chest freezer. If anyone entered the garage while he was away, they wouldn't notice anything. He could go away without worrying. His secret was safe.

He turned off the lights for the garage, locked it up, and went back indoors to get ready for the taxi which was picking him up.

An hour later, he was on his way. The driver of the taxi had sat outside the gates and hooted his horn to indicate he had arrived. William, with his wig and moustache in place, made his way outside with his suitcase and carried it slowly down the drive and onto the pavement. While the taxi driver placed it in the boot of his car, William carefully chained up his gate and padlocked it.

He didn't want any snoopers while he was absent. He had rung the Post Office and alerted them he would be away and they were going to hold onto his post until he returned so there was no need for anyone to want to gain access to his home ... unless the Police decided to pay a visit!

He got into the car and settled comfortably on the back seat as they journeyed along Peesdown High Street and onto the main road for the city centre and the railway station. He was on his way. It was time to go and have some fun elsewhere but he would be back in a few months and then he would really set his sights on

Miranda. He would ask her out, they would enjoy each other's company, he would ask her to marry him and then ....

THE END

REVIEWS

Thank you so much for reading Peesdown Park. I do hope you have enjoyed it and if so, would you please consider leaving a review and a star rating. These are so important for authors as it gives others a chance to decide if the book is for them and if we know readers are enjoying our books, encourages us to keep writing! Books sometimes take years to write and to know that our efforts are worthwhile can be a tremendous boost.

Just clink on the link below which will take you to the Peesdown Park page and scroll down until you see 'write a review'. Thank you so much.

www.amazon.co.uk/dp/B08193FHW5

www.amazon.com/dp/B08193FHW5

THE PEESDOWN SERIES CONTINUES:

PANIC IN PEESDOWN – BOOK 2

US: www.amazon.com/dp/B08W96FYR5

UK: www.amazon.co.uk/dp/B08W96FYR5

Following a winter cruising the Caribbean, serial killer, William Pemworthy, is back in Peesdown, his sights firmly set on Miranda, the popular, bubbly petsitter but he doesn't want to kill her, he wants to marry her! However, she has just become engaged to the gorgeous Army Major, Jeremy Cross. William is furious and is determined the marriage will not go ahead and if he has to kill Jeremy to prevent it, he will. William enlists the help of his mysterious cousin, Stephen, in persuading Miranda she is marrying the wrong man but his plan doesn't work and unbeknown to them, Miranda and Jeremy are now in terrible danger from both men. Can Miranda overcome the terror that awaits her, will Jeremy survive to rescue her and will William and Stephen escape justice once more?

PANIC IN PEESDOWN

PROLOGUE

JANUARY

Bob Watkins pulled on his jogging top and trousers, did up his trainers and left his rented terrace house on Unwin Street to the north of Peesdown. It was just getting light but was bitterly cold and he blew on his hands to keep them warm as he ran down the High Street, across Miller Lane, skilfully missing the icy bits of pavement, and into Peesdown Park. He kept to the grass as he was less likely to slip and headed down to the lake. It took around fifteen minutes to jog all the way round. He usually did five laps every morning and then headed home to shower, have breakfast and go to bed, having been at work all night.

He looked around with interest as he sped along. There were the usual early morning dog walkers, a couple of cyclists and three joggers, one male and two females. He recognised them all and nodded as they passed, no-one keen to stop and chat in the cold.

He reached the point where that woman had been found, raped and strangled a few months ago … Tanya something. The bloke who did it had never been caught and people, especially women, were very scared, not only in Peesdown but all the other parks in Leeds too … Roundhay, Meanwood, Golden Acre. Occasionally he jogged in one of them instead of Peesdown, fancying a change of scene but it was rare to see a woman alone since the murder. Most females now walked or ran in pairs or groups and kept a keen eye out to see who was around and even though the parks tended to be quieter in the winter, this year they had been almost abandoned during the week although busier with families at the weekends. Even so, everyone was on alert and little went unnoticed.

He wondered why the man had killed the woman. It was too extreme. He could understand the rape, the thrill of it, the power, the urgent need to dominate but to actually kill someone afterwards? That was too much. He could never go that far ... or could he? He could cheerfully have killed that stupid bitch he went out with last year who had declared her undying love, then stolen all his savings from under his mattress. Nearly £5,000 he had amassed. It had been his dream to travel the world so he had saved hard and had been intending to chuck in his job next year and go, starting off in America and Canada. He had spent hours planning his route and researching all the countries he wanted to visit; India, Thailand, China, Australia, New Zealand. He had intended working his way around and his savings would have given him a good cushion but that bitch had cleared him out and buggered off. He had tried to track her down but she had disappeared off the face of the earth. Rumour had it that she had hidden herself away in London but as that was like looking for a needle in a haystack and he didn't want to waste any more money searching for her, he gave up. However, if he ever saw her again, he would dearly like to place his hands around her neck and squeeze tight. Bitch!!

He supposed he could have just gone ahead with his plans anyway but she had taken every penny he possessed and he didn't want to depart on his big adventure with absolutely nothing to fall back on so he had started saving again but now his job was in jeopardy. The firm he worked for was folding and he would be out of a job next month with little in the way of redundancy money. He had a couple of interviews lined up but as there were so many looking for work at this particular time, he didn't hold out much hope.

Yes, he could kill that cow for what she had done to him, messing up his life. It wouldn't have even mattered about losing his job as he could have just gone now if he still had his savings. Blast women. He despised them all, starting with his useless prostitute of a mother and his needy, whiny, pathetic older sister who became a junkie and was found dead in her bed after an overdose. Bugger them all but especially that bitch who had cleaned him out.

He had gone a bit wild after her departure, convinced every woman was out to get what they could. She had utterly destroyed the little trust he had ever had in her gender. Women who went out with him were now treated with disdain and he used them for his own gratification, abusing them with rough sex when he took them home, threatening he would return and kill them if they ever breathed a word of it. He had convinced himself it wasn't actually rape, that they had wanted it as they had willingly gone out with him but in the back of his mind he knew it was wrong, especially when they cried "no!" and made it very plain it was what they meant.

He grimaced and concentrated on completing his final circuit of the lake and was just about to leave the park when he noticed a lone female jogger, running with little effort, almost gliding on the path. She wasn't even breathing heavily. Fascinated, he watched her coming towards him. She was utterly beautiful; her slim, long-legged body encased in dark pink lycra, her long dark hair pulled back into a ponytail and her face, oval, with high cheekbones, big eyes and a pert nose.

He stood aside to let her pass. She didn't even glance at him or say thank you. Snooty cow. He had never seen her before and wondered if he would again. It certainly looked as if she could do with a bit of rough sex to sort her out. He chortled and went on his way. He was tired and relaxed now and wanted his bed.

CHAPTER 1

JANUARY

William Pemworthy leaned over the railings of the cruise ship and looked down at the sea. It was calm, like a millpond ... virtually turquoise with the odd ripple of white. The sky was a perfect azure blue. It was all picturesque but, even with the sea breezes, it was hot ... too hot for him. He rubbed his handkerchief across his brow and pulled his white canvas hat further down over his sunglasses. He wanted to return to the cool of his cabin, to collapse on the bed under the air conditioning but if he did, he would miss seeing Tilly Pargeter when she came out of the dance class she was presently enjoying.

Line dancing. He pursed his lips and turned up his nose. Daft buggers. Shouting and hollering and waving their ridiculous hats around when they jumped up and down. Tilly had asked him to go with her but he had declined. There was no way he was going to be seen making a fool of himself.

He looked at his watch. The class would be finished soon and then they would all flood out, laughing and joking about how much fun they had had. Tilly would be hyped up too. She always was when she had been line dancing. She gradually calmed down though when they went to the Juniper bar for a drink afterwards. She would chatter on excitedly for a little while, and then listen to him, looking at him with adoring eyes, hanging on to every word that came out of his mouth.

He loved it. Her adoration. He wasn't used to it. It was a novelty for him. No woman had ever looked at him the way she did but it wasn't right. Something was missing and he knew what it was. She wasn't Miranda ... and she never could be. For a start, she looked nothing like her. Tilly was red-haired. It was

176

frizzy and coarse. Her skin was covered in freckles … her face, her neck, her arms … even her legs. She was overweight too and was always complaining about how much she was putting on since the cruise had begun but it didn't stop her ramming down as much as she could at every meal and the snacks between were large and frequent. He knew that because for the last two weeks they had spent most days together.

Just the sort of woman he had been looking for, on her own, lonely and looking for romance, he had targeted Tilly on first clapping eyes on her, sitting alone in the Juniper bar sipping slowly from a straw in her ghastly sickly lime-coloured cocktail. He had watched her for a while to see if anyone was going to join her but after half an hour and she had spoken to no-one, he decided to try his luck.

"Hi," he said, smiling down at her as he stood beside her and gestured to the barman that he would like to be served. "Interesting looking drink you have there."

She had smiled shyly. "It's a witches' brew."

"Glass of lemonade please … with ice and a slice of lemon," he said to the small, rotund, swarthy skinned barman. "Would you like another … witches' brew?" he asked the woman.

"That's very kind. Thank you … I shouldn't have too many though. They make me terribly squiffy."

She was right. Having downed two more during the evening, it wasn't long before she was slurring her words. They had left the stools at the bar and sat on the comfy seating overlooking the sea. It was getting late and they virtually had the place to themselves as most passengers had either gone to bed or were engaged in dancing the night away under the stars two decks above.

Their conversation had been mainly about Tilly. William had no desire to tell anyone much about himself and any questions she did have, he managed to field fairly well back to her. He did tell her two things though. He told her he lived in Peesdown.

177

He told her there was a beautiful park. He didn't tell her about Miranda.

* * *

"God, I'm fed up with this cold," moaned Miranda, blowing her nose loudly, disturbing Nellie, her chocolate Labrador and Charlie, her black and tan mongrel, who had been fast asleep on their red velvet sofas. They both opened their eyes and looked at her reproachfully. They were tired after a day running around the parks in Leeds with their groups of friends and needed their rest. How dare she disturb them?

"Never mind," Anna replied. "It will soon be spring. Then we'll all feel a lot better."

"Oh, Lord, Anna. It's only the end of January … we have February and March to get through yet. More snow, sleet, gales and rain … and as much as it makes my life a lot easier not having many people about when I'm walking groups of dogs in miserable weather, since poor Tanya Philips was attacked and murdered, I can't say I like walking in Peesdown Park much now. I was always careful before then but now I'm becoming paranoid, imagining murderers behind every tree, jumping at every movement, watching the dogs anxiously when their heads go up in the woods … and if they bark … well, my heart leaps into my mouth … and I have the protection of six dogs! Most people only have one or two and everyone I bump into, who still have the nerve to go to the park, are just the same. Everyone's scared and no-one wants to walk alone … or venture into the woods … they're staying out in the open."

Anna sighed. "I know. I have so many customers in the shop commenting on it and saying they're driving over to Roundhay or Temple Newsam instead and even then, they're taking precautions and walking with others … why don't you walk with Belinda or one of the other girls you have working for you?

Then you'll have twelve dogs for protection as well as each other."

"We can't unfortunately. Professional dog walkers aren't allowed to walk together as it's too intimidating for others ... which is understandable. It's difficult enough for some people to encounter six dogs, let alone twelve. No. We have to walk on our own but none of us are going to enjoy it very much until this damned madman is caught. Has your Sergeant Wilkinson any more news on that front?"

Anna smiled and blushed. "He's not *my* Sergeant Wilkinson."

"Oh, come on, Anna darling. I've seen how you look at each other ... and he's nice. I've known him for years and he's one of the good guys ... and not just because he's a policeman. He really is and I think you would make a lovely couple," Miranda teased. "Perhaps when Jeremy can get up from London next ... he won't have time this weekend with the party ... we can all go out for a meal together ... that would be nice, wouldn't it?"

She looked longingly and proudly at the photo of Jeremy in his army uniform on the sideboard. God, he was gorgeous. Every time she looked at him, either in real life or in a picture, she couldn't believe he wanted to go out with her ... and how hard she had fallen for him. She couldn't wait to see him this coming weekend. It was his birthday and his sister, Daphne, was throwing a party for him at her house in Headingley to which so many of his local friends and colleagues from his London barracks would be attending. It would be wonderful to be with him again but she was a trifle nervous, and that was putting it mildly, about meeting all those people who had known him far longer than she.

"Um, well," Anna blustered, wishing her cheeks would return to their normal colour, "anyhow, I'm not sure ... we'll have to see ... and no, in answer to your first question. No progress has been made on the murder investigation for weeks apparently.

179

No new leads, no new forensic evidence … but Andy assures me they're still working on it."

"Which means there's every chance they're never going to get this guy. Blimey. I'm beginning to wish I'd never decided to become a professional dog walker and have to risk life and limb every day. People have no idea that we do you know. They think we have a lovely life, swanning around the park in beautiful weather with perfectly behaved dogs and visiting cats to cuddle and pet them. They have no idea how dodgy it can be, what with weirdos in the parks and then having to enter people's homes when they're away to feed the cats, never knowing if someone has broken in or maybe still be there. It's not all it's cracked up to be, believe me … let alone the fact that it's damned hard physical work."

Anna grinned. "But you love it and you know perfectly well you wouldn't want to do anything else."

Miranda smiled back. "No. You're right. I wouldn't but sometimes I wish I was rich and could go off for weeks at this time of the year … on a cruise maybe … like William. I expect he's having a lovely time. I hope he comes home well again. He certainly looked very peaky when I popped round to see if he was okay before he went."

"He must be pretty wealthy," Anna remarked, slipping on her shoes. It was time for her to go home, having popped in after closing up Pampered Pets for the day to drop off the food for Charlie and Nellie which Miranda had ordered. They had spent the last hour chatting over two cups of tea and Miranda had offered her something to eat but Anna had a stew in her slow cooker at home and was looking forward to eating it.

"I should think so, with that huge old house of his in Miller Lane. The one next door is up for sale. Did you know?"

"Oh, is it? I should love one of those lovely old Victorian houses but it just wouldn't be practical … oh, by the way ... I've an appointment with an estate agent tomorrow evening. He's

180

coming to take details and photographs of the house ... I've finally decided I'm going to put it on the market and move into the flat above the shop."

"Good," sniffed Miranda before blowing her nose again. "You need to get yourself more settled. The shop is doing really well now word is getting around but you've been looking really tired lately and driving backwards and forwards every day in heavy traffic isn't exactly a stress-free occupation. Life will be so much easier once you are above the shop .... and get yourself a furry companion to keep you company," she finished with a grin.

Anna laughed. "You won't be happy until you see me with a dog, will you?"

"No. You said yourself you always wanted one. It's just a matter of time."

Miranda walked with Anna to the door while the dogs raised their heads and wagged their tails but were too comfortable to move.

"Bye dogs, bye Miranda. Get an early night. You look done in."

"I will ... and you do the same."

* * *

"Bastards!! Bloody bastards," yelled Sonia, throwing the phone down on the kitchen table where it nearly missed landing in a bowl of mushroom soup.

Josh, who was loading the dishwasher following their evening meal, jumped, as did the cats and dogs who had all settled down for the evening on the sofas and in their baskets.

"Who?" Josh asked, having a pretty shrewd idea of what his mother was going to say. It had to be something to do with

181

some poor abandoned or neglected animal from the venom in her voice.

"Someone's tied up two old dogs to a gate down a lane somewhere near Walton, you know that lovely village near Wetherby. Luckily, the farmer who owns the land just drove down there and found them, otherwise they would have been there all night. Poor little buggers. It's bloody freezing. They probably wouldn't have survived until the morning by the sound of it. He says they are terribly underweight and terrified. Anyway, he's bringing them here ... in about half an hour."

"Right," Josh said, putting on his coat. "I'll go and get the isolation room sorted for them and prepare some food."

Sonia nodded. "And I'll ring Jemma. I hate to drag a vet out at night but the dogs need to be checked to make sure there's nothing else wrong with them apart from starvation and cold. Jesus. I wish I could get my hands on the bastards who did this."

"You and me, Mum. You and me," Josh muttered, heading out of the kitchen door to stride over to the isolation room next to the dog kennels.

Jemma was happy to oblige. She was tired and had a date with her boyfriend later but she was as passionate about dumped and neglected animals as Sonia and always put their needs first.

"I'll be over in about an hour," she told Sonia. "I just have two more patients to see at the surgery and then I'll be on my way."

Josh returned to the kitchen, having turned on the heating in the isolation unit, made up two comfy dog beds with thick, woollen blankets and defrosted some rice and chicken which they always kept in the freezer for dogs who had poorly tummies and needed to be on a light diet.

"I think the farmer is here with the dogs," he said to Sonia. "I can see car lights coming up the lane. I'll go down and open the gate for him."

Sonia put on her coat and stood at the kitchen door, all the family cats and dogs now awake and raising their heads to see what was going on at this time in the evening.

All the outside lights were on and Sonia could see the van was dark blue as it pulled up beside her. A man with a beard and thick, curly hair got out and grimaced at her.

"John Marchant," he said, nodding his head in greeting. "And you must be Sonia. I've heard a lot of good things about what you do here at Happylands and it's good of you to take these two as you're probably full to bursting after Christmas with so many dogs being dumped. I could have taken them home but my old dogs would have given them what for and I think the poor little devils have had enough to contend with."

"It's no problem, John. We were up to capacity yesterday but today we managed to re-home four dogs so we have availability and we're all geared up for them. What breed are they? You never said on the phone."

"Bit of a mix-up really … might have a bit of Lab in them but see what you think."

He opened the side of the van slowly so as not to frighten the dogs more than they already were. They sat, a pathetic, heartbreaking sight, shivering at the back, their eyes wide with fear and misery.

"I gave them a couple of blankets and had the heating turned on full blast all the way here but I don't think it's done much good. I've no idea how long they've been tied to that gate. I haven't been up there for a couple of days and it was only by chance I did this evening."

He tried to coax the dogs out of the van but they refused to budge. Reluctant to pull them out, he turned to Sonia. "Any ideas?"

Josh had joined them and Sonia turned to him. "Josh, could you please get some of the chicken from the isolation unit. We'll have to tempt them out."

She talked to the dogs softly while waiting for him to return while John stood and watched her. One of the dogs began to respond to the sound of her voice and crept a little closer while the other remained where it was.

Keeping her tone gentle, Sonia looked up at John. "I think you're probably right. A bit of Lab and a bit of something else but not quite sure whether it's Border Collie."

The first dog responded to the smell of chicken Josh handed Sonia and after the first furtive nibble, gulped down a few handfuls, gradually growing closer and closer to the woman with the kindly voice and delicious food.

The other dog began to creep closer too and buoyed by the fact that her companion was growing in confidence, warily took a piece of chicken Sonia placed on the floor of the van.

"What sex are they?" asked Sonia. "Did you notice?"

"The first is a male and the timid one is a female," said John softly.

Gradually and slowly both dogs ceased shaking as Sonia kept up a soft dialogue, telling them how lovely they were and how they were going to be all right now.

It took nearly half an hour before they trusted her enough to allow her to clip on long leads to their collars and encourage them to leave the warmth and safety of the van. Josh and Sonia walked them slowly into the kennels, followed by a curious John who even though he had been well aware of the presence of Happylands, had never set foot in the place before. He was also intrigued with Sonia; her plain-speaking but inherent kindness.

When the dogs were settled into nice comfy beds, with a little more food in bowls beside them, Sonia looked up and smiled at him.

"Do come into the house for coffee, John. I think you've earned it."

"Well, I didn't do much apart from bringing the poor little devils to you. It's you who will have all the hard work … building them up and finding them new homes."

"I know … but at least they're safe now and no-one, over my dead body, will ever abuse them or their trust again."

John followed Josh and Sonia into the house and while drinking coffee and enjoying an enormous slice of chocolate cake, surrounded by several rescued dogs and cats Sonia told him she couldn't part with, decided he liked her more and more by the second. He made a mental note to pay Happylands a few more visits. After all, he had the excuse that he wanted to see how the two dogs were faring … and looking at the place, there might well be a few jobs he could help with in his spare time. Yes, this wouldn't be his last visit to Happylands.

* * *

Tilly was feeling exhilarated. Line dancing always made her feel like that. She had never done it before … until this cruise … but it was an activity she had always fancied having a go at and was pleased she had signed up for the classes. With a bit of luck, the exertion would help her lose a bit of weight … or at least work off some of the calories she was consuming. It was proving impossible to resist all the fabulous food which was set out in such a dazzling spectacle every day. Her taste buds were constantly being teased and Tilly had no will-power. None at all.

Anyhow, she wasn't going to worry about that as her new friend, William, didn't seem at all bothered by how tubby she was. Her new friend. Her new lover, hopefully. She had come on this cruise, a desperately lonely woman. She had never married, never had children and her parents had died in the last year, one after the other, her mother with breast cancer and her father from a broken heart as they had been inseparable. It had

185

left her devastated. Apart from her job as a librarian, she had never felt the need to have much contact with others and had very little social life. Her parents had been her world. She had lived at home with them, never wanting to leave the cosy bubble they had made for the three of them. Why would she have wanted to live in a flat by herself or with people she didn't know when she could have the closeness of a fabulous family life? She had barely socialised, preferring the company of her family and the books she devoured from the library but once her beloved parents had died, she had to think about what she was going to do with the rest of her life. Her colleagues had persuaded her to get away and enjoy herself on a cruise, meet new people, have some fun. So, she had gone mad and booked a long trip around the Caribbean, courtesy of the generous life insurance policy and ample savings her parents had bequeathed her.

She had embarked nervously and for the first twenty-four hours began to think she had made a big mistake. The hordes of jolly people, loving couples and happy families, had made her feel even lonelier and more depressed but on the second evening she met William and had been bowled over by his kindness, his interest in her and his olde-worlde charm. He had made the past few weeks more than bearable. He had shown her there was life after death and she could be happy again … if he was in her life. She knew she was falling in love with him ... had fallen in love with him ... and prayed he was feeling the same about her. She began to dream about a white organza wedding dress, a bouquet of lilies and pink roses … and best of all, the honeymoon … maybe another cruise.

CHAPTER 2

EARLY MARCH

William was on his way home to Peesdown ... and couldn't wait to get there. He had been away for the whole winter and was fed up with heat, ships and never being able to get completely away from the human populace. Now it was the beginning of March he wanted to be in England for the spring. He craved peace. He craved his lovely old Victorian home. He wanted to walk in Peesdown Park. He wanted, more than anything, to see Miranda.

His taxi pulled up outside his house at 2.00 a.m. so no-one witnessed his homecoming, which was just as well as he wasn't in disguise, although he now had the perfect excuse if someone did see him without it. He did a grin. He had been hatching a plot while away and couldn't wait to put it into action.

He paid the driver, who turned the taxi around quickly and sped back towards the High Street, desperate to get back to Leeds railway station to pick up another passenger. William stood outside his gates with his suitcases on the ground beside him and with the aid of the illuminated street lights, studied the road he lived on; Miller Lane, with the church at the far end, the Vicarage, the pub, the park gates. He noticed with interest a 'for sale' sign in the garden of the house next door. He had never had anything to do with the elderly couple who lived there as they were frequently away and if he had bumped into them, they only nodded and made no attempt to be friendly. That had suited him admirably. He certainly didn't want neighbours who bothered him repeatedly. He hoped the next lot would be the same. He didn't want to have to move. He liked his house and it was so perfect ... being right next to Peesdown Park. He breathed in the cool night air and could feel himself relaxing. It was a welcome relief after months of stifling heat, even when cooled down by sea breezes. God, it was good to be back.

With a smile on his face, he opened the new solid oak gates which he had ordered to be erected during his absence. They were perfect as no-one would be able to see up to the house at all now the wrought iron ones had gone but he would have to affix some good strong bolts on the inside as soon as possible to stop unwanted visitors intruding on his privacy. He walked up the drive, the security lights bathing him in a warm glow as he approached the house. He turned the key in the lock of the original Victorian wooden door and stepped into the hall. All was as it should be. Nothing out of place, nothing disturbed. He knew from experience that when the police searched a house, they weren't exactly fastidious about how they left a place when they departed so he was satisfied no-one had been inside during his absence and, therefore, he couldn't have been linked to that woman who had been raped and so tragically killed in the park before he left home in December.

He dumped his suitcases in the hall and grinned as he entered the kitchen and made a pot of tea, although he would have to drink it black as he hadn't any milk. He looked at the clock on the wall. It was only a few hours until morning and he could go for a walk in the park and see her … Miranda. They would have a lot of catching up to do. He had a lot to tell her about his cruise … where he had been and what he had done … although there was something in particular he could never tell her. That was his secret and his alone … and he had another trophy to add to his collection. In the morning he would have to retrieve his special box from where he had hidden it in the garage before he went away and enjoy an hour or two reminiscing on all his special activities. He chortled. 'Special'. He had never thought of it like that before.

* * *

"Will you stop kicking me, Charlie," groaned Miranda as she turned over in bed and pushed his legs away from hers. She never allowed the dogs on her bed normally but cheeky Charlie had decided during the night that she wouldn't mind for once. She had been vaguely aware he had joined her but had been too sleepy to resist. It was a surprise Nellie hadn't decided to join the party too but she could be heard snoring heavily downstairs in the lounge.

Miranda turned on the light and looked at the clock on her bedside cabinet. It was nearly 5.00 a.m. .and she had to get up soon so there was no point in trying to get back to sleep. She had to feed the dogs and let them out in the garden before heading off to feed four lots of cats before the traffic built up. If she could make a start while the roads were reasonably quiet, she could get it all done in about an hour and a half and then be free to crack on with all the dog walking and all the paperwork she had to do that day. Her business was expanding fast now and she was finding it difficult to keep up with the massive amount of office work and was thinking about hiring someone to help her on that front. She had considered turning the spare bedroom into an office but it was too much effort to move everything and she simply didn't have the time but she ought to as it made downstairs look so damned untidy. An office upstairs and someone to deal with all the different forms, letters and wages would be a real bonus. She hated being bogged down with it all. She wanted to be out and about with the animals. After all, that was why she had started the business in the first place.

Charlie thumped his tail on the bedding, always eager to get up and have breakfast.

"You're a very greedy young man," Miranda remarked, throwing her arms around his solid black and tan frame and kissing his nose. She had loved all her dogs but somehow this one was just a little more special. He was desperate to be a good

189

boy and always wanted to be as close to her as he possibly could, probably because he had such a bad start with some unkind person and now appreciated his good fortune. Darling Nellie, on the other hand, was a different kettle of fish. A confident Labrador, oblivious as to whether she was naughty or not and only behaved when it suited her. Naughty Nellie!

Miranda kissed Charlie on the head and headed for the bathroom to get ready for the day, throwing a desperate look at the photograph of Jeremy beside her bed. She thought, for the hundredth time, how it should be put away, thrown away even. She had picked it up several times to do just that but something always stopped her.

It had been taken on Boxing Day when they had taken the dogs up to Ilkley Moor and walked, hand in hand, for miles. The Army had generously granted him a few days leave over Christmas and although he stayed with his sister, Daphne, and her family, a good proportion of his time in Leeds was spent with Miranda. They had been so happy, getting to know each other, she actually dared to look forward to a future together but then he had been given the news he was going to be posted to Germany for an indefinite period. It had been a dreadful blow. His posting in London had been bad enough but at least he could get back to Leeds fairly easily and frequently but once he was in Germany, they wouldn't see much of each other at all. Miranda had been devastated and dreaded the day he would go and was desperately unhappy when he informed her that it would be at the very beginning of February, just a couple of days following his birthday.

Daphne decided his birthday party would double up as a leaving party, to which Miranda, as his girlfriend, was naturally invited. She would have much preferred to cook a delicious meal for him at her home, just the two of them and the dogs, and then curl up in bed together but it wasn't to be. Daphne had put in a lot of work organising the bash and there was nothing for it but to get through it as best she could.

She had been nervous, dreadfully nervous, at meeting Jeremy's old friends and some of his colleagues who were also on leave before their posting to Germany with him.

The evening was a miserable, heart-wrenching blur now and she could feel the tears welling up in her eyes as they did every time she thought of what had occurred.

She had managed to hold her own quite nicely to begin with. With Jeremy constantly by her side, she had been introduced to everyone and they had all been nice and included her in all their conversations. The only person she hadn't been keen on was a tall, willowy, blonde-headed woman who was introduced to her by Jeremy as Captain Karen Watkins. Miranda felt instantly at a disadvantage as Karen towered above her, the same height as Jeremy, her hair flowing beautifully over her shoulders and ample bust. She was dressed in a green velvet sequined dress and looked stunning. Miranda had held her hands instantly over her stomach to hide any kind of bulge, wishing she was inches taller and had stuck to her New Year's resolution of losing some weight.

"How nice to meet you," Karen had purred. "Jeremy has told us so much about you."

Miranda had been mortified to feel her cheeks turning pink, which would make her blusher look ridiculous. She had already wondered if she had applied too much. Excusing herself, she disappeared upstairs to the bedroom Daphne had set aside as a powder room for the female guests.

Her fears were realised. Her cheeks, thanks to Karen's remark and the two glasses of champagne she had consumed since arriving at the party, were ablaze beneath the blusher, making her look as if she were having an extremely hot flush. She took one of the tissues from the pretty pink box Daphne had left out on the dressing table and scrubbed at her face but it only made matters worse. She was just contemplating washing it all off in the bathroom when the bedroom door opened and the elegant, beautifully formed Karen Watkins entered with a smile which Miranda could only describe as somewhat triumphal.

"Oh, dear. Are you having a problem with your make-up, Miranda? I'm lucky, alcohol never seems to affect me in that way." She sashayed across the room and sat on the bed near to Miranda and crossed her long, slim legs.

"You know," she said quietly with just a hint of venom, "you're wasting your time. Jeremy won't stay with you. He's been seeing me on and off for a long time now and in that time, he's played the field … and so have I, come to that, but he and I have an understanding … and once he's sewn all the wild oats he needs to, it's me he's going to end up with … marry and have a family with … and you will be just another notch on his bedpost. So, if I were you, I wouldn't stick around too long to be humiliated … it really wouldn't do your self-confidence much good now, would it?"

Miranda had stood like a statue, unable to move, unable to believe what she was hearing. Her heart had been thumping wildly, she had felt nauseous and wanted to run to the bathroom and throw up but she wouldn't give the woman the satisfaction of seeing that. So, she hadn't said a word and concentrated hard on her breathing.

With yet another triumphal smile, Karen stood up and left the room, tossing her long tresses over her shoulder as she closed the door behind her.

Miranda had sunk onto the king-sized bed draped in thick gold brocade and tried not to dissolve into tears and ruin what was left of her make-up. All she had wanted to do was disappear, to get home, to get back to Charlie and Nellie who loved her unconditionally and would never let her down. All the old feelings of rejection the Beastly Bastard had left her with returned with full force. Her marriage had never been a particularly good one, fraught with money problems due to Barry's need to spend every penny both of them made as fast as possible and then rack up thousands of pounds of debt, but his final betrayal with her best friend, Charlotte, had been the most humiliating and traumatic end to their relationship. It had taken a long time to recover and push all those feelings away and regain her self-confidence and self-esteem and stupidly she had placed her trust in another man and found herself back in the same position ... well not quite. Although mortified, thanks to Karen flaming Watkins, she had been spared any further heartbreak and she should probably thank the woman for preventing the relationship from continuing. Better she should find out now what Jeremy was really like than further down the line.

She could have kicked herself. She hadn't wanted to get involved with another man, had always said she wouldn't but when she had set eyes on Jeremy that day outside his father's shop which she and Anna had turned up to view a few months ago, she had been utterly smitten. How stupid she had been. Stupid, stupid, stupid. She had known deep down she would never be good enough for him. They were worlds apart. It was ridiculous and she had to extricate herself from her predicament as fast as possible.

She hadn't felt able to face him again that evening. Taking her coat off the hanger from the rack of guests' coats in the bedroom, she had hurried downstairs and praying she wouldn't bump into anyone, crossed the spacious hall and slipped out of the front door.

She had arrived at Daphne's in a taxi, not wanting to drive because she would be drinking. It was a long walk home and the silly high heel shoes she was wearing would cripple her. She walked around the corner, out of sight of the house and called a taxi on her mobile. She had cried while waiting for it to arrive, uncaring if her make-up was utterly ruined. The taxi driver wouldn't care and neither would Charlie and Nellie, who would be the only other eyes set on her that night.

She sent Jeremy a text. "I'm sorry, I had to leave. Terrible headache. Enjoy your party, good luck in Germany and please don't contact me again."

He didn't reply. More than likely his phone wasn't switched on but even if it had been, he probably didn't hear the ping of the text arriving due to the high volume of the music. Still, he wouldn't care too much about her departing. He would have Karen to keep him happy ... and they would be off to Germany in the morning and that would be that. She would never see him again. It was over.

She arrived home in the taxi half an hour later, still with no answer from Jeremy. She collapsed onto the floor with Charlie and Nellie, who realising she was distressed, tried their best to comfort her by licking her and cuddling as close as they could. She had wrapped her arms around them and wept, resolving that she would never, never fall in love with a man again. It just wasn't worth it. Her entire focus in the future would be her business and her dogs.

CHAPTER 3

MARCH

The phone was ringing as Anna opened up the shop and stepped inside. She dropped her handbag on the counter and answered the phone.

"Pampered Pets," she said cheerily. The name rolled off her tongue now she had become used to it and as the shop was doing so well, she was immensely proud of it too.

"Mrs Stapleton?"

"Yes."

"Hello, good morning. It's Rendell's, the estate agents. We have a couple interested in your property and were wondering if you would be available to show them around this evening ... around 7 pm?"

"Oh, brilliant. Yes, that's perfect," Anna smiled. "What are their names?"

"A Mr & Mrs Merridew ... they're cash buyers so if they like your residence, you could be moving fairly quickly."

"Right," Anna said as her tummy lurched. This really could be it. The house had been on the market since early February and two other couples had viewed it but failed to put in an offer but perhaps this time she would be lucky. "Gosh. That's good. Thank you ... I'll look forward to seeing them."

She put the phone down and perched on the seat beside the till and stared into space. She wanted to sell the house, of course she did but now someone might actually be wanting to buy it, it felt strange. She and Gerald had bought it when they had married and never wanted to move as they loved it so much ... and now she was doing just that. She felt like a traitor ... guilty ... as if she was turning her back on their old life ... but that was just silly. She was moving on ... doing the sensible thing, moving into the flat above the shop to save time and money and make life a lot easier.

After all, what did she want with a three bedroomed house and large garden now? The flat here was perfectly adequate for her needs and there was the gorgeous garden outside which she was looking forward to caring for now the winter was over.

She stood up and went through to the back, through the pretty garden room and into the kitchen and made herself a cup of coffee. She had an hour before the shop was due to open and Emily, her new member of staff was due to arrive for her first day. It would be marvellous to have real help at last and enjoy a proper lunch hour. Since opening the shop a few months ago, she had struggled more or less on her own, working all day, keeping a sandwich and a flask of coffee beneath the counter and darting to the loo for a few minutes while she locked the shop door and put a 'back in a few minutes' sign on it. She could have shut the shop at lunchtime but that would have been silly as that was often the busiest time when people were shopping in their breaks. She had taken on a couple of people but neither had suited. One had lasted a month, another about seven weeks but they had been young and became bored easily of the chitchat, mainly about customers' pets. She had learned her lesson since then. Emily was in her forties. She hadn't worked for years, having stayed at home to bring up her three children but they had now fled the nest and she wanted something to occupy her.

"My George, he's a fireman," Emily had said proudly at her interview, "he's quite happy for me to have a little job and I've always loved animals ... we have our little Sammy, our Chihuahua, and adore him ... in fact, I think we might have seen you in Peesdown Park when we were walking him ... you were with Miranda from Four Paws ... we like her very much. She looked after Sammy for us when we had to go to a funeral in Scotland last year ... it was George's cousin ... died of a stroke ... poor man. My George was really upset."

It was difficult to get a word in with Emily. She certainly liked to talk but she was nice, kind and friendly and Anna was more than willing to give her a chance and was looking forward to her arriving today. It would be possible to pop into the park for a walk with Miranda too once Emily had been shown what was what.

That would be a refreshing change.

Anna smiled. It was going to be an interesting day, having Emily join her, the Merridew's looking over the house this evening ... and a walk with her best friend, who no doubt would talk about nothing but Jeremy. Miranda was still suffering badly from the trauma she had suffered at Jeremy's birthday party and it was hard to jolly her along as she was sunk in despair that she would never see him again and he would probably marry the beautiful, clever, posh Karen Watkins. Poor Miranda. Anna felt so sorry for her. She liked Jeremy enormously and was disappointed he hadn't been straight with her best friend that he had another woman in tow.

* * *

Freddie Fletcher was looking forward to today as his replacement as park keeper, Bob Watkins, was joining him on his rounds of Peesdown Park so he could be shown the ropes before Freddie hung up his uniform and took a much welcome retirement.

Beryl, Freddie's darling wife, with whom he could not live without, had finally persuaded him to hand in his notice two weeks ago. He had intended to stick it out until he retired but had never recovered from that awful day when he found that woman's body in the lake ... Tanya Phillips. He simply couldn't forget it. Every time he closed his eyes, he could see her again ... and it wasn't pretty. The poor, silly woman, must have had a terrible end. He hadn't known it at the time but the police had informed him afterwards, and it was soon common knowledge, that she had been raped before being strangled. Stupid, stupid woman. He could feel deep anger towards her at times, even while feeling deeply sorry for her. Why the hell did she have to be so crazy as to walk around the park at night? He had warned her that there was a rapist about who had never been caught and she had just shrugged it off, totally oblivious to her own safety and welfare ... but she had paid the price ... and so had he.

He had enjoyed his job for years but since that awful morning he hadn't. It had become a nightmare, wondering who could have done such a dastardly deed. He had always been observant, after all, you had to be, in charge of a place such as Peesdown Park with all the goings-on, especially in the summer with the younger generation and their antics but now he studied everyone more closely, engaging more than he normally would in conversation, trying to get an idea if they could be capable of such a terrible act.

It all played on his mind, day in and day out, night in and night out. Who was it? Was it a park regular? Was it someone he knew well? Had he missed something? He kept having nightmares if he did manage to get some sleep and frequently woke Beryl. She was looking more and more drawn and tired as time went on. It wasn't fair on her ... and on him. They had talked it over a couple of weeks ago, both at the end of their tether with it all.

"I don't think you have any choice, Freddie," Beryl insisted. "You have to hand in your notice. It's going to make you ill, going to the park every day, walking around the lake, never being able to forget or put it to the back of your mind and then not sleeping properly. You ... we ... simply can't go on like this."

"I know you're right," he had agreed "but it's a while before I can claim my pension. We need the money, Beryl ... I can't give it up ... not yet."

198

"Nonsense. If we don't have a holiday this year ... have one of those staycation thingies people are talking about ... you know when you just remain at home but go out for days, we can save a lot of money ... and we have those premium bonds Aunt Mary bought us for our silver wedding anniversary. They've only netted us twenty-five pounds so far. We could cash them in, which will help. Then there are our savings and my job ... and then perhaps you could find something part-time ... gardening maybe. We'd manage, Freddie."

He had felt a huge weight being lifted off his shoulders at her words. "Oh, Beryl. If you're really sure."

"Yes, I am," she had said determinedly. "I want my old Freddie back and once you're away from that park, you can start forgetting what happened ... at least not forget exactly but put it to the back of your mind and find something else to think about. We could start planning a holiday for when you do get your pension ... somewhere we've never been ... we could splash out and go abroad ... see some of the sights we've always wanted to before we're too old to enjoy it ... so ... hand in your notice today.

Promise me, Freddie, you will."

He had. He rang Reginald Barrington Senior from Barrington and Barrington, the solicitor who looked after the affairs of the Pee family who owned Peesdown Park, and informed him of his decision. Mr Barrington had expressed his disappointment but was most understanding when Freddie explained how he felt after finding Tanya Philips and the effect it was having on him.

"I'll find a replacement for you as soon as I can," Mr Barrington had said. "I'll try and get someone to start as soon as possible so you can familiarise them with the park and your duties before your notice expires."

He had been true to his word. Young Watkins was commencing this morning which made Freddie look forward to going to work himself for a change. It would be good to have someone with him, someone to chat to and rely on if there was any need for backup ... and the best bonus of all was that there weren't many days left before he could hand in his uniform and be free of Peesdown Park and all who entered it for good.

* * *

Robert Watkins, Bob as he liked to be called, was looking forward to his first day at work in the park. He hadn't been able to believe his luck when he saw the advert for a park keeper for Peesdown with a decent salary and the prospect of working only during the day and being in such a beautiful and clean environment. With his job as a security guard on the construction site coming to an abrupt end, he hadn't hesitated in applying for the park keeper's job and was chuffed to bits when he was told it was his.

He knew the park well and not just from using it for jogging every day. He had hung out there a lot with school friends, using his free bus pass to get there from the horrid little back-to-back in Harehills where he had lived with his mother and sister. It had been good to escape into the fresh air and get away for a few hours from the seedy life his mother lived, bringing man after man back to have noisy sex in her bedroom, right next to his and from where he could clearly hear every grunt and groan. God, it had been good when he had finally grown up and could leave and find a place of his own. He had shared a house with two other lads for a few years while he worked as a labourer on a building site but when he found the security job, which paid much better, he rented his little terrace in Peesdown, pleased to be living so near to the park where he could jog every day and use it as a garden when he wanted to just sit and watch the world go by in nice weather.

However, using the park for recreational purposes rather than working there was going to be a different kettle of fish and he was looking forward to it, getting to know everyone who used it regularly and making sure everyone behaved themselves. He certainly wasn't going to stand for any nonsense from anyone, that was for sure... and there was the added bonus of all the women to meet and ogle, especially in the summer when they appeared in their skimpy outfits, lazing around on the grass, or running around the lake and walking their dogs. He looked good in his dark blue uniform ... smart and trustworthy ... and women liked a man in uniform. Yes, he had high hopes for a few more interesting encounters before he swanned off on his travels next year.

* * *

William woke up, opened his eyes and had to think for a moment as to where he was. It seemed strange not to be in his cabin on the ship and feeling some kind of motion. Everything was still and calm and instead of seagulls, he could hear garden birds twittering and tweeting outside his window.

He looked at the picture of Miranda by his bed and smiled. He would see her today. He would walk with her, talk to her, smile at her. He could feel the butterflies in his tummy at the mere thought. He wondered what she had been up to in his absence. Probably expanded her business as she was very ambitious ... and hardworking. He would give her that. It couldn't be easy taking six dogs at a time to the park and keeping control and at the same time making sure her employees were doing their jobs properly.

He thought about some of the other people he knew from the park. Freddie Fletcher, the park keeper. He had found the body of Tanya Phillips floating in the lake, which must have been a hell of a shock for the poor old boy. William felt quite sorry for him.

Then there was Anna from Pampered Pets. No doubt her shop was doing well as she was such a warm-hearted woman and easy to like. He would pop in later and say hello if she wasn't in the park today.

He also had something to tell them too ... an exciting plan he had been working on all winter and today he was going to start putting it into action. 'Operation Miranda' he was going to call it.

He grinned, got out of bed and looked out of the window at the gate at the far end of the garden. Yes, it looked good. Nice and solid and provided total privacy with the high hedging all the way around. He would pay a visit to the ironmongers along the High Street and buy a couple of solid bolts and fix them later ... and he had to go to the post office and collect his mail ... and he needed to retrieve his trophy box and scrapbook from the garage ... after all, he had more things to add to the collection now ... and a photo

... of a very drunk Tilly Pargeter, just before she so tragically died. He remembered that day clearly. Their ship had docked in St. Lucia early in the morning where it was going to remain until the following day. They had gone ashore and hired a speedboat to take them to an uninhabited island a couple of miles out to sea. He had found out about it from a tour guide on their ship who had visited on a previous cruise. Apparently, the beach was particularly beautiful but it was rare for anyone to visit as there was nothing but deep, dangerous forestation in the middle and it was impossible to arrive or leave unless by boat so there was every likelihood visitors wouldn't be disturbed for hours.

William had told Tilly about it, enthused about how lovely it would be to get right away from the world for a few hours, to be alone on their own private island to swim, have a picnic, relax and soak up the sun.

Tilly thought it was an excellent idea, seemingly bowled over by the thought that he wanted to be totally alone with her for a few hours. Her eyes had widened and her smile had been broad as she nodded her assent and talked of nothing else but how she was looking forward to it.

The tour guide booked the speedboat and arranged a luxury picnic hamper, which included a few shots of Tilly's favourite Witches' Brew and a couple of bottles of champagne. An hour after they docked in St. Lucia they were being whizzed across the water by a charming young Rastafarian and deposited on their own, private island, William pleased as punch that no-one else from the ship had considered the trip worthwhile and had remained in St. Lucia soaking up the sights.

Tilly had jumped out of the red and white speedboat, her face wreathed in delighted smiles as she waited for William to come ashore with the hamper. They waved goodbye to the young man who grinned in acknowledgement and swung his boat and dreadlocks as he sped off again, having said he would be back to collect them around 5.00 p.m. As it was only 10.00 a.m., they had many hours to fill.

William put down the hamper in a shaded spot beneath some trees, while Tilly paddled happily in the sea.

"I do wish I could swim," she said sorrowfully. "It looks so enticing. I should have had some lessons on the ship."

"I could teach you," he said, "We could start your lessons now and then continue when we get back on board."

He stared at her. He could feel the old itch. It had been bothering him for days ... just as she had ... and now he had her ... completely at his mercy ... with no-one around to come to her aid. It was a completely different scenario to what he normally did. Usually, he carried out his attacks at night and didn't hang about but today it was going to be different. It was the morning, in brilliant sunshine and he had hours in which to play with his victim. Stupid woman, trusting him ... just as they all did.

Suddenly she whipped off her top and skirt to reveal a green swimsuit beneath. "Come on then. No time like the present," she giggled.

He removed his outer clothing to reveal his black swimming trunks and noticed her gulp as she looked his body up and down. She wanted him ... and it was going to be easier than he thought. He might actually have sex with her normally, without force. It would be interesting to see if he could manage it properly for once before he finished her off ... because that was the real thrill. The ending of the life, hearing the last breath, the final closure of the eyes, the relaxation of the body. He felt the excitement in the pit of his stomach. He couldn't strangle her though. He couldn't leave any signs that he had murdered her. It had to look natural ... like an accident. He stared at the water and then at her as she grabbed his hand and led him towards the stunning blue sea and they entered it together.

TO CONTINUE READING PANIC IN PEESDOWN,
GO TO:

UK: www.amazon.co.uk/dp/B08W96FYR5

US: www.amazon.com/dp/B08W96FYR5

PASSION IN PEESDOWN – BOOK 3

US: www.amazon.com/dp/B0BNCD2J87
UK: www.amazon.co.uk/dp/B0BNCD2J87

Nothing seems to go right for long for Miranda, Peesdown's bubbly petsitter. While her ex-husband, the Beastly Bastard, is desperate to patch up his relationship with her, she and new husband, Jeremy, have a more pressing problem with Karen Watkins, Jeremy's former army colleague. Karen is determined to split up Miranda and Jeremy and will stop at nothing to achieve her aim and when Miranda and her unborn child are put in danger, will Jeremy resist Karen's charms and save his family from disaster? Meanwhile, what exactly is the Beastly Bastard up to? Then there is Bob Watkins, the disliked park keeper. What major crime has he committed, causing him to leave Peesdown in a hurry? Yet again, it's all happening in Peesdown!

POISON IN PEESDOWN – BOOK 4

DUE FOR RELEASE 2023

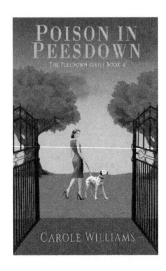

The stunningly beautiful Cassandra has purchased one of the gorgeous Victorian dwellings in Miller Lane, leaving several questions to be answered.

The ground floor is being turned into a beauty salon but the new resident has set up home in the granny annexe with her Dalmatian, Rolly, so what will the expensively decorated top floor bedrooms in the main house be used for? Why is Cassandra recruiting female escorts to work as beauticians? Why is she 'interviewing' the muscular, good looking Danny? Finally, why is she more than friendly with a Police Superintendent, a Judge and a Barrister?

Then there is the poor Vicar with a bad shoulder and in need of a massage. He might receive a bit more than he bargained for when visiting Cassanda!

There's certainly a lot going on in book 4!

FURTHER BOOKS BY CAROLE

THE CANLEIGH SERIES
A chilling psychological family drama

THE CANLEIGH SERIES is set between 1950-2003 at Canleigh Hall near Leeds and moving to London, Oxford, Scotland, the Caribbean and America. A Yorkshire family drama packed with passionate love, intrigue, suspense, blackmail … and murder!

www.carolewilliamsbooks.com

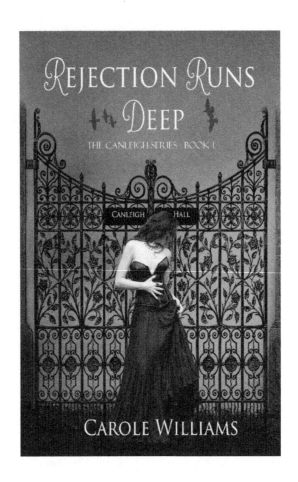

REJECTION RUNS DEEP

www.carolewilliamsbooks.com/the-canleigh-series

My mother was a slut and I despised her. My father ignored me when I most needed him and I think I killed my grandmother. The only bright lights on the horizon were my deep friendship with Philip Kershaw, the boy next door, my wonderful, crazy horse, Demon, and my deep love for Canleigh, where I had been born and which I never wanted to leave.

However, even though I am the elder, my twin, Richard, will inherit the estate which makes me livid and has caused many a row between us but we have come to an agreement that he will give the estate to me when the time comes as he wants a medical career instead. I shall marry Philip too and he will live with me at Canleigh and we will hold major equestrian events and live our lives surrounded by animals.

So, I had it all planned. Life was going to be rich and satisfying … but then they destroyed me. In one weekend, I lost my lover, my home and my beloved horse. I can never forgive them … and although I have to leave Canleigh now, I will return and they will all begin to wonder if I am mad … or just very, very bad.

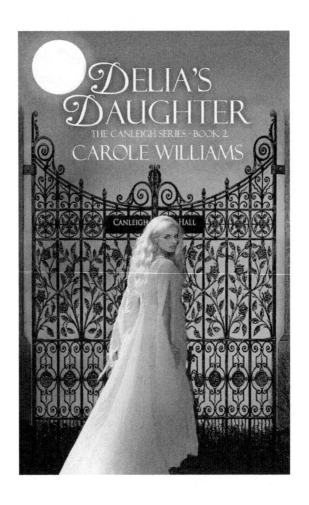

DELIA'S DAUGHTER

www.carolewilliamsbooks.com/the-canleigh-series

I'll never forget seeing my mother, Lady Delia Canleigh, trying to kill Granny Ruth. I was only four years old at the time and have grown up knowing my mother is evil. It's been difficult, dealing with the mixed feelings I have for her as even though she was so wicked, I love her deeply. However, due to new circumstances now I have reached adulthood, I am forced to reassess my relationship with her and I don't know what to do. Do I finally reject her or not? I also have another worrying problem. I am deeply in love with Jeremy but since our marriage he is behaving oddly. You see, I have inherited Canleigh Hall and a fortune to go with it, which was a total shock and a massive responsibility for both of us but I really don't like the way Jeremy is behaving now we are living there. I can't quite put my finger on it but something isn't right, especially when his friend, Matthew, is around ... or when he is near Felix, our butler. Both men make me very uncomfortable, even a little scared and I don't know why and now I have seen a dangerous glint in Jeremy's eye, just like my mother's, which is highly unnerving. Surely I shouldn't be frightened of my own husband. Or should I?

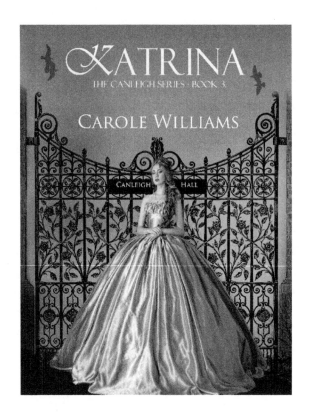

KATRINA

www.carolewilliamsbooks.com/the-canleigh-series

I have always been fascinated by my evil, stunningly beautiful Aunt Delia, especially her obsession with Canleigh Hall and all those terrible things she did to try to attain it. I've always envied Lucy, her daughter, who ended up with Canleigh, even though she suffered badly when she first lived there with her husband, the traitorous Jeremy. My mother, the saintly Lady Victoria, is next in line if Lucy doesn't have any children … or dies … and then, after my mother, it will go to me but that could be a very long time in the future, if ever, and I'm not sure I want to wait that long.

Since a small child I have imagined myself, beautiful and rich, swanning around in a gorgeous gold dress at a ball I will hold as chatelaine of Canleigh Hall and now I have grown up, I still like the idea. I like it very much. However, I also have another obsession, to be a famous film star and now I have to choose which path to take. Do I concentrate on getting to Hollywood or push Lucy and my mother into the next life by being as evil as my Aunt Delia and succeed where she failed with Canleigh? Hollywood or Canleigh. Decisions, decisions!

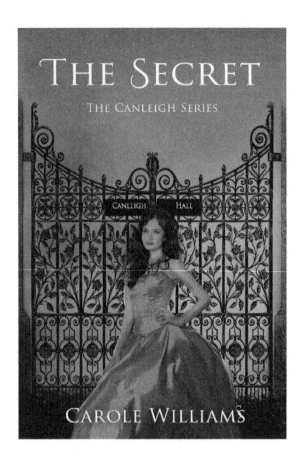

THE SECRET

www.carolewilliamsbooks.com/the-canleigh-series

I'm bored stiff at Canleigh. I'm bored stiff with my husband, the sainted, stuffy old Duke of Canleigh. We've been married for 12 years but it seems like a lifetime. I should never have married him but I had to, for his money, for the status, for respectability but I've made sure to keep a life of my own, away from his gaze and his constant, pathetic puppy dog looks.

But I've slipped up … big time … with my lover and my maid. One already knew my secret and is threatening exposure, the other has found out by accident. It could mean curtains for me and I could lose everything. So, there's nothing for it but to go on a cruise, with both of them in attendance. However, I shall have to go home alone and explain what has happened to them but the Indian Ocean is very deep … and the sea should swallow the evidence!

I am now working on **DARNFORTH**, another thrilling family drama which begins in Normandy in World War II just as the Germans are invading France.

To hear when Darnforth and future books are to be released, head over to my website, www.carolewilliamsbooks.com, leave your email address and you will be sent details as soon as they become available and don't forget to claim your FREE copy of **THE SECRET** and a thrilling short story called **YES DEAR.**

You can also follow me on Facebook –

www.facebook.com/carolewilliamsauthor

or email me at carolewilliams.author@gmail.com

Many thanks for reading Peesdown Park … and please don't forget to leave a star rating and/or a review. These are so important for authors as not only does it help sell our books, it rewards us for all the thousands of hours of hardwork, pounding our laptops, and spurs us on to continue.

Thank you so much and happy reading.

Carole Williams.

Printed in Great Britain
by Amazon

24058540R00126